MUDDY WATER
ROMANCE AND MURDER
IN HENRY COUNTY

A Novel By

Tom Steele

D0064543

LLUMINA ☆ STARS

ISBN: 1-933626-18-6

Printed in the United States of America by Llumina Stars

Library of Congress Control Number: 2007905910

For Linda, Jenny, Teresa, and Mark

CHAPTER ONE

I f there had been witnesses to the altercation that was taking place between the two men, they would have questioned the sanity of the smaller man, who foolishly scuffled with the six-foot, four-inch tall police officer. Closer observation would have caused the witnesses to understand that the small man was drunk.

"Dumb ass small town cops!" Scott Miller bellowed. "You got the wrong man. You screwed up. Ya all screwed up...and I'm gonna let everybody know about it."

Miller's breath reeked of whiskey and his clothing emitted the foul stench of tobacco smoke, heavily layered over his unwashed garments. Miller fell against Deputy Lambert's body, and he used Lambert as an anchor to keep from falling off his own wobbly legs. Just as Deputy Lambert's patience started to wear thin, Miller's eyes rolled back into his head and his threats began to recede into an inebriated tangle of words.

"I...gonna be the one...be the one...bring that new suriff dow," Miller slurred.

"Damn it, Scott! Sit down and shut up!" Deputy Lambert ordered. "You're drunk again. Don't make me hurt you."

The powerful deputy grabbed Miller and easily wrestled his intoxicated assailant down onto a jailhouse bed.

"Stay down on that bed, Scott!" Deputy Lambert warned.

Shaky and tired, Miller fell back on the bed and then rose up again.

"Yeah...I'm drunk, Joe," he said. "But, I'm right. Armstrong messed this one up. Ya all screwed up on this one. You got...wrong guy locked up in Joliet...there's killer...killer walking free in Kewanee. Walking free and laughing at all of ya. I know. I got proof. I'm...gonna tell everybody about suriff Armstrong."

Miller's body crumbled back on the thin, jailhouse mattress. He slowly raised his arm up and started to say more, but collapsed back on the bed, silenced by the same whiskey that had given him the courage to shout out his protest to the deputy.

Deputy Lambert looked at the drunken mass sprawled out on the bed. He knew Scott Miller had never liked Sheriff Armstrong, and he knew Scott was not a favorite of the sheriff, but tonight's outburst crossed a dangerous line and put Joe in a difficult spot. Miller was Joe's friend, but Sheriff Mike Armstrong was Joe's boss.

Scott's always been a character, Joe mused.

Deputy Lambert grabbed the thin, olive drab blanket lying at the end of the jailhouse bed and threw it over Scott. He shook his head and remembered a time when he and Scott were young boys.

Man…me and Scott used to raise a lotta hell in Kewanee, the deputy thought. The problem is Scott just never quit raising hell. That's why he'll be locked up in this cell tonight and why I'm standing over him in this uniform.

A loud snoring noise burst forth from the bed as Deputy Lambert left the cell and slammed the heavy steel door behind him. Joe looked through the barred window into the darkness and immediately felt good about being the one who had brought Scott to the county jailhouse.

Somebody had to bring Scott in, the deputy thought. It's better for Scott that it was me. Scott wouldn't have been so lucky if Deputy Rogers had run across his path tonight. If Rogers had caught up with him, Scott would be more than just sleeping off his drunk in a cell. Rogers would never cut Scott any slack…that's for damn sure.

Joe shook his head, but smiled slightly as he watched Scott sleeping on the cell bunk.

Because of their shared childhood experiences, Deputy Lambert had a soft spot in his heart for Scott. Harbored in the back of Joe's mind were memories of a younger and very different Scott Miller.

Walking down the narrow, concrete jailhouse corridor, Joe debated whether or not he should mention Scott's rambling outburst to the sheriff. Joe knew Scott Miller had enough grief in his life, and he did not want to add any more.

Scott's just blowing off steam and trying to act important, Joe thought. There's nothing to that line of crap he's babbling about. But, I gotta at least tell the sheriff about it, and the sheriff's gonna be pissed when he hears what Scott has been saying. God, I'd rather not rat on him, but Mike needs to know, and I'd better tell him. It's gotta be bullshit anyway. There can't be anything to what Scott's saying.

But, Miller's words weighed heavily on Joe's mind. He knew Scott's drunken gibberish was directed towards the murder of Katie Karver and, whenever Joe was confronted with any information about the Karver case, it always caused him to shudder. This time was no different. It wasn't long before Joe began to feel a sickening sensation rolling up from his stomach and moving to his chest.

What if Scott is right? Joe anguished to himself. What if we got the wrong guy locked up? Goddamn it! I don't wanna think about all of that again. I don't want to think of Katie being murdered. I can't think about it any more. God, it's hard being a cop in a small town…there's no place to hide…nowhere to escape. It was bad enough that I was always running into Larry Karver before he left for Phoenix and now Scott lays this in my lap.

Larry Karver had been a high school classmate of Joe and Scott. All of the guys in high school had envied Larry because his family was wealthy and powerful. Larry seemed to get everything he wanted, and he never paid for anything. When Joe and Scott had raised hell in Kewanee, they always paid the consequences, but Larry always got a pass. And, Larry had gotten the one thing Joe wanted; Larry married Katie Summers, the girl who had been coveted by every boy in Kewanee High School. Katie was long, tall, and beautiful. Every high school boy found it a pleasure just to watch her walk into a room.

A picture of Katie's sweet smile popped up in Joe's head. Images of her beauty raced through his mind, time spun backwards and he found himself unable to continue walking any farther down the hallway.

When will I ever get over Katie? he thought.

In high school, Katie and Joe had just been friends. But, for a short period of time, while they were attending community college together, they became lovers. At first, Joe had felt guilty about their love because Katie was engaged to Larry Karver. But that guilt faded rapidly. Joe never really liked Larry and he would have continued making love to Katie if only she had consented.

God, Katie was good, Joe desperately remembered. She was so good. Making love with her was the best thing I have ever done,

The deputy leaned back against the wall in the narrow jailhouse corridor and felt an emptiness beginning to gnaw away at his gut.

Joe had connected with Katie in ways he never experienced with anyone else. Holding her had always made the world seem right. When she had come into his life, Joe felt complete. Without her, he felt out of place and alone. Katie and Joe had not made love in over seven years, but he could still feel her arms wrapped around him. He could smell her presence and his memory could readily invoke her taste.

Moving to escape the hallway, Joe ducked into a small, empty jailhouse office. He knew he had to tell the sheriff about Scott, but right now he just wanted to be alone with his thoughts of Katie. Everyone considered Joe to be a strong man, but memories of Katie always disabled him. He had loved her deeply.

Joe closed the office door and sat down behind a desk that was the communal property of any deputy who needed it. The office was dark, and Joe wanted it that way. He leaned back in the desk chair and stared into the obscure shadows that filled the tiny room and surrounded him. The murky darkness pulled him back to the time when he first made love with Katie. He recalled a day over seven years ago when Larry Karver had phoned him and made an odd request. The Karver family had all been gone for more than a week, and Larry had called from Chicago, where he and his family were visiting Larry's uncle.

3

"Hey Joe, this is Lar. How ya doing?" Larry Karver had said into the phone.

"I'm good, Larry. You back from Chicago?"

"Nah, I'm stuck here for a few more days," Larry answered. "That's why I'm calling you. I need a favor, and I'm hoping you can help me out."

Joe laughed into the phone.

"Sure, Larry. What'd ya need? Ya know I'm here to serve."

"I want you to take Katie out. She's been sitting home doing nothing, and I want you to take her skiing on the Mississippi. You can use my dad's boat at the marina. You know where everything is."

"Hey, wait a minute," Joe responded anxiously. "Will Katie want to go skiing with me?"

"Come on, Joe," Larry pleaded. "Of course she will. She likes you, and I trust you. That's a great combination, and I want you to do this for me. I already promised her I would take her skiing this coming week, and now I'm stuck being a good nephew at my uncle's house. I can't get away from here, and I don't want her being mad at me all summer. And, I don't want her bored. Show her a good time. Do this for me."

"Alright, Lar, but you're taking a big risk. I mean, putting your girl alone on a boat with a handsome stud like me."

"Yeah, right!" Larry shot back. "I'm more worried about the damage you'll do to the boat. Katie *is* my girl. I'm not worried about that. And listen, I think the gas tank's full on the boat. If it ain't, just tell the dock people to fill it and charge it to my dad. And, take some food with ya. I'll pay you back when I get home."

"You're sure about this Larry," Joe asked. "I mean it's alright with your dad if I use the boat?"

"Yeah, yeah! Don't worry about that. Dad lets me use it all the time. I never ask anymore."

"And you're sure Katie wants to go skiing with me?"

"Hey, you're the best skier in Kewanee," Larry replied. "Why wouldn't she want to go with you? Do this favor for me, Joe."

What was that stupid bastard thinking? Joe wondered as he sat in the small jailhouse office. Larry was a dumb ass back then, and he's still a dumb ass.

CHAPTER TWO

Joe remembered that he was nervous on the day he dialed Katie's phone number, but he was thrilled over the idea of talking with her. Joe had feelings for Katie that went beyond her appearance, and he knew it would be dangerous for him to be alone with her on a boat.

When the phone stopped ringing, Katie's voice boomed cheerfully into Joe's ear.

"Hello!" Katie said.

The sound of her voice both frightened Joe and compelled him to want to hear more.

"Hi, Katie! This is Joe. Larry asked me to give you a call," he blurted out.

"Hey Joe! How are you? I know why you are calling. I told Larry I needed to go skiing sometime this summer, and I told him to ask you to take me. So I hope you're calling to say yes. You're not gonna disappoint me, are ya?"

Joe's heart melted as he listened to Katie's voice on the phone. He tried to image what she was wearing and where she was in her house. He had been in the Summers' home twice, once while attending Katie's graduation party and once at her twentieth birthday party, and ever since those visits he had fantasized about being alone with Katie in her home. He imagined her curled up on a big couch in the family room wearing shorts and a t-shirt.

"Who could disappoint you, Katie?" Joe replied. "Besides, I can't wait to get out on the water. You don't mind going with just me?"

"I'm tired of crowds, and Larry tells me you're the best skier in Kewanee. Maybe you can show me some of your techniques?" Katie giggled into the phone. "Skiing techniques, I mean."

"You're funny, Katie. Very funny."

Katie knew she was sexually attractive. Her flirtatious overtures to Joe were an attempt to escape the burden of her good looks by using suggestive humor. Joe knew Katie was only kidding when she flirted with him, and he admired her sense of humor. Her ability to poke fun at her sex appeal broke through the awkward tension he always felt when he talked to her.

"But I hear that you're a pretty good skier, too," he said. "Maybe we can both learn something?"

"Hmmm, maybe," Katie replied.

Without skipping a beat, Katie quit being flirtatious, and her voiced switched to a tone of genuine adolescent excitement.

"What day are we going, Joe? Do you want me to drive?" she asked. "This is really nice of you to do this for me."

"Yeah, right," Joe replied. "It's real nice of me. Let's see, I get to drive one of the best boats on the river and I have the pleasure of skiing with the prettiest girl in Kewanee. Sounds more like selfish to me."

"Oh…so I'm the prettiest girl in Kewanee, huh? Why Joe, I didn't think you noticed such things."

"We all think you're pretty, Katie. I'm just saying what all the guys say."

"My, this is interesting," Katie coyly replied. "You talk about me with all of the guys, huh?"

"Katie, I'm just saying that it's…I'm just saying it'll be…I'm just saying, I get to go skiing with the prettiest girl in Kewanee, and I'm really looking forward to taking you," Joe confessed.

"And I get to be with the nicest boy," Katie said. "Pretty good looking one, too. You know all of the girls like you, Joe."

"Well, when you see all those girls, tell them I like them too," Joe calmly replied in an effort to hide his embarrassment. "What day do ya want to go skiing? I'm gonna suggest we ski on Thursday. I don't have to work that day and the weather is supposed to be hot. We should have the river all to ourselves on a weekday. Is Thursday good for you? You can drive if you want. Doesn't matter to me."

"Thursday it is," Katie said. "I'll pick you up at 7:00 a.m. I'll make sandwiches and bring snacks for us, but you get the drinks. Is that O.K?"

"That's great, Katie. Sounds like a plan to me."

"Hey, Joe," Katie said. "Thanks for agreeing to do this. I promise we'll have a good time. I'll see you on Thursday. Now, don't forget."

"I won't forget," Joe replied. "I'll be waiting out front of my house at 7:00 a.m. See ya then."

After he hung up, Joe sat sideways, sprawled out in an overstuffed chair next to the phone in his house. He smiled to himself and thought about the phone conversation. A big grin appeared on his face each time he thought about Katie saying he was good looking. He decided that Thursday could be real dangerous, and he couldn't wait for Thursday to arrive so he could be with Katie.

CHAPTER THREE

Katie Summers had always been attractive and admired for her beauty. When she was a little girl, she was an effervescent child who greeted everyone with a radiant smile. Adults raved over how cute "Little Kate" was, and Katie would always beam in response to the praise she received. By the time she was three years of age, Katie had emerged as a social butterfly.

Being a pretty child was a simple and joyful time for Katie, but like all little girls, her childhood was torn away from her between her 13th and 14th birthdays as her body began to blossom into womanhood. Katie's mother told her that a girl's body changes as she moves towards adulthood and Katie imagined the changes to be magical.

"Katie," her mother had said. "You are a very pretty girl. Soon, you will grow up and become a beautiful young woman. You will meet a handsome man who will propose to you, and you will have beautiful children of your own."

Katie believed her mother. She believed all of the stories she had been told about beautiful women and handsome men. She believed the changes in her body would transport her into a fairy tale world. She watched her body change and wondered who would be her prince.

As a teenager, Katie continued to be outgoing and social. She was a popular girl at Kewanee High School, and she was frequently the center of attention. No one would have suspected from her appearance or her actions that Katie regretted the loss of her childhood and was becoming uneasy about life. Outwardly, she appeared confident, happy, and assured, but there was no intellectual depth in her thinking processes and she found no comfort in the academic pursuits of high school.

It was in high school that Katie became worried and a fear began to surround her heart. What she feared was social rejection. Being social had always been an anchor for her; it was what she was good at and what she enjoyed. But as she grew older, her own human frailties and the mysteries of life began to fill her with doubt and insecurities.

Katie remained a social butterfly, but the joy of being liked had now become a *need* for her. She aggressively sought the acceptance of the high school's popular crowd in order to allay her insecurities. She remained overtly friendly to everyone, but she ignored forming any relationships with people who had little social standing, and she buttered up to those who were part of the social elite. All of her actions and comments at school became calculated to please people. She showered compliments on all of the right kids in order to gain their friendship and company. She never disagreed with the popular mindset, and she often floated from one point of view to another in order to never offend anyone. Her view on any issue always depended upon whom she was with when the issue was being discussed. If there was division on the issue, Katie fled the company of those who were talking about it and waited for a more neutral atmosphere to prevail before she returned.

To become an integral part of the elite circle, Katie learned to promote herself by being the person who knew everything about everyone. She became obsessed with rumors and social nonsense. She was the person to go to if you wanted scoops or the latest dirt, and she could always be found in the middle of the group she called "the cool crowd." But the more Katie anchored herself with the popular crowd, the more insecure she became. She knew that many of the kids she hung with were self-absorbed and shallow. They fed on the need for approval, but would gossip about another person without mercy or forgiveness.

Although Katie was an important part of the "in-crowd", she constantly feared the possibility of them turning on her. Katie did not have the courage to stand alone in the world, and she knew she needed continuous approval just as much as the other cool kids did.

But, Katie's greatest fear was romantic rejection. She had developed a passion in her heart for romance. It was a passion in search of her prince. The idea of finding the right man became a goal for her, but she worried about that process too. Katie viewed boys as one of life's great ambiguities, and she learned that dating boys was a dangerous game. She had seen young girls crying hysterically over the loss of a boyfriend, and Katie came to fear the personal closeness of a female-male relationship. She knew her dalliances into the social circles of school were light excursions compared to a romantic relationship; her friends might be mean to her, but a boy could break her heart.

Despite her apprehensions, Katie dated early in search of her prince. At fifteen, she was dating Jim Easton. Jim was two years older than Katie. He was considered to be "cool" by Katie's girlfriends, and he was popular with the crowd of kids Katie hung with. Jim had a car, a part-time job, and was the starting quarterback on the high school football team. Jim was tall and lanky and good-looking. Unfortunately, much of Jim's popularity was due to his disruptive antics. Jim was the proverbial bad boy whose adolescent foolishness was an allure to many young girls. In school, Jim was brash and disruptive. He lived for Friday nights when football made him the star of Kewanee, but he had no interest in school and no plans for the future. Jim was going nowhere fast.

Katie did not see Jim's faults. Through her adolescent eyes, Jim was seen as an idol. She hung on him in the hallways and talked incessantly about him to her girlfriends. Katie's girlfriends were envious of her and many of them resented her successful conquest of Jim.

"Do ya know what the senior girls are saying?" Rhonda said one day.

Rhonda Logan was a sophomore at Kewanee High School and one of the "cool kids." Although Rhonda could not name an Eastern European nation or cite a line from Shakespeare, her head was filled with the kind of dribble that appealed to Katie's friends.

"What?" Katie anxiously asked. "Are they saying something about me?"

"Yeah, they're talking about you and Jim," Rhonda said.

"What about me and Jim?" Katie asked. "What are they saying?"

It was lunchtime at Kewanee High School, and Katie was sitting across from Rhonda at a cafeteria table. The room was abuzz with the noisy clatter of a multitude of conversations that spilled forth from three hundred students who, having avoided the academic discussions of their classes, were now babbling incessantly about nothing.

"Well, you didn't hear it from me," Rhonda said. "They're saying that Jim's looking around. They're saying that no sophomore virgin's gonna hold on to him. They're saying, if you don't put out, he's gone."

Katie could feel her heart sinking. People were talking about her. They were analyzing her life and finding it unsatisfactory. She felt tears welling up in her eyes.

"Jim'll never leave me," she said softly.

But Rhonda could tell by the look on Katie's face that the news had hit her hard. Moments like this excited Rhonda and put her in the driver's seat. She was conveying bad news, juicy gossip, and waiting to glean personal information from her victim. If Rhonda was lucky, Katie's defense mechanism would fail and Katie would confide in her, giving Rhonda more information that she could use later in order to maintain her status as a person in the know.

"Do you, Kate?" Rhonda asked. "Do you and Jim do it?"

Moisture blurred Katie's vision.

"We do everything but that," she said slowly. "Jim told me we don't have to do that. Jim told me we could wait...until later. We're going to get married after high school. You know that."

Katie felt a swirling sensation in her head. She saw a group of older girls heading her way and she immediately smiled and waved at them, pretending to be happy.

"Hey! You guys going to the game tonight?" she shouted cheerfully.

The girls smiled back and sat down at the table with Katie and Rhonda.

"Sure, Kate. We're all going. How bout you?" Shelby asked.

"Course I'm going. Gotta see Jim play and help him celebrate afterwards. Me and Jim always celebrate after the games."

"Oh…you and Jim are still going together then?" Sandy asked.

"Yep," Katie replied in a bubbly tone of voice. "I think Jim's gonna give me his ring after the game tonight."

Katie abruptly stood up and dislodged herself from the long bench, which was attached to the cafeteria table. She picked up the brown plastic tray that held the remains of her half-eaten lunch and purposely smiled broadly at all of the senior girls sitting at the table.

"See you girls at the game," she said and quickly walked away.

Rhonda rushed to join Katie's hasty retreat from the table. She walked shoulder to shoulder with her as Katie fled from the cafeteria.

"Is he really gonna?" Rhonda said. "Is Jim gonna give you his ring?"

"I'll make sure he does," Katie replied. "I won't be coming to school Monday without that ring on my finger."

CHAPTER FOUR

Friday night was the first in a series of heartaches for Katie. She gave herself completely to Jim that night. She surrendered her virginity to him on the floor of a parked and empty school bus.

"I love you," Katie desperately whispered to Jim as he pulled at her clothing.

"I love you too," Jim said hurriedly.

Katie stretched her arms under the seats of the bus and held on to the cold metal legs as Jim pushed inside of her. His performance was over in just a few minutes, and what they did in the bus that night did not make her feel loved. Instead, she felt separated from Jim during the whole procedure. All of his actions on the floor of the bus were directed toward providing him with a single, short moment of pleasure. There was nothing romantic about the incident and no climatic joy for Katie. In fact, what they did that night was cold, painful, and clumsy. Katie walked away from the ordeal vowing she would never do it again.

There was no offer of a ring from Jim that night, and he spent all of Saturday working on his car. They saw each other again on Sunday, and Katie was the one who suggested that Jim give her his ring.

"Hey, why not?" Jim said. "I mean, after Friday night, we should let people know you're really my steady girl now."

Katie dated Jim for twenty months. Those were unhappy times in which she constantly hoped for more from him. Jim always disappointed her.

Often, Jim let her know he had sexual needs, which had to be fulfilled and she wound up reneging on her vow of abstinence.

"Everyone's doing it," he told her. "All of the junior and senior girls do it."

Jim's insistence and Rhonda's lunchroom warning hung over Katie's relationship with him like a wrecking ball. She understood what she had to do to keep Jim as her boyfriend. They became sexually active, and Katie discovered she was good in bed. But, she initially mistook Jim's desire for sex and her own passionate abilities to be signs of commitment toward a stable and mature relationship. However, she soon discovered that Jim would never be stable or mature.

Jim was fun and exciting, but Katie arrived at the conclusion that he was no prince. His social status changed when he graduated from high school and continued to work part time. There were no Friday night football crowds after graduation and, without schedules or external discipline to confine him, Jim was always involved in trouble. Katie's circle of girlfriends quit raving about him. She was a junior in high school when Jim was arrested for being drunk and disorderly. She secretly sold some of her jewelry to help him pay a court fine. Katie cared about Jim and she tried to talk to him about the future and about settling down, but he remained wild and immature. After much pain, Katie finally gave up on being with him, and she stopped seeing him the summer before she became a senior.

Katie learned a lesson from the time she spent with Jim. She learned to guard the passion in her heart, and the search for her prince became guarded, too. She admitted to herself that she had enjoyed Jim as a lover. They were good in bed, but she needed someone who was safe and secure. Katie wanted a prince who would provide her with a palace and social standing, and she decided social position was more important than personal love. She would never get close to one man, and a man would never hurt her again; instead, she would find a man who she could dominate. She replaced the fear in her heart with a cold and calculating approach to finding her new prince.

Katie's new hope settled on Larry Karver, and she found him to be all she was looking for. Larry's family was wealthy and Larry was the heir apparent. Girls did not rave about Larry, but they did admire his financial future, and he moved in the right social circles.

Katie found Larry to be an easy conquest. He was egotistical, privately awkward, and star struck over her beauty. She had dated Jim Easton, the most popular boy in school, and she had been chosen as the duchess of the Junior-Senior Prom. There was no doubt she would be the queen of the prom during their senior year. Larry saw Katie as a beautiful trophy. He was proud to be seen with her and proud to have his father know that she preferred him to all of the other boys.

Katie easily manipulated Larry, who was drawn in by her charms and the flattery she directed his way. She complimented him constantly and dressed up for him, allowing him to show her off wherever they went. Then slowly she began to dominate their relationship.

In order to be assured she was in charge of their relationship, Katie tested Larry periodically. She would purposefully pick fights with him and then wait for him to apologize to her. Every time she walked away from him, Larry came crawling back. Whenever he thought about ending his relationship with her, Katie's nature would change from calculating to kind. She would revert back to the sweet girl who had pursued him in high school. She would agree with everything Larry said and shower attention on him. Her strategies worked well. Larry stayed with her, always hoping for those moments when she would be kind and loving. Katie enjoyed the control she was asserting over Larry. He was the man she was looking for. He was her new prince.

But there was one unhappy aspect of Katie's new plan, which left her feeling empty. Katie discovered that men who can be dominated in a relationship are not very good in bed. Larry's romantic moves were clumsy and did nothing to arouse Katie's desire for him. She tried to teach him everything she had learned about sex, but he remained a novice. She longed to be stimulated, but when he touched her, his fingers moved quickly over her body, groping rather than caressing her. He would always start making love to her before she was ready, and he would finish with a whimper, not with a climax. He seemed unmoved by sexual passion, and he refused to engage in sex more than once a week. Larry was never able to satisfy Katie, and he always left her in need. Larry Karver was not a prince in the bedroom.

To placate Larry's fragile ego, Katie learned to compliment his less than mediocre sexual performances and she faked her orgasms. She lied about her sex life to all of her friends, except Robin Thompson. Robin and Katie were close friends and they talked openly about their desires and their misgivings. But, privately Katie convinced herself that her sex life was no different than a majority of women. She replaced her feelings of sexual passion with a passion for romantic control. She continued to smile at everyone and pretended to be happy.

The day Katie spent on the Mississippi River with Joe momentarily disrupted her plans for the future. Joe had been a quiet boy in high school, but he was very good looking. Katie had flirted with him a number of times. She liked his broad shoulders, his dark hair, and his smile. Katie also admired Joe's quiet courage and his solitary nature. He never seemed to care about his social status. He was always friendly, but independent, and he never judged anyone. He didn't engage in gossip or ask questions about people. What was in Joe's head was a mystery to Katie, and she found his stoic personality attractive and intriguing.

Even though Joe was never really in the popular circle at high school, both Katie and Robin had a thing for him. She and Robin would mention Joe when they talked about boys they would like to do. Robin was the first person Katie had called after her phone conversation with Joe.

"Hey Robin, guess what?" Katie said into the phone.

"You know I don't like guessing," Robin replied. "Just tell me the news."

"Alright, I'll tell you. You'd never guess it anyway. This Thursday I'm going water skiing with Joe. Just me and Joe and the river. All day long."

"Wait a sec. Whoa," Robin exclaimed. "Slow down. What about Larry? Where will Larry be? And, Joe doesn't have a boat."

"We're gonna use one of the Karver boats," Katie answered. "Larry's stuck in Chicago, and he doesn't want me to get bored. So, he asked Joe to take me skiing on one of their boats. I'm really looking forward to it."

"Yeah I can tell you are," Robin laughed. "Maybe looking forward to it way too much. You'd better be careful on that boat. Still waters run deep, you know. God! Is Larry nuts or what?"

"Phhhht! Larry's just trying to please me. You know how he is," Katie said. "Plus, Larry doesn't look at Joe as competition. I told Larry he should have Joe take me skiing."

"Geez, you do have Larry in the palm of your hand. That's for sure. But God, Katie, this is way overboard. I mean Joe's a real good-looking guy. He's hot!"

"I know," Katie replied. "To tell you the truth, I'm a little nervous. You know what I mean?"

"Oh yeah, I know exactly what you mean," Robin said. "Joe is hot! I told you he's been hitting some of the bars with me, didn't I?"

"Yeah, you told me that. But nothing is happening between you two. I mean, he hasn't made any moves on you. Has he?"

"No. Joe's a complete gentleman, damn it," Robin laughed. "But then I'm not wearing a swim suit and alone on a boat with him all day long. Which swim suit you gonna wear?"

"I don't know. I think my red two-piece," Katie said. "What'd you think of that?"

"I think you'll be hot! I already feel sorry for Joe," Robin laughed again. "He won't be able to keep his eyes off of you."

"That's what I figured, too," Katie laughed. "The poor guy."

"Really Katie, what's the purpose of all this? I thought your mind was set on Larry."

"My mind is set on marrying Larry. But, it's not my mind I'm worried about. It's been a long time since I felt like a woman."

"Well, just be careful out there on the river," Robin warned. "I'll tell you…I don't think I could resist Joe if he made a move on me."

"Now look who's talking. Remember you've got good ole Frank."

"Good ole Frank and good ole Larry," Robin laughed. "How did two hot girls like us wind up with those guys? We should have had more fun first."

"I was just thinking the same thing. Poor Joe, lucky me."

"Just remember this," Robin said. "Friday night we're getting together and I want a full report. Promise me."

"You're the only one I could tell, Robin. You're my best friend. Whatever happens, I'll need to tell someone and you're it. Does it bother you that I'm thinking this way?"

"No it doesn't, Katie. I envy you," Robin confessed. "Just protect your heart and try not to hurt Joe."

"I'll do both," Katie laughed. "I really am looking forward to this. I like Joe. I don't wanna hurt him though. I just wanna have some fun. I hope he does, too."

"Joe's a big boy," Robin replied. "And he knows you're with Larry. Maybe nothing'll happen but skiing."

"I promise you this, Robin…when we meet on Friday, I'll have more to talk about then just skiing."

"Oh God help Joe," Robin laughed again. "Have fun and I'll talk with ya on Friday."

CHAPTER FIVE

The Karvers owned three boats; they kept one at a lake in Wisconsin and the other two were at a marina on the Iowa side of the Mississippi River. One of the Mississippi boats was a thirty-two-foot luxury liner with a cabin and sleeping quarters. Since it was doubtful that Larry had gotten his father's approval for this outing, Joe wanted nothing to do with the larger boat. Besides, he wanted to be able to see and talk to Katie while they were out on the river. The Karver's twenty-foot, V-8 ski boat would be perfect for that. The ski boat was white with red trim and it was outfitted with a passenger compartment that would allow him to always keep Katie in view.

Katie was fifteen minutes late when she arrived to pick up Joe. She made up for the lost time by racing over the roads that took them to the river. It would normally take more than one good hour to drive from Kewanee to Le-Claire, Iowa, but Katie got them there in fifty-five minutes. They pulled into the marina parking lot at 8:10 a.m., parked the car and walked toward the boat dock. Katie was carrying a small cooler containing the food she had promised to bring. Joe carried a larger cooler filled with ice and beer. They both had backpacks slung over their shoulders, which were stuffed with towels, extra clothing, and a variety of sun lotions.

"See, I was right," Joe exclaimed proudly while walking down the wooden ramp that led to the boat slips. "The sun is shining and there's no one here. We'll have the river all to ourselves."

"I hope you have a key to the boat," Katie teased back at him. "Otherwise 'no one' will include us."

"Not a problem," Joe responded. "Larry always hides a key in a box under the dash. He told me it would be there."

When they got to the Karver boat slip, Joe hopped from the dock onto the boat. Katie handed him the coolers and backpacks, kicked her sandals into the boat, and then leaped on board landing next to Joe. The boat wobbled in the water, throwing the two together. Joe grabbed onto Katie and pulled her to him.

"Whoa. Steady there," he said laughing. "Are you OK?"

Katie laughed and smiled at Joe.

"Yep, I'm fine. I just haven't been out in the boat for awhile. You find the key and I'll store our junk."

Joe was happy to find the key where Larry said it would be. He inserted the key into the ignition, turned it one notch to the right and watched the gas needle move up to the full mark.

Well, those are two things Larry was right about, he thought. I got the key, and the gas tank is full. I guess Larry is not a total fuck up.

Joe turned the key fully to the right and smiled when he heard the engine kick in.

"Katie, untie the rear ropes and push us away from the dock," he said while revving the engines. "We're going to head up river away from the locks. We'll cruise up to the Cordova Islands and get the skiing gear out there. That plan OK with you?"

"Great," Katie replied. "Let's get going. I wanna spend the whole day out here."

Joe watched as Katie pulled her white, college t-shirt up over her head, stuffed it into a small cargo hold, and turned to face him. She was tan and wearing a two-piece, red swimsuit. She flashed a knowing smile and struck a model pose.

"Hope you like my suit," she said.

Without waiting for a reply, she turned and began pulling on the rope that tied the rear of the boat to the dock.

Who wouldn't like your suit, Joe wondered as he watched her unhitch the boat.

Katie finished untying the knots and threw the ropes into the boat.

"OK, the boat's free," she shouted.

Joe carefully backed the boat out of its slip and then cruised slowly as he maneuvered out of the marina waters and into the channel of the river. Katie moved to the front of the boat and took over the passenger seat.

"Do you know how deep the water is here, Joe?"

"Its only about six feet deep here, but the channel's very deep. You know the dams keep the water depth in the channel at nine feet or more so the barges can go up and down the river. The dams make the river wider than it would normally be because they hold back the water in order to keep that depth. You see those buoys over there? They mark where the edge of the channel is on this side of the river. If you go outside of those buoys, you can run into shallow water."

Katie looked closely at Joe while he talked about the river. She admired the sharp features of his face and, she was impressed with what he knew. Larry never seemed to know anything and his eyes were definitely not as attractive as Joe's.

"How do you know so much about the river? she asked"

Joe slowly pushed the boat's acceleration lever forward and felt the power of the engine pulling the boat's stern down into the water.

"My dad and I fish out of another pool south of here, and my uncle has a small ski boat there. I learned to ski with my uncle," he responded. "See that barge coming down the river? The water will get real rough when we cross his wake. That's why we are going to go to the islands and find some backwaters to ski in. We'll find some place where we don't have to worry about those big guys."

Joe scanned the shores of the river and pointed out the beautiful homes that decorated the water line on both the Iowa and Illinois sides to Katie. He had fished in the two river pools further south, but he preferred this pool because of the turn the water made centuries ago when the river had forged its route, constantly pushing toward the Gulf of Mexico. The unique turn in the river caused people who were not familiar with the area to suffer some directional confusion because, at this location, the Mississippi River flows east to west for thirty miles before rushing back to its typical north-south flow. The east-west flow of the water is perfect for recreational boaters. The early morning sun rises up from the river and shines brilliantly on the waters of the "Mighty Mississip". Throughout the day, the sun positions itself directly over the channel, warming the water and adding sparkle to the array of ripples that dance back and forth across the river's powerful current. One of the most spectacular attributes of the east-west stretch is being out in the middle of the river at sunset and watching a brilliant, red sun slowly descend into the water as it changes the blue sky to pink.

Joe was looking forward to sunset. Sunset, in a boat, on the Mississippi River with Katie. He couldn't imagine that life could get any better than this.

"Hey, Katie," he said. "Open up the cooler and get us a beer, will ya?"

Katie grabbed two bottles from the cooler. She brushed the crushed ice away from the sides of the cold bottles, twisted the tops off, and handed one to Joe while taking a small sip from hers. She watched Joe lift the bottle to his lips, tilt his head back, and take a long swallow of the cold beer.

"Kinda early for beer, don't you think?" she asked.

"It's gotta be afternoon somewhere," Joe smiled. "Maybe it's afternoon in Paris or Rome? Let's pretend that we're there."

Katie stood up and faced the bow of the boat. She leaned forward on the windshield, letting a light spray of river water caress her face. She took another sip from her beer and turned around to look at Joe. He had shed his t-shirt and his tennis shoes and was wearing a blue swimsuit. His body was a deep tan from working outdoors at his dad's painting business. His long, black hair was being swept back by the wind. His chest and his shoulders were broad and encompassed in a muscular body. He was standing behind the wheel of the boat looking over the windshield, enjoying the blast of the wind, spray, and sun against his body.

"Yeah, Joe," she casually responded. "Let's do that. Let's pretend we're in Paris."

19

Katie reached out and pressed her cold bottle of beer against Joe's bare shoulder.

"I've never been to Paris. Maybe you can show me around?" she said.

Joe felt the chill of the bottle against his skin and smiled at Katie.

"Then Paris it is," he said. "But for our skiing, we'll stay on the *Mississip*."

For Joe, one of the great joys of life was being in a boat heading up river with the morning sun shining on his partially clad body. He knew such an outing on the river was an extravagance because the high-tech boats were expensive. Certainly he would not be able to do it if it were not for the Karvers' wealth or his uncle's generosity. Joe's dad was a hardworking painter who would not be able to afford such lavishness. Whenever Joe was able to be out on the river, he always wished that everyone could experience the wonder of it all. There was a magnificent, primitive feeling that engulfed boaters; a feeling of unabashed freedom and a oneness with nature. When he was on the river, he felt connected to all life forms and he always experienced a compulsion to strip naked and jump into the water, allowing it to surround and engulf him.

Joe's eyes scanned Katie's body, and he watched the wind whipping her blond hair around her long, brown neck. He wondered if she felt the same way as he did.

Maybe life could get better, he thought. Today I am a lucky man.

Joe was unaware of it, but this day on the river with Katie would define the rest of his life. It became what he wanted life to be.

Joe and Katie skied all afternoon. They played on the river and bumped into each other on the boat, laughing about their awkwardness and enjoying every clumsy moment. Each time they "accidentally" touched, the length of the moment became longer, breaking down the inhibitions that had made them just friends and drawing them closer. Katie's smile was enthralling, and Joe was enjoying being able to talk to her without any distractions. The river was theirs, and they made it their playground.

When evening approached, the setting sun shone brightly on the river, turning the murky Mississippi water a fiery red. Katie wanted to ski one more time before it got dark and Joe agreed. He stood backwards at the helm of the surging boat watching the tight ski rope lift Katie out of the water and then pull her along the top of the river. Katie skimmed effortlessly across the water, jumping back and forth over the boat's wake and waving at Joe. After fifteen minutes, she waved one more time and then let loose of the ski rope, causing her to sink slowly into the river. Joe circled the boat around and pulled along side of her as she bobbed up and down in the water.

He quickly moved to the stern and stood on the small rear deck of the idling boat as it swayed gently in the middle of the river.

"You look great on skis," Joe shouted to her. "But, let's get you outta there. It's getting too dark to be skiing."

Katie pushed the skis up out of the water to Joe and swam to the boat's ladder. Joe shoved the skis in a storage bin and reached for Katie's arm, pulling her up into the boat.

"Wow, that's fun!" she exclaimed. "The water is so smooth. It's like glass.

Katie was beaming with exhilaration and dripping wet. She unbuckled her life vest and dropped it on the deck of the boat. She picked up a towel, threw it in Joe's direction and pivoted on her bare feet, turning her back to him.

"Dry me off," she said.

Larry. That stupid bastard, Joe thought as he caught the towel and looked at Katie. *That stupid bastard.*

Joe rubbed Katie's hair roughly with the towel.

"You know…you got your hair all wet," he joked.

Katie pushed her head back against the towel and laughed.

"You don't like my hair, Joe?" she teased.

Joe moved the towel to Katie's slender shoulders and tenderly kissed the top of her head.

"Oh, I like your hair. I like your hair very much," he whispered.

Joe reached around Katie's slender waist and patted her tummy with the towel. He felt her body move back against him.

"You have a nice touch," she said.

Joe dropped the towel and tightened his arms around her body. He pulled her body close to him. He was strong and he stood a full head taller than Katie. He tenderly kissed her shoulders and his hands moved to caress her breasts. He felt her body tremble and heard her moan with delight as his fingers found her nipples. His hard body pressed against the wet bottom of Katie's swimsuit. She tilted her head upward, and their lips met briefly. Katie turned in Joe's arms, reached behind his head, and pulled his lips to hers. They kissed passionately; hungrily tasting each other until Katie gradually pulled away from Joe's lips and stepped back from him.

Her eyes steadily scanned the man standing in front of her. She smiled at him coyly and reached out to touch the bulge in his swimsuit. Her touch made him feel both dizzy and strong. His heart raced. He closed his eyes and gasped slightly as he felt his trunks being pulled off his hips. He opened his eyes and stepped out of his trunks while watching Katie gracefully peel her swimsuit from her body and drop the two pieces on the floor of the boat. She straightened up and stood naked in front of him. The sun was a blazing red fireball shining behind Katie, illuminating her beauty. She was a vision. She appeared to be a gift of the sun. Her young, tan body was athletic. Her legs and her arms were long. Her blond hair fell on her shoulders in tousled, wet strands. She smiled brightly and stared at Joe. She was confident and sure of herself.

"You know, Joe, sometimes Larry can be very stupid," she said moving slowly toward him.

Joe could not match Katie's calm composure. He rushed to embrace her. He lifted her up into his powerful arms and covered her lips with his as her body wrapped tightly around him.

Joe and Katie spent the rest of the evening making love. They made love on the boat and in the water and on the beach. They made love standing and sitting and lying down. Joe exhausted Katie and demanded more. Katie hurt, but felt good about it and always matched Joe's craving. The river rejuvenated them. The power of the river became their power; it surged wildly through their bodies. Their lust for each other flowed like the river. Nothing could stop their desire.

They made love the remainder of that summer, a time that became precious in Joe's memory. Whenever Larry would go out of town, they would steal away into their passionate, private world. Time together was limited for them, but they used it well. They made love all over the county – sometimes in Joe's house, sometimes in Katie's house, often in cars, and in motels; they made love under the stars, in the sunshine, and in the rain. Any time Joe saw Katie, he wanted her. There were times when they would meet while Larry was still in town working at his dad's store. There were hurried moments that were supposed to last only a few minutes, but were always extended longer by their lust. And there were those wonderful occasions when they spent their time in beds and in showers, hugging, kissing, sharing and looking at each other. Joe treasured those times the most. His focus was entirely on Katie. They were two lovers in a swirling universe, which empowered them with an explosive energy, energy they used to fuel the passion they felt for each other. Joe's desire for Katie never diminished. Nothing could match the excitement he felt when he and Katie were feverishly wrapped together. During those times, everything in the world disappeared. Only Katie existed for him, and he used the time to thoroughly explore her.

CHAPTER SIX

Katie's reaction to the time she was spending with Joe was quite different than the way he felt. Katie knew she was falling in love with him, and her feelings for Joe frightened her. She talked with Robin about her feelings after her skiing adventure. She continued to talk with Robin throughout the summer.

"I'm confused," Katie said as they sat sipping mid-afternoon beers at Governor's Tavern. "I don't know what to think."

"Joe's turning your heart, huh? I told you to be careful," Robin replied.

"Yeah, you did," Katie said with a distant look in her eyes.

Robin sighed and squeezed Katie's wrist gently.

"I'm sorry. I'm not rubbing it in, Katie. You got real problems, huh?"

"Yeah I do," Katie replied. "I got real problems."

Robin could see tears in Katie's eyes.

"What are you gonna do?" Robin asked.

"I'm gonna keep seeing Joe. You don't know how it is. When I'm with him, I just surrender. I love how he does…everything. And Robin…the guy does everything, and he never stops."

"You're right. I don't know how that is. Remember, I've got good ole Frank," Robin laughed. "Remind me again, why am I supposed to be feeling sorry for you?"

"Because this is a mess," Katie laughed in desperation. "I've got this hunk lover doing me, and I'm supposed to marry one of the richest guys in Kewanee."

Katie and Robin looked at each other and then burst out in laughter.

"You're right," Katie managed to say. "Why are you supposed to feel sorry for me?"

After controlling her laughter, Robin reached for Katie's hand.

"We've had one too many beers," she said. "But I do understand. What are you going to do? I mean we need to talk about this seriously."

Katie sighed and composed herself.

"Yeah, we do. I am going to see Joe more," she said. "I gotta give that a chance. I bond with him so intensely when we make love. And Joe…well, I know he feels it, too. I really like him. He's so different than everyone I hang around with."

"Joe's a man, Katie. I see it too," Robin said. "And he's a romantic man. That's very dangerous. Wherever he is right now, you can bet he's thinking about you."

Tears welled up in Katie's eyes again.

"Yeah, I know he is. I think of him, too. But God, he has messed up my plan."

"Did you ever think that your plan was not a very good one," Robin said.

"What do you mean?" Katie asked. "I thought we both had the same plan. Find a secure man…one who's blown over by us, and marry him. Wasn't that the plan?"

"I always thought it was kind of a dumb plan, especially when you put it that way!" Robin blurted out laughing again. "We need to think over the plan. Let's get another beer."

The girls laughed more and ordered two draft beers. They sat in momentary silence, waiting for the waitress to bring their drinks. They dared not look at each other for fear of laughing out loud or crying. After the waitress left their table, they both took a gulp of beer, and went back to discussing the men in their lives.

"Robin, you know what I mean by the plan," Katie said with a noticeable sigh. "Damn it, I admit the plan does sound shallow, doesn't it? Especially now…and Joe seems so…so…so…"

"So NOT shallow?" Robin interjected.

"Yeah, he's real and loving. He could hurt me. I can't let him do that."

"Maybe he wouldn't," Robin offered. "Maybe he'd stay with you always."

An expression of doubt came over Katie's face.

"Like a fairy tale prince, huh?" she responded sarcastically.

"There are guys like that. At least, I think there are. I admit I've never met one, but Joe's a gentleman. And Katie…keep this in mind…that plan was made when we were in high school. Haven't things changed for you by now?"

"Changed? How do you mean?"

"Listen, a lot of our so called friends in high school were jerks. I know we had some good times then and we hung with all the right people, but I gotta tell ya, I really never cared for a lot of those people and I got tired of sucking up to them. Who needs it and who needs them?"

"I don't know," Katie said. "I mean...yeah, you're right, but the thing is….I can't get hurt. Not again. I can't. But, I've got to think about it more and give it a little more time. I confess…I ache for Joe. I love being with him. I want to see him again."

At the end of that summer, Katie and Joe lay naked in bed. They were wrapped in each other's arms with Katie's warm body draped across Joe's broad chest. Her soft breasts pressed against Joe and he could feel her heart beating rapidly. His mind was filled with passionate images of the things that they had just accomplished. His eyes slowly scanned her body. He inhaled deeply through his nostrils in order to smell her fragrance. He used two fingers to gently follow the curvature of her spine up and down her smooth back. He felt her finger tenderly tracing a circle on his shoulder.

"Katie," he whispered. "I love you."

"I love you too, Joe," she softly replied.

"Katie. Why do you stay with Larry? Be with me."

Katie lifted her body up off of Joe's chest, bent down and gently kissed his ear. Her long, perfumed hair fell across his face. Then she laid her head on his shoulder.

"Joe," she said softly. "I'm engaged to Larry and I am going to marry him."

"Why Katie? Why?" Joe pleaded. "We love each other. Don't you like being with me more than him?"

"Larry will never leave me, Joe. Larry's a safe and secure man. I need that. I have to have that."

"Katie," Joe replied in hushed desperation. "I'm safe, too."

Katie's lips tenderly kissed Joe's chest.

"No, Joe," she said. "You are insatiable. I love you for that, but you are not safe and secure. Any man who can make love like you cannot be safe. Larry is safe…safe and secure."

Although Joe attempted to communicate with Katie again, that was the last time they made love.

Joe sighed as his mind slipped back into the present. His body collapsed into the jailhouse office chair. He shook his head, took a deep breath, and stared upward at the dark office ceiling.

God, I miss Katie, he thought. How can she be dead? There can't be anything to what Scott was saying. The case is closed. I gotta forget about it. I don't want to think about it anymore. But, what if Rogers' investigation of her death was sloppy. That damn Rogers is such a kiss ass…he could've messed it all up. I know he was in a big hurry to get a conviction just so he could please the sheriff and the Karvers. That Goddamn Rogers…I've never trusted that son of a bitch. Damn Scott for bringing all this up again. Damn him all to hell!

Joe felt tears welling up in his eyes. He got up out of the office desk chair, hoping the movement would break his current concentration. He knew he had to regain control of his emotions. He adjusted his jacket, rearranged some of the equipment hanging from his belt, and decided that he would go see Sheriff Armstrong to tell him what Scott had said.

CHAPTER SEVEN

S heriff Armstrong's office was part of a newly constructed jailhouse complex, which had been duped "the rat maze" by the deputies of the department. In order to get to the office, Deputy Lambert had to negotiate a labyrinth of hallways and then enter a large outer office space that contained a cadre of clerks, a large glass cage for dispatchers, and a reception area for anyone waiting to see the sheriff. The sheriff's main office was designed to be an inner sanctum, and access to it required that a person walk through a waist-high swinging gate in the middle of the outer office and then enter by way of a security door.

"Hey, everyone," Joe shouted out in a perfunctory manner as he entered the outer office area. "Hey, Joe," came the polite obligatory response from a smattering of office workers who then diligently returned to their work-a-day world.

Still hesitant to report what Scott had said, Joe decided to check on his mail before going in to see Sheriff Armstrong. He took a short, hard right and walked toward the office mailboxes. As he approached the mailboxes, his attention was drawn to thirty, bright-red, six-inch high letters painted conspicuously on the west wall of the office, which spelled out the motto of the Henry County Sheriff's Department: 'Protection, Service, and Dedication'. Below the motto, and painted in black, three-inch high letters was a chronological list of all the sheriffs who had served the county, along with the dates of their service.

Joe absent mindedly sorted through the collection of material in his mailbox while glancing at the record of service for all of the sheriffs.

You gotta give Armstrong credit, Joe thought. He took on the longest serving sheriff in the county and beat him in the primary election, and when he won the job, he hit the ground running. Mike's only been the sheriff for eight years, but he's a twenty-four/seven cop. He's done a lot for this department and I know he'll be elected sheriff again.

Deputy Lambert admired Armstrong's commitment to expanding the sheriff's department and was proud of the fact that in his seven years of service as a deputy, he had become the sheriff's right-hand man. He respected the sheriff's successful record of law enforcement, and he was hopeful the sheriff would be able to ferret out the causes for Scott's inebriated accusations. Joe wanted any doubts he had concerning the investigation and conviction in the murder of Katie Karver to be dispelled by Armstrong.

Dumping all but one piece of mail into the trash, Joe threw the remaining letter he had salvaged back into his mailbox, which he also used as a filing cabinet. He knew he would eventually throw the lone surviving letter away, too. But for now, he would keep it unopened in his mailbox just in case he later deemed the letter important enough to examine further.

Well, let's get this over with, he decided.

He turned away from the mailboxes and headed toward the sheriff's office. He knocked once on the sheriff's security door, which was constantly left ajar, and entered the office.

Sheriff Armstrong looked up from behind his cluttered desk, peering over the top of his reading glasses.

"Hey Joe," the sheriff said. "What can I do for you?"

"Hey, Sheriff. I just brought Scott Miller in and put him in a cell for overnight."

The sheriff removed his glasses and held them in his right hand. He leaned back in his chair and sarcastically stroked his chin with his left hand.

"Let me guess," the sheriff said. "Miller's drunk, right?"

"Yeah, of course," Joe confirmed. "But I got him before he was able to even start up his car. So, technically there's no DUI here."

"I hope Miller appreciates you, Joe. You know, he really is a pain in the ass. I know he's your friend and all, but he's a pain in the ass."

"I know, Mike. I know," Joe agreed. "But I didn't come here to plead his case or anything. I just wanted to tell you something Scott said to me when I was putting him up in his cell. It's nothing important, but I thought you should know about it."

Pointing to a stack of papers on his desk, the sheriff frowned slightly.

"I gotta tell you, deputy…this had better be good, cause I'm really not much interested in what comes out of Scott's head…and these papers are way overdue."

Armstrong placed his glasses down on his desk and rubbed his fingers through the stubble of his brown, crew cut hair.

"But, let's hear it. Tell me what Scott's been up to," he said.

Deputy Lambert proceeded to inform the sheriff about the rambling comments Scott had made just before he passed out in his cell.

"Well, it's like I said," Joe began. "I doubt that it's important. But, Scott made some comments about the Karver case. He's got it in his head that we arrested the wrong man. He even claims to have proof that someone else was involved."

Deputy Lambert was startled to see the sheriff's manner rapidly change as he revealed the conversation he had had with Scott. Quickly, the sheriff's face became contorted with anger and frustration. He got up out of his chair and pounded his fist down on the desk. He straightened his back and rose up to the full measure of his five-foot, eleven-inch frame. The sheriff was not a huge man, but his body was well proportioned from years of dedicated exercise.

"Miller, that son of a bitch!" the sheriff shouted. "How long has Scott been here? Do you know if he has talked with anyone else?"

Deputy Lambert stared at the sheriff, surprised by his outrage. Joe had always known Armstrong to be a quiet man who digested information slowly and had never responded to any news with such an outburst.

"Mike, slow down a little," he said. "He hasn't talked to anybody. I'm sure of that. I'm sure Scott's only talked with me."

The angry look on Sheriff Armstrong's face confused and alarmed Joe.

"I'm the only one who has seen him," he assured the sheriff again. "And he's drunk, you know. I doubt that Scott will even remember what he said."

The sheriff sat back down in his chair and exhaled heavily, attempting to release the demons that had taken away his normal tranquil demeanor. He was silent now, but Joe could tell that he was boiling inside. His hands were clasped tightly around an empty coffee cup and his body rocked nervously in his chair.

"Mike, you know we have all sorts of idiots in jail who are always making weird statements," Joe said. "Why should Scott be different?"

Joe tried to make eye contact with the sheriff as he spoke, but he could tell that Armstrong was oblivious to everything in the office. His mind seemed consumed by the information his deputy had just provided.

"I want that son of a bitch isolated," the sheriff said sternly. "I don't want him talking to anyone. You understand?"

The words seethed slowly out of the sheriff's mouth like volcanic steam. He did not look at his deputy; instead, his eyes were fixed on the wall behind Joe. The deputy was glad that he did not have to face the sheriff's glare.

"You see to it personally, Joe!" the sheriff ordered. "No one is to talk to that bastard except me. You understand?"

Instinctively, Joe came to a semi-attention stance in front of the sheriff's desk and immediately felt strange about it. He almost saluted the sheriff, but caught himself before doing it.

"I'll make sure of it, Mike," Joe promised. "Scott's sleeping off his drunk right now. When he wakes up, he'll be kept alone."

What's going on here? Joe wondered.

"No one is to talk to him. No one!" the sheriff repeated.

Armstrong stood up from his chair. He stared directly at the deputy.

"I'm trusting you on this, Joe. I'm going to drive over to the Geneseo football game. I'll be back in a couple hours and then I'll have a talk with Mr. Miller. You take care of him while I am gone. Just you!"

The sheriff's eyes locked on Joe's face and the deputy was caught in Armstrong's gaze. Joe did not like what he saw. Sheriff Armstrong looked worried and frightened. Joe wanted to put his hand on the sheriff's shoulder to comfort him, but he knew that was a very bad idea.

"I will take care of it, Mike," Joe said. "You can count on me. Always."

"I know I can, Joe," the sheriff said.

Sheriff Armstrong moved hurriedly from behind his desk, rushed passed Deputy Lambert, and disappeared out the office door.

That was odd, Joe thought. What the hell was going on there? Why is Mike so upset?

The deputy moved behind the sheriff's desk and reached for the phone. He dialed four-seven-four and waited as the inter-office phone system rang two times.

"Deputy Marshall," the voice of the watch commander responded.

"Bob, this is Joe. You know I put Scott Miller in cellblock C a little while ago?"

"Yeah. I just walked by there two minutes ago," Bob replied. "He's sleeping like a baby."

"Good," Joe said. "Just leave him alone and let him sleep it off. The sheriff's got a couple of questions to ask him when he wakes up, but I don't want him talking to anyone else. So don't put anyone in that cellblock. You understand?"

"Sure. Scott's never been any problem," Bob said. "We'll leave him alone until we hear from you guys."

Deputy Lambert hung the phone up and sat down in the sheriff's chair. The sheriff's desk was cluttered with a collection of papers, some needing filing and most needing to be dumped. Joe dutifully began to stack the papers into two piles with the largest stack being designated as trash. At the bottom of the clutter, he found a note written in the sheriff's handwriting. *Re-elect Sheriff Armstrong,* the note read. Below the slogan was a big question mark and the words, *why re-elect.* Joe picked the note up and stared at it.

This must be the reason why the sheriff is so jumpy about Scott running off at the mouth, Joe concluded. Its election time and he's worried about Jim Taylor running against him. Taylor really is his first serious opponent, and I know Taylor's an ambitious guy and getting a lot of funding from the Democrats. But Mike's done a helluva a good job these last eight years. I can't imagine him getting beat. Mike ought a know that.

Joe put the note back down on the desk and scrawled the following words at the bottom of the piece of paper, *because Sheriff Armstrong's the best law and order man in the state.* Below that he wrote, *the pile on your right should be trash, but you decide. I told Marshall to leave Scott alone.*

I wonder if Taylor could beat the sheriff, Joe thought as he looked at the note. Taylor's got a lot of experience, he sounds and looks good when he speaks, and he's got a lotta friends in the eastern part of the county, especially in Colona. That stuff Scott was saying is nonsense…has to be nonsense, but it would be dynamite if it were true. Can't be true though. Can't be. The sheriff will straighten it all out. I'll talk to him more about it after he's calmed down some.

Tired of thinking about what Scott had said and fearful the thoughts would immobilize him again, Deputy Lambert left the sheriff's office in search of company and work.

CHAPTER EIGHT

Sheriff Armstrong climbed into his squad car to make the short drive to Geneseo. He headed east, driving slowly through the streets of Cambridge. It only took three minutes to reach the edge of town where the sheriff was able to accelerate up to highway speed for two miles before having to turn north towards Geneseo on route 82. As his squad car glided along past corn and soybean fields, Armstrong reviewed how he had behaved in Joe's presence and he was immediately upset with his behavior.

Joe's a good man to have on board, the sheriff thought. He's intelligent, strong as a horse, and he's always been loyal to me. He's a good-looking kid, too. I was smart to take him under my wing. And it's been good for Joe, too. I know he looks up to me….kinda like a younger brother would. Joe's become a good cop. I knew he would work out well the first day I met him. Of course, there's such a thing as being too good of a cop. Hell, he should forget all that college training in psychology and sociology. He's always analyzing other people too much when he should look at some of his own weaknesses. His problem is he's too honest and has a big heart. He's too good of a guy to be in this line of work, but he's lucky to have a guy like me watching over him. Still…I gotta remember to apologize to him when I get back to the office. I shouldn't have flown off the handle like that. It's that goddamn Scott Miller's fault. It's hard to believe he and Joe were once so close. Miller is a worthless drunk. Joe should see that. I'll apologize when I get back. Shit, he's gotta know I've got a lot on my mind.

Just inside the Geneseo city limits, the sheriff spotted two huge John Deere tractors parked in an empty lot next to McDonald's. A large sign supporting the Geneseo football team had been erected between the two tractors. The sign read *Beware! Green Machine Country! Go Leafs!*

Should be a helluva a game, the sheriff thought.

Geneseo football is a sacred institution in western Illinois, and Sheriff Armstrong was proud to be a part of it. The football team, known as the Green Machine, routinely mows down their opponents. Attendance and enthusiasm at Friday night home football games rivals anything that can be found in Texas. Hundreds of adults would be attending this first game of the season and, with a dependability that is often a mark of middle-class rural areas, ninety-five percent of the adults in attendance would be voters.

The sheriff parked his squad car inside the steel, wire fence, which surrounded the football stadium. The parked squad car was a noticeable reminder to the crowd of the sheriff's presence. And while the squad car announced the sheriff's attendance to everyone seated in the stands, Armstrong personally worked the football crowd by shaking as many hands as possible.

During his eight years in office, the sheriff had become a consummate politician and this election year was of utmost importance to him. Nine years ago he successfully unseated his predecessor in the Republican primary. Back then, Armstrong had only been in law enforcement for twelve years. In order to unseat the former sheriff, Armstrong's campaign message had stressed that he was a fresh face with new ideas. Once he had been elected sheriff, he initiated a number of new policies in the sheriff's department. Winning the upcoming election would be a stamp of approval for his ideas and would signal a permanency for the personal brand he had placed on the department. And Armstrong felt certain that success in this election would catapult him into a life-long career as the Sheriff of Henry County. It was his dream to stay in office longer than any other sheriff. Being a visible presence at the fall football games was part of the sheriff's re-election strategy.

It was getting close to kick-off time for the varsity game and a large crowd of fans streamed into the stadium, sweeping by Sheriff Armstrong, waving as they passed. It was time to start campaigning.

"No problems tonight, folks. Our backfield is fast and this Chicago team has no discipline," the sheriff said to a group of enthusiastic fans.

"Those guys will never get through our defensive line," he shouted while patting the back of a parent of one of the players.

"Hey, Sheriff Armstrong! Thanks for coming to watch our son play," a grateful parent hollered.

"Hope you got some emergency vehicles ready just in case some of those Chicago city boys need medical assistance," another parent kidded to the sheriff.

"There won't be enough equipment to handle what our boys will be mowing down tonight," Armstrong joked back.

As usual, the Friday night football scene was filled with hoopla. Booster clubs hawked everything from Green Machine blankets to food and chances to win a Chrysler convertible. The fans screamed incessantly over victorious plays, bad referee calls, and coaching mistakes. Cheerleaders bounced up and down and squealed with delight each time a small Geneseo cannon shot off a blast, trumpeting a Green Machine touchdown. The one hundred members of the high school band, splendidly dressed in green and white uniforms, beat drums and sounded horns to recognize the successes of the home team. Their music blared in concert with the blast of the cannon, the squealing of the cheerleaders, and the roar of the excited fans.

Armstrong decided to stay at the game through half-time; doing so would give him another opportunity to work the crowd, which spilled out of the stands in search of popcorn, hotdogs, pork sandwiches, and a change to rehash how the high school football coaches had done in the first half of the game.

"I know we'll be going to state with these players," Sheriff Armstrong commented as four men approached him.

Doug Bennett reached out and shook the sheriff's hand.

"Yeah, they're great," Doug said. "They're always great, but the coach should have Murphy playing in the backfield. I know the guy's big, but he's fast too, and he'd do a lot better than Kent."

"Well…yeah," the sheriff agreed. "Murphy's a tremendous athlete. He's got a lot of talent, that's for sure."

The sheriff looked at the four men and noticed a slight, uncomfortable pause in the sports banter. It was obvious the men had more on their minds than Friday night high school football.

"If you've got a minute, Sheriff, I want to introduce some of my neighbors," Doug Bennett said. "We want to talk to you about the quarry expansion on Wolf Road."

"Sure, Doug. I was wondering how people out your way felt about expanding the quarry," the sheriff replied.

"We don't like it, Sheriff," the man standing next to Doug blurted out. "How would you like a rock quarry sitting one hundred yards from your home with those goddamn huge piles of rock blocking your view?"

"And you know, Sheriff," another man chimed in, "the quarry owners are also asking the county for a special use permit so they can build an asphalt plant up on top of the ridge. That thing's gonna stink to high heaven and be as noisy as a steel mill!"

"We don't want to live in a home that sits downwind from an asphalt plant!" Doug declared. "No one said anything about this when we were buying our homes out here. Quiet countryside. Clean air. Good schools. That's how they sold us on moving here. This expansion idea isn't fair to us homeowners."

"You're at the county seat every day, Sheriff," a man in the back of the small group said. "You know the county board members and the zoning people. We want someone to talk to them and let them know how we feel."

For the next fifteen minutes, the scoreboard clock ran down the seconds left in halftime, and as the clock ticked away, Sheriff Armstrong found himself trapped in the middle of a growing crowd of voters sternly objecting to the quarry's expansion plans and demanding that he support their opposition to the project. The sheriff's normal Friday night working of the happy football crowd had turned into a disaster. After being assaulted by one complaint after another, the sheriff attempted to sooth the apprehensions of the aggravated group of men.

"You guys know I'll do what's right here," he declared. "I'm glad to hear from all of you about this issue. You can be sure that I'll be looking into this expansion idea. I got a letter from River Bend on my desk right now asking me to examine what impact their expansion plan will have on road safety. Me and a couple of my deputies are going out there tomorrow to make some measurements on the roads. I'm concerned about how the intersection of Wolf Road and Cleveland Road will be affected by this idea. A lot of school busses go by there in the morning and in the early afternoon. I can't promise anything right now, but I'll let you know how it turns out."

"I'll tell you, Sheriff, you're right about the traffic," Doug affirmed. "All that truck traffic out there colliding with school busses and commuters is gonna be a mess. You look into it and we'll be waiting to see what's gonna happen. We want some help on this thing. We don't want any rock quarry in our front yards."

CHAPTER NINE

The rock quarry in Henry County was a product of geological evolution, and geology had been good to most of Illinois' 102 counties. Five hundred million years ago, a primordial, shallow sea covered the area that would become the State of Illinois. Simple organisms lived and died in the ancient waters, causing the sea floor to become a fossil graveyard, which, over enormous spans of time, resulted in the formation of thick layers of limestone. As the ancient seas receded, dense tropical swamps grew and fell for millions of years, leaving rotted vegetation strewn under the prehistoric land. Time and compression turned the massive piles of vegetation into vast sheets of coal that are buried twenty-five to one thousand feet below the surface. The rich veins of coal stretch for three hundred and fifty miles from northern Illinois to the Ohio River.

Above the surface of the land, other powerful forces worked to mold Illinois' geological future. For one million, six hundred and fifty thousand years, four distinct Ice Ages covered Illinois with enormous frozen mountains. The advance and retreat of the glaciers flattened the terrain, allowing for the development of wide prairies and the eventual growth of abundant timberland. Ten thousand years ago, the glaciers made their last retreat, leaving Illinois at the mercy of massive dust storms that dropped a deep layer of mineral-rich topsoil across the land.

The richness of the soil attracted settlers who began to arrive in the area in 1720. The settlement of Illinois accelerated when an act of Congress promised frontier land to any American male who volunteered to fight the British in the War of 1812. The congressional act produced the requisite volunteer militia and resulted in a massive influx of settlers into the Illinois territory. In 1818, the territory was organized into the 21st state to enter the national union. But taming the Illinois frontier was not easy, and early attempts by Americans to settle on the land resulted in a number of conflicts with the indigenous Pottawatomie, Winnebago, Sauk, and Fox Indians tribes. The issue over who would control the land was settled when the Indians were defeated in the Black Hawk Wars of 1832 and forced to move west of the Mississippi River.

Henry County, Illinois, was officially formed in 1837 and is located near the northwestern edge of the state's boundary line. The county is no exception to the benefits the entire state derived from its geological history. Henry County's 5.4 million acres of land is blessed with a fertile layer of topsoil, which has won world acclaim for is productivity. The fruitful soil of Henry County is on par with rare, high-quality farmland that can only be found in Argentina, the Ukraine, and the Yellow River Valley of China.

Eighty-seven percent of Henry County's land is used for agricultural purposes, which has kept the county's population prosperous and small. The 1870 census registered a population of 37,506 people. When the 21st century arrived, 50,644 souls called Henry County their home. The smallest village in the county has a population of 125. The largest city holds a mere 13,000 inhabitants. The people of Henry County are proud of the county's rural nature, and they are adamant about protecting their rural style of life.

The Henry County Board of Directors – the County Board – is also sensitive to the interests of the agricultural community and is protective of the county's rich topsoil. Any plans to rezone property from agricultural to residential or commercial use are scrutinized by the county's Building and Zoning Commission and the Planning and Development Committee. The twenty-four members of the County Board often vote down schemes that would substitute the agricultural use of the land for other commercial adventures.

One of the biggest and oldest commercial industries in the county is the River Bend Cleveland Rock Quarry. Limestone blocks from the quarry area were used to build the Henry County Courthouse in 1880, and the quarry was officially opened as a gravel pit in 1927. The quarry is located on the northern edge of the county's border and is a notable exception of the desire to keep the county land tillable and void of heavy commercial development. The quarry's survival is a consequence of the vital services in crushed rock it provides to the area. Aware of the negative images a rock quarry can create in the minds of its neighbors, the quarry's corporate owners annually distribute a brochure that proclaims the continual need for the quarry's existence.

The most recent commercial enterprise in Henry County is the booming housing industry. "Where People Long To Be", is the motto of the Henry County Tourism Bureau. Housing developers plaster the motto throughout their advertisements and promote Henry County as a haven for people who want to escape the large metropolitan area that exists in neighboring Rock Island and Scott counties. Henry County's ninety-seven percent white population and its prosperous median household income are subtle, delicate sirens that also help to beckon new homebuyers. The wooded hills, which border the vast farms of the county, have become subdivisions inhabited by middle-class families, who are glad to enroll their children in the county's rural, homogeneous schools. To the delight of the subdivision developers, the rock quarry was located in a heavily wooded area at the bottom of a valley that had been carved out over thousands of years by the steady flow of the Rock River. The quarry's inconspicuous location kept its operation noiseless and invisible.

But now the delicate mix of farmland, subdivisions, and the rock quarry was about to become an explosive issue for the residents of Henry County. The owners of the quarry, River Bend Quarries Incorporated, proposed that fifty-nine acres of agricultural land be rezoned as commercial so that the quarry operations could be expanded to the top of the valley. They also requested two special use permits be granted by the county. One of the special use permits would allow River Bend to store piles of crushed rock on the newly rezoned land, and the other special permit would allow them to build an asphalt plant on four acres of the land.

The fifty-nine acres of land are located one hundred yards east of the Barker Housing Addition and just twenty yards north of Billy Wolf Road. Billy Wolf Road is the main corridor for most of the commuters who purchased homes in the county's recently developed bedroom communities. The commuters enjoy driving through the tranquil countryside on their way to and from work. But if River Bend had its way, they would be forced to drive by a very different scene. Farmland and gently rolling hills were to be torn up and replaced with ten, forty-two foot high piles of crushed rock and an asphalt plant. The quarry's expansion plans were threats to the aesthetic nature of the land, and nearby homeowners believed the expansion threatened the real estate value of their property.

The football fans, who were confronting Sheriff Armstrong during the halftime activities, were homeowners who lived near the proposed quarry expansion site.

CHAPTER TEN

T he score at the beginning of the third quarter of the football game was typical for the Green Machine; Geneseo was three touchdowns ahead of their opponents. Sheriff Armstrong knew it would be politically safe to leave the team in the hands of the hometown fans. He decided to head back to his office in Cambridge.

Driving south on route 82, the sheriff pondered the new information he had received during halftime. Of course he had heard of plans to expand the quarry, but he had not anticipated this degree of opposition to the project. He speculated that the grumbling he heard at the game was just the tip of the iceberg, and he wished that the issue had waited until after the election. Armstrong wanted this race for office to be a carefree and sweeping victory that would affirm his record as a superior law enforcement officer.

Damn! I wonder what my worthy opponent's stand is on this issue, the sheriff thought.

As he turned his squad car west and drove into the Village of Cambridge, the sheriff saw the first yard sign supporting the man who was running against him. *Time For a Change! Jim Taylor for Sheriff* the sign read.

That son of a bitch has already started campaigning, Sheriff Armstrong said to himself. Time for a change my ass!

Armstrong made a mental note of the home that displayed the sign and then vowed to swamp Taylor's puny campaign effort with a thousand yard signs of his own.

I'll take care of this Miller thing first, he thought. And then, I'll light a fire under my campaign workers to blanket the county with my signs. That goddamn Taylor'll wish he never took me on.

The sheriff parked his squad car behind the jailhouse and while walking toward the entrance to his office, he reminded himself to apologize to Joe. Entering the outer office complex that surrounded his office, the sheriff motioned to one of the dispatchers.

"Tell Joe that I want to see him right away."

Four minutes later, Deputy Lambert knocked twice on the sheriff's door, opened the door, and walked inside.

"How was the game, Mike?" Joe asked.

"Well, there were a lot of voters there, and Geneseo was way ahead when I left. Those are two things I like to see in a local football game," the sheriff replied. "I see you cleaned up my desk for me. Anything new here that I should know about?"

"Nah. Everything's been quiet. Hey speaking of voters, I see Taylor has some signs up out on Smith Street. He's kinda early on that, don't you think?"

"In an election year, you can never be too early," Armstrong countered. "I saw that damn sign too. It's in Baker's yard. Time for a change my ass! What the hell did I ever do to Baker? Baker ever complained to you about anything I've done?"

"Nope. I've never heard him complain," Joe replied. "But, you can't please everybody, Mike."

"Yeah well, I don't want to please all of 'em….just eighty-nine percent. Oh say, you took care of Miller, right?"

"I did," Joe responded, ignoring the political comment. "He's sleeping right now. I told the guards to leave him alone. What're you going to do with him? You don't believe any of his bullshit, do you?"

"No, Joe, I don't. But as the sheriff, I have an obligation to check his story. Sorry I got so upset. I have a lot of things on my mind…you know with the election and all. I don't need Miller babbling nonsense all over Kewanee. Hell, the Karver Case is one of the top achievements of this office. We don't need a drunk taking that away from us. Right, Joe?"

"Sure, Mike. I understand. You're right. Want me to release Scott?"

"No. I'll check him out first. More than likely he'll be leaving here after he sleeps off his drunk. The man is worthless. He'll just go get drunk again. Someday we will be scooping him up off the highway. Why don't you go home? Get some sleep. You look tired."

"Yeah, I could use some rest," Joe agreed. "And I know you're right about Scott. My problem is I still see him as a high school boy. But, I don't take anything he says seriously. Scott's a good guy though."

"He still is a high school boy," the sheriff said. "You grew up. He didn't. I see it all the time. Still, when he makes comments about a murder case, I gotta at least talk to the guy. I'll talk with Scott in his cell, but I'm sure it's nothing."

"I expect you're right," Deputy Lambert said. "Well, I'll see you tomorrow. Don't stay too late, Mike. You've already spent over ten hours here."

"Hey, I know how many hours I've been here," Armstrong shot back. "Christ, what are you, my wife? But, let me ask you one more thing before you leave. Have you heard anything about the quarry expansion? I mean have you heard people talking about it?"

Deputy Lambert stood holding onto the sheriff's open door with a thoughtful look on his face.

"You know I live pretty far away from the quarry," he said. "But, I did hear a couple of guys talking about the expansion while I was having a beer with Harlo at Bud's Tap. They weren't happy about the quarry getting so close to Wolf Road. Those guys kept calling the idea a blight. You know how everyone sees the western end of Billy Wolf as the entrance to God's Country. But, that was just a couple of guys talking in a bar."

"Let me tell ya, a bar's a good place to find out what people are thinking," the sheriff replied. "But thanks, Joe. If you hear any more about the quarry issue, let me know. It's an election year and I gotta stay on top of everything."

"Hell, Mike, the voters love you. You know that. The only way you could get beat is if someone has some lewd pictures of you," Joe said, laughing. "They don't, do they?"

"If anyone's gonna get caught with lewd pictures, it'd be you," the sheriff fired back. "You're the only single guy in this office, deputy. Now get home before I arrest you for insulting an officer of the law."

"You're not really worried about Taylor are you, Mike? I mean, I know he has lots of experience in law enforcement. But come on, Mike…you won the last two elections with sixty-eight percent of the vote. No one could beat you."

"Yeah well, that's just when a guy should worry. Anything that seems like a sure thing is trouble."

Sheriff Armstrong leaned back in his chair, cupping both of his hands behind his head. A reflective mood appeared on his face.

"You know, Joe, I think that's how I won this sheriff's badge. Hell, my predecessor was in this office for 28 years, that's seven terms of office. He was in this job longer than any other sheriff. Everybody's always telling me what a great sheriff he was, and I know he wanted to be elected to an eighth term of office. But, he got complacent. He didn't expect a primary election challenge and he wasn't ready for it. 28 years is a long time, but I beat him and I'm gonna beat his record. I'm never gonna take anything for granted. Some people called me ruthless when I took on my "icon" predecessor, but ya gotta always be ruthless when you're campaigning for office, and ya gotta always protect your ass. There's lots a people out there just waiting for me to make a mistake, but that's not gonna happen to me. I'll be the most successful sheriff this county has ever seen."

The sheriff tilted his chair forward and dropped his hands back down on his desk. The reflective mood that had provided a brief insight into the sheriff's private ambitions quickly disappeared from his face.

"Now you go home, Joe," he said. "Get out of here and get some rest."

"Alright Mike. See you tomorrow," Joe called out as he departed.

Deputy Lambert left the jailhouse complex and walked directly to the deputy's parking area. He stood by the side of his squad car and purposefully took time to admire the ornate marble trim that wrapped around the top of the large 19th century courthouse building. Then he climbed into his car and pulled out of the jailhouse parking lot.

Could Mike be right about me growing up, Joe wondered. Sometimes I wonder if I did grow up. I'm not a drunk like Scott, but I did buy the same house that I grew up in. And the sheriff's right, I don't have a family. All I do is take care of myself…that's not grown up.

CHAPTER ELEVEN

J oe's drive back to Kewanee from work was a thirty-six minute journey. Two months ago, he took the time to figure out that he had driven this route five thousand times over the last seven years. He had calculated the total driving time to be over three thousand hours. Initially, when he had been hired on as a deputy, he thought of ways to make the driving time more productive. He decided to look at one of those foreign language tapes and use his driving time to learn Spanish. He had even gone shopping and purchased a tape entitled *How to Learn Spanish in Thirty* Days. The tape had been sitting inside of a blue plastic Wal-Mart bag on a closet shelf in Joe's house ever since the date of purchase.

In the end, what Joe would do with his driving time was settled not by any philosophical wrenching of the soul or by any desire to improve his life; instead, he forgot about the issue and simply settled into a routine. While going to work, he would organize his thoughts concerning the upcoming day's challenges. On the way home, he would use the time to unwind and to reflect upon his life. Now he was driving east, heading home toward Kewanee on Illinois 81, and it was time to reflect.

I guess I've done better in life than Scott, Joe decided. I've got an associate's degree in law enforcement. I'm a good cop and a responsible person. Robin always says I'd make a good catch as a husband. And Robin's a smart cookie. I trust her judgment.

Robin Karlson was a classmate of Joe's and had been Katie Karver's best friend. Robin's maiden name was Thompson, but she became Mrs. Robin Karlson when she married a man who taught economics in the Rock Island School District. Robin had obtained an associate nursing degree from Black Hawk College, and she was a health care assistant for Trinity Hospital where she was considered to be a valuable and reliable employee. The Karlsons had purchased a home in a subdivision of houses that were affordable starter homes. Robin's husband, Frank, was a frugal man who saved their money in order to buy a new home. The Karlsons were beginning the process of settling down, but Robin did have a wild streak in her, which was manifested during her college days.

As college students, Robin and Joe would go drinking during the weekends. They always made sure to look out for each other when they caroused in the bars. They were good drinking buddies, and they had set a goal to drink in all of the popular bars in the area. Joe liked having a woman to talk with, and he loved being seen with Robin. She was pretty, and it felt good to walk into a bar with her. Robin liked Joe, too. She liked being able to tease him and grab at his ass without having to worry about him coming on to her. If it had not been for Katie, Joe would have pursued Robin. If it had not been for Katie, Robin would have pursued Joe. Katie had brought them together and had kept them apart. They had both loved her, and they were the only two people with whom Katie had dropped her guard and allowed them to know her.

After they both graduated from Black Hawk, Robin and Joe remained friends, and they made it a habit of keeping in touch by meeting in some of the old haunts they frequented in their college days.

"Why don't you find a girl and get hitched?" Robin asked Joe the last time they had caught up with each other. "Any woman would be lucky to have you. You still have a great ass."

Robin and Joe were seated at a small table, sipping beers on an outdoor tavern patio in Moline, Illinois. Joe stretched his neck, bent his torso sideways, and looked around the table.

"You still have a great ass, too," he said leering at Robin, who was sitting on a decorative wrought iron chair.

"You can't tell what my ass looks like while I'm sitting down," she laughed.

Joe flashed a complimentary smile at Robin.

"I checked you out when you walked in here," he replied. "I always look at your ass."

Robin rolled her eyes back and shook her head. Her full, chestnut brown hair gently swirled around her long neck.

"You need a woman. I am going to have to find you one if you don't get busy," she said while acknowledging Joe's compliment with her own radiant smile.

"Problem is…all the good ones are taken," he said while touching the wedding ring on Robin's hand. "For sure the two best have been taken."

"The problem is you can't get over Katie," Robin teased.

Taking a sip of cold beer and peering over the mug, Robin saw the expression on Joe's face sadden. She immediately regretted making the comment and reached to hold his hand.

"I'm sorry. I shouldn't have said that. I know Katie meant a lot to you," she said in an apologetic tone. "You know what, Joe? You're too nice of a guy. That's the real problem. Hey, do you ever see Larry?"

"He moved to Phoenix. Let's forget about all of that," Joe said while he held onto Robin's hand. "Tell me about this new house you guys are building."

Robin avoided Joe's question. "Whatever happened to you and Shayna? I thought that was going somewhere."

"It did. It went nowhere. We almost got engaged, but...I don't' know...I wanted something else."

"I promise I won't bring it up again, Joe...not unless you ever want to talk about it. But just so you understand, I know what you want. You want someone like Katie."

Robin gripped Joe's hand firmly and felt her eyes becoming moist. She was the only person who knew about Katie and Joe.

Joe laughed defensively and squeezed her hand.

"I'll make a promise, too," he said. "You tell me about the new house you're building, and I'll buy all of the rounds."

Joe saw Robin about four times a year. In the winter, he would meet her for a couple of drinks at a tavern that had a huge fireplace, and they would sit by the hearth drinking and chatting. In the summer, they met at a tavern on the river that had an outdoor patio where they would sit and watch the sun fall into the water while they drank and joked with each other. When they first started meeting, Robin would bring Frank with her, but after two such meetings, Frank informed her that he did not enjoy Joe's company.

"Hey, three's a crowd," Frank told Robin the last time she invited him along. "Why don't you just go by yourself?"

"You don't mind? I mean if it really bothers you, I wouldn't have to meet him at a bar. I guess if some of your friends saw me with Joe, they might become suspicious," Robin speculated. "I mean, Joe is just a good friend, but he's pretty good looking too."

"Yeah right," Frank replied. "Joe's a small time cop from Cambridge. Big deal. He doesn't even have a real college degree."

"Joe graduated from Black Hawk, and he has an associate's degree in law enforcement," Robin shot back defensively. "He's a smart guy, and he lives in Kewanee, not Cambridge. I graduated from Black Hawk too, you know."

"I know you did and I'm proud of you," Frank said. "But did Joe have a four-point average in college? Did he get a bachelor's degree in three years? I did. Is he working on his master's in economic theory? Who would think that you would choose a guy like that over me? Come on Robin...I know he's just a friend from your past. Enjoy seeing him. Soon you'll get tired of it," he smugly stated. "Plus, I've got a lot of important things to do."

Robin knew she should have been upset with Frank's reply, but instead she felt a sense of relief. She did like seeing Joe. He always made her feel important and special. More and more she understood that the most special thing in Frank's life was Frank. Initially she had been attracted to him because he seemed so confident, but in living with him she discovered she had been mistaken. She now believed Frank was an egotistical man who hid behind his arrogant nature, afraid to expose himself to the world. Frank was a coward, and he used the inflated sense he had of himself to hide that fact. In the end, they agreed that Robin would see her old friend, alone, and Frank would find something else to do on those evenings.

Joe also preferred meeting Robin without Frank present. He did not like crowds and he had decided he did not like Frank. He did enjoy listening to Robin talk about her life though. He envied the fact that she had found a mate and settled down, but he noticed she avoided talking about Frank except to say that he was busy and often gone during the evenings. To keep herself busy, she belonged to a local YMCA and participated in a number of sports leagues that were associated with her work place.

Robin liked listening to Joe, too, and she always enjoyed flirting with him and watching him laugh. Often she wondered what would have happened if she had met him before he had known Katie.

After they gulped down their fourth round of drinks, Robin confessed that she was tipsy.

"I can't go home like this, Joe," Robin confessed. "And neither one of us should drive. We better go for a walk along the river, or it will be the jail-house for us."

"Oh oh, I don't wanna be locked in a cell with you," Joe laughed.

He pushed back his chair and stood up.

"After all, if I was locked up in a cell with you, who would protect my ass?"

Robin put one arm around Joe's waist and snuggled up against him as they walked out into the warm summer night, heading toward an asphalt path that wound its way along the south bank of the Mississippi River. Walkers, runners, bikers, and roller bladers shared the walkway with them as they strolled west toward the setting sun.

Joe affectionately kissed the top of Robin's head and softly whispered into the night air.

"Ever wonder what would have happen if we had met each other before we knew Katie? Do you ever wonder that, Robin?"

Robin pulled Joe closer.

"Yeah, sometimes I wonder about that," she replied.

Robin stopped walking, turned toward Joe, and kissed his cheek. She caressed his rugged, handsome face with her soft fingers and peered into his dark eyes. Joe placed his strong arms around her long body. He held her gently at a distance with his hands resting on her slender hips. His face beamed with a warm smile.

"You're quite a temptation, Deputy Lambert," Robin purred. "I admit that my timing was way off on meeting you."

She tenderly thumped Joe's nose with her index finger.

"But, I guess I'm lucky," she continued. "I did marry a safe man."

Joe frequently thought of Robin on his drive home. Today he laughed quietly to himself while remembering Robin's comment about Frank being a safe man.

As he entered the outer western boundaries of Kewanee, he slowed his car down to comply with the Kewanee speed limit.

What's a guy have to do to be safe, Joe wondered. You always hear about girls being attracted to bad boys. Seems like all of the girls I care about want safe guys. You would think a man who became a cop, bought his parents' home, and lives with a cocker spaniel would be safe enough. What the hell am I doing wrong?

CHAPTER TWELVE

Deputy Neil Rogers stood next to a splintered and broken guardrail that up until now had curved along highway 81. He watched his patrol partner, Deputy Thomas, carefully making his way down the side of a steep hill, inching his way toward the driver's side of an overturned car.

"See anybody in the vehicle?" Deputy Rogers called out.

The car sat mangled and torn at the bottom of a deep crevice. A trail of tattered turf and uprooted brush marked the car's reckless path. The vehicle had plunged seventy-five yards through some heavy undergrowth only to be abruptly stopped and flipped over when it crashed headlong into a small tree. Both the car and the tree had been losers in the deadly impact.

Earlier that morning, Deputy Thomas was finishing his third shift detail, when he spotted the car off of the highway. A late August sun had just risen and its rays were piercing through a humid, midwestern morning sky.

Son of a bitch! It's going to be hot as hell today, and now I'll be climbing down that damn hill, Thomas said to himself when he first spotted the car.

Thomas dutifully radioed Deputy Rogers for assistance and waited for him to arrive on the scene. Rogers arrived in less than five minutes and immediately assigned Deputy Thomas the task of climbing down to the wreck.

"Yeah, I see the driver," Thomas shouted back up the hill. "You were right. It's Miller. You'd better get down here."

"Coming," Rogers shouted back. "Wait for me and don't touch anything."

"Looks like he's been here a couple of hours," Deputy Thomas noted when Rogers approached the overturned vehicle.

Deputy Thomas rested both of his hands on his hips and stared up the steep embankment toward the broken guard railing.

"Maybe the sheriff was wrong in letting Scott out so early," he said.

Deputy Rogers took off his sunglasses, tucked them in his front shirt pocket and stared at the wreckage. Scott Miller's crumbled body was sprawled across the top of the overturned car's passenger compartment.

"It's not easy to know when to release a drunk," Rogers said. "But, I do know two important things about this accident."

"What's that?" Thomas asked.

"Well, one. It's a long way down here from the road. It must have been one helluva a ride Scott took. And two," Rogers said firmly poking his index finger into Deputy Thomas' shoulder. "You had better keep your mouth shut about questioning the sheriff's judgment. Sheriff Armstrong doesn't make mistakes."

"I know that," Deputy Thomas shot back. "Anyway, Scott must have tied another one on right after he left the jail. He wasn't one for letting much time elapse in-between his drinking. He drank more than anyone I've ever seen."

Thomas walked around to the other side of the vehicle and peeked into the car through the busted passenger-side window.

"Scott wasn't wearing his seat belt," he said out loud. "Wooee, Scott!" Thomas exclaimed in a hopeless conversation with the deceased. "How many times have I told you to wear your seatbelt? You drink way too much to be out on the road without a seatbelt."

Rogers knelt down and pressed two fingers against Scott Miller's jugular vein. He felt only coldness as he moved his hand to the lifeless man's chin and turned Scott's face upward. He stared momentarily into the dead man's face, then let Scott's head slip back down onto the ceiling of the car.

"Yep, and drinking killed him," Rogers said. "Looks like this was the weapon of choice."

Deputy Rogers held up a half-empty bottle of whiskey to show Thomas.

"It smells like a brewery in there."

"Guess I missed the bottle," Thomas confessed. "Well, Scott's long past giving advice to. Let's get the wrecker and the coroner out here to clean up this mess. And, someone should tell Joe. Scott and Joe were good friends in high school."

Deputy Rogers dropped the whiskey bottle in a plastic bag and moved away from the wreckage. He pulled his sunglasses out of his shirt pocket and pushed them back against his sweaty face.

"Yeah, I'll tell him," Rogers replied. "Joe is living in his parents' old house, right?"

"Yeah, that's right. I can go with you if you want. He may take this hard."

"That's OK," Rogers replied. "I can tell him…but first I'll tell the sheriff. The sheriff has to be the first to know. Chain of command, Thomas. Always follow the chain of command."

The two deputies made their way back up the hill and got into their separate vehicles. While Thomas sat in his squad calling for assistance, Rogers used a cell phone to call Sheriff Armstrong. The sheriff's cell phone rang at 7:05 a.m. Sheriff Armstrong had worked late the night before and was still in bed, but he was not asleep.

"Morning Sheriff" Rogers calmly said. "Hope I didn't get you out of bed."

Deputy Neil Rogers had been with the sheriff's department for six years. Rogers' had quickly learned how to keep legal bullshit from hampering good police work, but he always made sure to protect himself and the sheriff's office. His written reports were pieces of art that were envied by other deputies and admired by prosecutors. Rogers had a way of obtaining the right results, and he always made his investigation stick. The sheriff considered him an efficient, level-headed man.

With the exception of Deputy Lambert, Sheriff Armstrong normally maintained a sensible distance between himself and his deputies. But over the years, he began to allow Rogers to be a little less formal with him, too. The sheriff knew Rogers was a suck up, but throughout the years they had both benefited from their relationship. Although nothing was ever said between them, Rogers and Armstrong had an understanding; what was good for one of them was good for both.

"You know I'm in bed, Neil," Sheriff Armstrong growled. "Cut the crap and tell me why I'm hearing your voice so early in the morning."

"Thomas and me just found Scott Miller," Rogers reported. "His car was at the bottom of a drop off on Illinois 81. You know…that curve just before heading into Kewanee? You know where I mean?"

"Yeah, I know," the sheriff replied.

"Scott's dead. It was an accident," Rogers continued. "I'm sure the tox report will make it a DUI. I found an open bottle of Seagram's in Miller's car. Just wanted to keep you informed."

"Too bad," the sheriff replied. "I guess we all knew it would happen someday. Miller drank his life away. You write up the report, Neil. I want to see it when I get to the office, and I want that report flawless. Oh, and I want you to call on Joe and let him know about the accident. Joe liked Scott."

"I'll take care of everything, Sheriff." Rogers said. "See you at the office."

Sheriff Armstrong placed his cell phone back on the nightstand next to his bed. He sat up on his elbows and looked at the glaring red numbers on the digital clock.

7:06 a.m.

The sheriff laid his head back onto his pillow and listened to the slow breathing of his wife, who was laying in their bed less than twelve inches away from him. She had slept through the whole conversation, exercising a talent she had acquired during Armstrong's first term of office. The sheriff's sleeping patterns were irregular, and she had learned to adjust to them without jeopardizing her own need for rest.

The sheriff put both of his hands behind his head and stared up at the bedroom ceiling.

One less problem, Armstrong reflected. Scott Miller was a goddamn, loud-mouthed drunk. Well, the bastard's dead now, and there's nobody to corroborate what he said about the Karver case. The dumb son of a bitch…and he wanted to be on the force at one time! What a joke that would've been. I was right in refusing him a job. Hell, Miller spent more time in the bars of Kewanee than he had in his own residence. He had more time in at Shelly's Place than any of the bartenders. Everyone knows him to be a drunk, and there is nothing to that rambling nonsense he told me last night. That bastard was just making it all up to get at my nerves.

Sheriff Armstrong knew he had to get up, but he decided to take just a few minutes to collect his thoughts and to begin planning his strategy for the day. Lately he had been feeling older, and he enjoyed the leisure of lying back into a warm, early morning bed. But after only a few seconds, the sheriff frowned and hurriedly rose up out of bed. He was still thinking of Scott's jailhouse story, and those thoughts were overriding any pleasant value that could be found in spending a few more minutes resting on his back. The sheriff decided to begin his normal morning routine and tried hard to put Scott Miller out of his mind.

While Armstrong was shaving, he paused to look into the bathroom mirror, recalling the time he had spent with Miller in the jailhouse cell. The sheriff looked deep into the mirror, hoping to find solace in his own facial reflection concerning the doubts that were swirling in his head.

Scott's dead and so is any threat from his accusations, the sheriff concluded. And that story of his was all bullshit. I just gotta let all that get behind me now and concentrate on my campaign.

Armstrong left the bathroom, walked into his kitchen, and began to prepare a light breakfast. The smell of toast and fresh coffee filled the air, causing his wily mind to jump into high gear again.

What if Scott was telling the truth, the sheriff thought? What if Taylor got hold of any of that information? Taylor would take something like this and splash it all over the county. He'd do anything to beat me in this election. Taylor…that son of a bitch…why couldn't he wait a few years to run for the sheriff's job and give me the chance I need to prove myself? What the hell did I ever do to him?

CHAPTER THIRTEEN

L ike all serious politicians, Sheriff Armstrong never took an election for granted, and the up-coming election worried him. Henry County had been a bastion of Republicanism for many years, but ten years ago a new Democratic Party Chairman began to organize the county party and was able to achieve a number of significant victories. The Democrats won control of the Henry County Board and they were able to win the Treasurer's Office and the County Clerk's Office. Now, they were conducting a movement to win the Sheriff's Office by fielding a Colona police officer, Jim Taylor, as their candidate for sheriff. Jim Taylor was a vibrant young man who was experienced in law enforcement, exuded confidence, and was running an excellent campaign.

Being a policeman in Colona was a political plus for Jim Taylor's candidacy. Colona's population is composed of middle-class, working people who had consistently been a base of support for the Henry County Democrats. Sheriff Armstrong always felt a tinge of discomfort when police work called him into Colona. The city was Ted Chapman's territory, and the sheriff's reputation in Colona was the product of Ted's observations. Ted Chapman was a Democrat, a dynamic force on the Henry County Board, and a strong critic of Sheriff Armstrong. Jim Taylor's experience as a Colona police officer was fertile soil from which to launch his campaign

After completing high school in Chicago, Taylor served a tour of duty in the Army and had become a staff sergeant in the Army's military police. Upon his discharge, Jim earned an associate's degree in law enforcement, moved to Henry County, and became a police officer with the Colona Police Department. Jim Taylor was well respected in the community and his eight years on the police force had earned him a reputation as a good cop. When he thought of his future, Jim wanted to take on more responsibilities in law enforcement and was considering leaving Colona in search of promotion and advancement.

Jim's desire for advancement and the Henry County Democrats' desire to put a Democrat in the sheriff's office meshed one evening in February. On that evening, Jim was engaged in the routine duty of being a visible presence to people. He was sitting in his squad car watching the evening traffic flow east and west on Colona Road in the hopes that the sight of his squad car would make the commuters act in a reasonable manner while they headed home from work. It was while performing this duty that Ted Chapman approached Jim Taylor to ask him to run for the position of Henry County Sheriff.

"Hey Jim," Ted exclaimed while getting out of his pick up truck and walking toward Taylor's squad car.

"Hi, Ted," Jim responded through the open window of his squad car. "Anything wrong?"

Ted waved both of his hands, palms up, in front of Jim.

"No, no, Jim," Ted replied. "I just saw you sitting here and thought I should tell you about a conversation a group of us guys had last night. We were talking about you."

"About me, huh? That can't be good," Jim laughed.

Ted beamed back at him, slowly shaking his head up and down.

"Oh, but it is good, Jim. It's real good," Ted said. "You know you're well thought of here and throughout the whole county."

"Oh, oh, this sounds political to me," Jim guessed.

Ted placed both of his hands on the top of the squad car and looked intently into Jim Taylor's face.

"It is political, Jim," he said in a serious tone. "We need a good man to become the Sheriff of Henry County, and we think you can do that. We want you to be the Democratic candidate for sheriff."

Jim reached for the squad car's steering wheel and held onto it tightly with both hands.

"Whoooa, Ted," he said. "I gotta tell you, that's asking a lot. I'm not sure I'm the best candidate for you. Have you asked anyone else?"

"You're it, Jim," Ted said, pointing a finger at Taylor. "We considered a number of people, but you're the one we're asking. And, Jim, I want you to run. I know you can win. Hell, you would sweep Colona and Kewanee even without campaigning. We got lots of people who will help you, and we're willing to put a good amount of money behind you. So, what'd ya say? Do you want to be the sheriff? You'd make a great one."

Ted could tell that Jim was interested, but he also knew he had dumped a lot on him in a short amount of time.

For a brief moment, Jim stared into the windshield of his squad car, reflecting on Ted's request. Then he looked back into Ted's face.

"I'll tell you what, Ted, I am interested," he said. "But, this is a big step for me, and something like this won't be easy. I'd be going up against the man who beat an icon. And Armstrong's been in law enforcement for twenty years. Why hell, I only have thirty years total on the face of this earth."

Yeah, yeah," Ted groaned, "Twenty years. Big deal. He's been sheriff for eight years. Well, it's time for another change. We need a Democrat in that office."

"Maybe so," Jim replied, "but Armstrong's built up quite a reputation, too."

"Hell, Jim, you of all people should know Armstrong has picked up a lotta negative baggage over those eight years. I tell you he's vulnerable. There are people who don't like him. He's a brash s.o.b. This is the time to take him and you're the guy who can do it."

"You really think so? I mean I put a lot of stock in your judgment. We all do. You really think Armstrong can be beaten?"

"Listen, Jim," Ted answered. "If you are interested in becoming sheriff and you wait four more years, Armstrong will get a lock on that office. You wait another four years and you'll be facing a juggernaut that'll roll right over you. This is the time to strike."

"Well, that's a good point," Jim observed. "And, who knows where I'll be in four years."

"Damn right," Ted encouraged. "You have to seize the moment. And this is your moment, Jim."

"You know I'd have to talk to my wife about this. I can't make a decision like this without involving her."

"Sure, Jim, sure. Of course you gotta talk with your wife," Ted agreed. "We all understand that. And I'll bet you Carol will support this idea."

"Well, let me talk to her about this and I'll get back to you tomorrow. I mean that's the best I can do tonight. I can't make a commitment without asking her first, and I'm not going to guess what she will say. I'll talk with her after my shift ends tonight."

Ted smiled and reached inside the squad car for Jim's hand. The two men shook hands while Ted laughed lightly.

"I can't ask any more than that, Jim," he said. "But I will tell you this...we are a little under the gun here. If you're going to run, we only have three days to file the necessary papers. I know this is short notice, but we'll help you get the petitions signed and the papers filed, but you gotta let me know first thing tomorrow morning. Can you do that?"

"OK, Ted," Jim promised. "I'm pretty sure Carol will agree with me. I'll tell ya, I'm pretty excited about all of this. But for now, you'd better move on and let me do my job here."

"Tomorrow, Jim. Tomorrow we will start planning your campaign and come November you'll be the newly elected Sheriff of Henry County. You have a good evening and tomorrow I will introduce you to some guys who will help us get you elected."

Ted waved his right hand in Jim's direction while he hurried back to his pick-up truck. Jim sat in his squad car looking through the windshield, but his focus was no longer on watching the evening traffic; instead, he was looking into the future and dreaming of political success.

Sheriff Taylor, Jim thought. I gotta admit, it sounds good, and it's just the direction I have been looking for. If Carol says yes to this, I'm going to give it everything I've got. I'm going to be the next Sheriff of Henry County. I know Carol will support me on this."

CHAPTER FOURTEEN

Jim and Carol Taylor were in the fourth year of their marriage and they were renting a small house in the southwest section of Colona. Carol Taylor was a teacher's aide in the Colona School District. It was her dream to buy a home in the country and raise two children. She knew the dream would require more income than she and Jim made, but she had faith in Jim. She knew he had ambition and ability, and she knew he shared her dream.

On the evening Ted asked Jim to run for sheriff, he was working a truncated, second-shift patrol schedule. No matter what shift he worked, Carol always waited until he was home to eat supper. It was nine p.m. when she heard the garage door opening, signaling that Jim was home for the evening.

"Hi, Hon!" Jim called out as he walked into the house.

"Hi, Jim!" Carol responded. "How was the shift tonight?"

"It was fine. All's quiet in Colona and all's right with the world, now that I'm home. Something smells very good. Is that lasagna?"

"It is," Carol answered. "Wash up and sit down. I'll bring it to the table."

Jim washed up at the kitchen sink, and dried his hands on a small, cloth towel, which hung down on a rack that was attached to the bottom of the kitchen cabinets. As he rubbed his hands dry on the towel, he watched Carol place the hot lasagna platter on the table.

"Something special did happen tonight," he said. "Not work stuff, though."

"You sit down and start your supper, Jim. Then you can tell me all about it."

Jim sat at the kitchen table, as his wife scooped out a large square of lasagna and placed it on his plate. She put a smaller portion on her own plate and then sat down with him.

"OK," she said. "Now tell me what was so special about tonight?"

"Ted Chapman stopped by and talked to me. You know Ted?"

"Everyone knows Ted," Carol responded. "If he stopped by to talk to you, it must have something to do with politics, right?"

"Right," Jim answered.

"Taste your lasagna," Carol said. "I made it a little different tonight, and I want to know what you think of it."

Jim dutifully tasted his lasagna.

"It's delicious, Hon. I love it."

"Good," Carol said. "Now tell me what Ted wanted."

"Ted asked me to run for sheriff," he said. "I told him I'd have to talk with you about it."

Carol put her fork down on her plate. Her heart and her mind had collided when she heard Jim's words. She could tell he wanted to run. She knew he was asking her permission, but she also knew he had already made up his mind, and she did not want to stand in his way. Her thoughts rushed to the dream she and Jim shared. If he became the sheriff of Henry County, the money they needed to fulfill their dream would be there for them. But what would be the price? Her eyes misted over.

"How much time," she asked.

"How much time for the campaign or the job?"

"Both."

"It will take a lot of time for both, Hon."

While he was driving home from work, Jim had mentally gone over the conversation he thought he would have with Carol. He had made up his mind to run for sheriff, and he wanted to be able to call Ted that very night with an affirmative answer. But, as much as he wanted to run for the job, he knew he could not do it without his wife's blessing.

"Jim," Carol said. "I've always supported you. I've never complained about you being a police officer. But, I've always been afraid."

Carol's words stung. Jim knew being a cop's wife was a lot to ask of any woman. He loved her and he understood the sacrifices she had made in order to be his wife.

"You know why they're asking you to run, don't you?" Carol asked.

"Ted said I'd make an excellent sheriff, and he thinks I can win."

"I think you can win too. But I mean the other reason they're asking you."

"Yeah, I know," Jim said. "I know I wasn't their first choice. You're talking about Chase Blair. Chase would've been their first choice."

"Yes," Carol said. "And Chase is dead. I remember when he got killed…run over by some pothead idiot he had pulled over on a traffic stop. I remember going over to Chase's house to comfort Breanna and their kids. Listen…this is going to sound strange, but I want you to run."

"You do?" Jim responded, wrinkling his brow. "I don't get it. It sounded like you were gonna say no."

"I want you to be sheriff," Carol said. "I stay at home worried that I'll get a call like Breanna did. I worry all the time about you. But, I know I would worry less if you were sheriff. I don't want you out on the road alone anymore. Sheriffs don't get killed. I want you to run, and I want you to win. It would help me a lot. I don't want to have to worry about you getting killed any more."

Jim looked at Carol's face. There were tears in her eyes. He reached for her hand and held it in his.

"Hon," he said. "I'll win. I promise you that. It's like Ted said...Armstrong's picked up some baggage during his eight years in office. There are a lot of cops who don't like him. I can beat him. I know I can."

"We'll both work hard. We'll work hard and you'll win," Carol said. "I'm proud of you. You're a good man."

Jim called Ted that very night and told him he would run. After calling Ted, Jim sat in a reclining chair in his living room and thought about the choice he had just made.

This is right, he concluded. Now I know I will win. I'll win this for Carol. She's right about the sheriff's position being safer. She shouldn't have to worry about me getting killed.

Jim's love for Carol became the motivating factor in his desire to win the race for sheriff. He never told anyone about the conversation he had with her, but he used his commitment to her to muster the strength he needed every time he had to make a speech or talk one-on-one with people in order to gain their support. Whenever he felt inadequate or apprehensive, he remembered his promise to his wife; then, his nerves were steadied and he focused on what he needed to do to beat Sheriff Armstrong. The love and the support that Carol had given him shaped Jim into the most viable opponent Sheriff Armstrong had ever encountered.

CHAPTER FIFTEEN

Death is a part of every police officer's job. Deputy Lambert had seen death from accidents, natural causes, suicides, and murders. For him, a death was a mystery to unravel. The corpse was a part of the mystery, a piece of the puzzle. It was his job to study the scene of the death, interview interested parties, read the coroner's report, investigate the cause of death, and write a report explaining how the death occurred.

In rural Henry County, most deaths appeared ordinary and easy to explain, but Joe had learned early in his career that the investigation of a death could quickly become extraordinary. With only two weeks on the job, Joe had been sent to help investigate the death of Albert Coffee. Coffee had reached the age of eighty-six when a mailman found his body lying face down on the kitchen floor of his dilapidated, small farmhouse. The mailman immediately called the sheriff's office for help.

After dismissing the mailman from the scene, Deputy Wachtel, the senior officer who was giving Joe on-the-job training, stepped over the corpse and sat down on a kitchen chair. The chair was part of an old chrome kitchen set, the type of kitchenware that was popular in the late 1950s. A three-inch strip of silver duct tape ran down the backing of the chair, hiding a vertical tear on the upholstery. Three other chrome chairs surrounded the kitchen table; each bore prominent signs of aging patched with strips of duct tape in a variety of patterns. A small box of glazed donuts sat unopened on the table and an empty juice glass sat next to the box of donuts.

Deputy Wachtel motioned toward Deputy Lambert and pointed at a chair.

"Have a seat Joe," Wachtel said. "Mr. Coffee's not going anywhere. I think he just took his last trip."

Joe pulled one of the chairs out from under the table, turned the chair around, straddled his long legs around it and sat down with the front of his body facing the back of the chair. He scanned the small kitchen area slowly. A frying pan, a carton of eggs, and a stick of margarine sat on a grime-covered stove. Directly across the room from the stove, the kitchen refrigerator door was partially opened; the light inside revealed the bleak contents of Albert Coffee's supply of food. Only four items were stored in the refrigerator, all were clustered together on the refrigerator's top shelf. A half-eaten piece of cake sat alone on a large glass plate. Surrounding the large plate was a quart of milk, a pitcher of orange juice, and a half-empty jar of black olives.

Coffee's body had fallen between the table and the stove. A metal spatula rested on the floor three feet away from Coffee's outstretched right arm.

"Doesn't look like any foul play here," Joe said to Wachtel.

"Nah...nothing foul here," Wachtel replied. "Looks like the old boy finally bought the farm. Heart must've quit when he was making breakfast. See the refrig open and the donuts on the table? The old man was probably gonna have a donut while he was making eggs. Bet he was reaching for juice when his heart went out. Yep, you might say those donuts killed him sure as any gunshot wound would've. Cops aren't the only ones killed by donuts, huh Joe?"

"Guess not," Joe replied. "It looks like a heart attack alright."

Joe looked out a kitchen window and watched an emergency vehicle screaming down the dirt road that led to Albert's house. Wachtel leaned back in the chair he had commandeered and placed both of his hands on top of his head.

"Yeah, this one's easy for us," he said. "Old guy dies of a heart attack. That's what the autopsy will say. Neat and clean. Hell, I'd have one of those donuts if I knew the old guy didn't cough on them before he croaked."

But Wachtel was wrong in his assessment of the situation. There was nothing ordinary about Albert Coffee's death. The toxicology report found poison in his system, and an investigation determined that Albert's son, Matt, had been poisoning his father over a six-month period. When questioned, Matt Coffee eventually confessed to the crime.

"I've been waiting for that old man to die for fifteen years now," Matt Coffee said when Joe interrogated him. "Hell, he had a good life. When do I get mine? And, you know....he was dying anyway. I mean, he would've spent the next few years in an old folks home."

"Matt, you've lived and farmed with your dad since you were a boy," Deputy Lambert said. "He's always been there for you. Why would you want him gone?"

"Shit," Matt replied. "You were in the house...it's a goddamn pit. My old man was a miser. He kept all of his money in the bank. 'Saving it for a rainy day. Gotta take care of the farm.' That's what he always said. God damn it! It's been raining all my life, and the farm's nothing but work. I don't like living way out there on a muddy-ass farm in a broken down, old house."

"I can understand that. But did you ever tell your dad that?" Joe asked. "Why didn't you just leave?"

Matt Coffee's face took on the look of a pouting boy.

"I needed money to leave," he said. "How the hell was I supposed to leave without money? And there wasn't any talking to him about money. Dad didn't care about money. All he ever wanted to do was farm and work hard. He didn't even know how much money he had. All he could talk about was farming. God damn it, I have a right to a life you know! I shouldn't have to do just what he wanted. I mean, what about me? What about me?"

"You have a right to a life, Matt. It must have been hard living there all those years and wanting to be somewhere else," Joe said. "I can understand that."

"You're damn right it was hard!" Matt exclaimed. "I put up with it longer than most people would've. You know, I carried him for the last four years. He couldn't have made it out there without me. I was taking care of him twenty-four, seven ever since he turned eighty-two. A lot of people would've put him in a home a long time ago. But I knew he wouldn't want to be in no home. He told me that."

"What'd he tell you, Matt?"

"He told me he'd rather be dead than be put in one of those old folks homes. You know, I had dreams of my own. Shit, everyone was always saying how agile and healthy Dad was, but they didn't know. They weren't with him twenty-four hours a day like me. He owes me for all of the help I gave him. I gave him my whole life, you know. And, he told me he didn't want to be put in one of those homes."

"I'm just curious," Joe said. "What'd you want to do? I mean, if things were different, where did you want to go?"

"South," Matt sighed. "I want to go south to the ocean. It's too fucking cold around here. And there was plenty of money to do that. I could've been living down there and just enjoying life. I told him I wanted to leave, but he wouldn't part with any of his money. 'Gotta take care of the farm.' That's all he could talk about. All work and no play that was Dad's life. All I needed was some money. Christ…I'm fifty-five years old, and I've never had a day off, or took a vacation. I watched my mom die in that old farmhouse without ever having anything she wanted. He never bought her nothing. I could've had a good life living on the beach somewhere on the Gulf. There's plenty of money."

"So you started poisoning him?"

"Hey, why should I have to wait for that old man to die?" Matt cried out. "I've been waiting for ten years now! I got tired of it all. Christ, he was going to die soon anyway…another five years for sure. I doubt he had that much time left in him. I just helped him along a little. This way he didn't have to go to one of those homes, and his death was neat and clean. Hell, one of those nursing homes would've taken all his money anyway."

Deputy Lambert sat staring at Matt Coffee. He could tell Matt meant what he said. Matt believed he had done his father a favor. The callous nature of Matt Coffee taught Deputy Lambert a lesson in police work.

If sons will kill fathers, then it's a ruthless world, Joe surmised. You can't take anything for granted.

From then on, Deputy Lambert purposefully adopted an analytical approach to death. He incorporated a cold, professional shield into his being; he used the shield as a protection between himself and the sting of death, enabling him to do his job and to retain his sanity. But after almost seven years of experience as a cop, a gapping hole had been torn in Joe's protective shield by Katie Karver's murder. Now, another hole was about to rip through that protective barrier by the news Deputy Neil Rogers was bringing to Joe's home.

CHAPTER SIXTEEN

Deputy Rogers knocked hard four times on the front door of Joe's single-story ranch home. Joe had just finished breakfast and was thinking about getting dressed for work when those thoughts were interrupted by Rogers' unexpected appearance. Dressed in an old crumpled pair of jeans and a t-shirt, he looked out a window and saw Rogers standing on his front porch. He knew immediately that Rogers' presence could only mean ill tidings.

Neil Rogers and Deputy Lambert were professional associates, but they were not friends. Joe had never been invited to Deputy Rogers' home, and he had never invited Rogers to his house.

"Hey Joe," Deputy Rogers hailed as Joe opened the door.

Rogers could tell from the expression on Joe's face that he knew he was about to receive bad news. Joe motioned for Rogers to enter his home.

"Neil, come on in. How can I help you this morning?"

Joe was expecting bad news, but he knew there was no need to press the deputy with anxious questions. Rogers would tell him why he was there in due time, and Joe did not want to give Rogers the satisfaction of thinking that he was curious about any information Neil had, or that he was in need of Rogers' help. Joe knew Rogers would lay everything out in front of him. Rogers would be succinct and complete while he used the news to surgically tear away at Joe's flesh. And, Joe knew that Rogers would enjoy the process.

Rogers entered the house and the two men stood in Joe's living room. Joe made no offer for Rogers to be seated.

"Mind if I sit?" Rogers asked.

He saw a slight, knowing smile appear on Joe's lips.

"Please do. I suspect I should sit too, right?" Joe replied.

Rogers sat down in an old, comfortable armchair, and Joe sat five feet across from him on a sofa, but more than five feet separated the two men. Joe had analyzed Neil during the years that they had spent together as deputies and Joe had found serious shortcomings in Deputy Rogers.

While it was true that the sheriff viewed Neil as an efficient and success-ful cop, Joe found him to be a cross between CHIPS and Barney Fife. Neil was an authoritarian person and, as a professional law enforcement officer, Joe did not like how Neil emphasized order over law. Neil was the type of man who chose a career in law enforcement because he enjoyed being in charge of people. He rubbed the law in the face of those who were unfortunate enough to cross his path. He lectured and berated people; even minor vehicle code violators, whom he had caught on the fringe of illegal acts. Rogers enjoyed catching people in illegal acts, and he enjoyed punishing people.

Deputy Rogers' approach to law was the exact opposite of Deputy Lambert's. Joe had become a police officer because he wanted to make the world a safer place. He looked at his job as an opportunity to help people, not to control them. Often Joe's quiet demeanor and hard, handsome appearance caused people to believe he was arrogant, but in reality he was a humble observer of the world. He was a good cop, who always earned respect from those who came to know him. And, Joe was always courteous and accommodating in his professional interactions with Neil, but early in their work relationship he had decided that he did not like Rogers, and he resented Rogers bringing him any bad news. He resented having to share anything so personal with a man whose actions and philosophies were so diametrically opposed to his.

"Joe, I have some bad news for you," Rogers began.

Joe sat in stoic silence waiting for Rogers to dislodge the information he had brought. It was evident from the expression on Rogers' face that he enjoyed being in the position of dumping bad news into Joe's living room.

"Scott Miller is dead," Rogers continued. "Thomas discovered his car off Highway 81 this morning. I was called to the scene. It looks like he had been in the car for a couple of hours before we got to him. He was dead at the scene, so there was nothing we could do for him. I found an open whiskey bottle in his car. Sheriff Armstrong has asked me to write the report up. We all know Scott was a friend of yours."

Joe kept the expressionless mask on his face, but his heart began to race. He had learned how to remain composed from his many years of police work. Now he was learning how to fake composure.

I will not give this pompous son of a bitch the satisfaction of seeing me crack, Joe thought. I will not share my feelings with such a man. Why the hell didn't Mike come and tell me about Scott? I deserve better treatment than this.

"I know the tox report will confirm that he was DUI," Rogers said. "Scott drank way too much, Joe. You know, all those years of hard drinking had changed him. He wasn't thinking straight any more, and he was talking crazy. I know you were his friend, but he was a drunk and it killed him. End of story."

Joe looked into Rogers' face as if he were calmly staring down a combative defense lawyer. He tried to think of the proper way to respond to Rogers' cold report. He did not want Rogers thinking he had control over any aspect of his life.

"Do you want anything, or do you have any questions for me?" Rogers interjected in an effort to break the silence surrounding the two men.

"No. Nothing. Thanks for coming, Neil," Joe impassively replied. "Everyone knew that Scott drank too much. I'll look at the report when I come in later today. Is Mike out of town?"

"No," Rogers replied. "I just talked with him on the phone. He was getting ready to head in to the office, I think. He told me to drop by and tell you about Scott."

Deputy Rogers rose up from the armchair. Joe remained seated. Rogers moved towards the door and then turned to face Joe.

"You sure there's nothing I can do for you?"

"No. I'm fine," Joe replied with a forced smile. "I might be a little late for my shift."

Rogers opened the front door and then turned to face Joe again.

"Sure. Everybody will understand that. Take some time…and Joe…don't worry. Things will get better." Rogers said.

Joe watched Deputy Rogers exit out of the front door. He was glad to have Rogers out of his house, and he was glad to be alone. He felt drained by the news he had just heard. He remained seated on his sofa and decided to let the news sink into his soul.

Rogers is a bastard, Joe decided once again. End of story, huh? Drinking didn't kill Scott. Rogers couldn't investigate his way out of a paper bag. Scott's been dying for ten years. All that asshole did was pick up the remains. End of story, my ass! Rogers doesn't know the real story.

CHAPTER SEVENTEEN

S cott Miller was a boyhood friend of Deputy Lamberts'. The two men had grown up together in the *Hog Capitol of the World*, Kewanee, Illinois. Joe was a year younger than Scott and he had hung out with Scott and his best friend, Bob Popp. As kids, the trio had wandered around downtown Kewanee, ducking into stores, theaters, and restaurants in search of adventure. The proprietors of the establishments that they had most frequented labeled the boys "The Three Musketeers".

Most everyone would consider Joe's hometown to be small, but Kewanee is the largest city in Henry County, and it has a number of cosmopolitan attributes. During the hay days of America's manufacturing, Kewanee acquired an industrial base when a boiler manufacturing plant located there. The factory's need for a large labor pool caused the city's population to become the only area of racial and ethnic diversity in rural Henry County. Several ethnic restaurants flourished in the city and, annually, Kewanee was host to a four-day festival that celebrated the city's diversity and drew tourist from all over the United States.

In many ways, living in Kewanee was like living in a neighborhood that had been scooped out of a large city and placed in a rural county. Nevertheless, a child growing up in Kewanee did not accrue any credit for being cosmopolitan or rural. Kewanee's metropolitan nature was not large enough to impress anyone outside of the county, and the rural folk of Henry County looked with disdain upon the blue collar and diverse character of the city. Although unwarranted, Kewanee's sorted image only increased in the mid-1980s' when the industrial base of the city collapsed, leaving Kewanee economically desperate and crowded with more taverns per capita than any other city in a three-county radius. The Karver Hardware Store, a huge downtown furniture store, the headquarters for a national hamburger franchise, a large sport store emporium, a Super Walmart, and several smaller retail stores were now the driving forces of Kewanee's economy.

As Joe sat on his sofa and processed the terrible news that Deputy Rogers had just delivered, thoughts of his boyhood days in Kewanee began to flood his mind. He stared out the window of his small home, focusing his gaze on the beautiful oak tree that engulfed his front lawn. As boys, the "Three Musketeers" had spent time climbing trees in the Kewanee City Park. They would sit in the trees and eat food out of the lunch sacks they had hauled up with them. A summer tree was a good place to hide out, the leaves concealed them from the adults on the ground, and they could spy on everyone without being discovered. In the treetops, the three boys would each sit, on their own private limb, lean back against the tree, discuss the mysteries of life, and expound upon their plans for the future. In his mind, Joe saw Scott Miller and Bob Popp dropping out of the oak tree and leaving him sitting alone.

Bob and Scott had been close to each other ever since second grade when the Popp family moved from Chicago to Kewanee. "The Three Musketeers" were all good friends, but there was a special connection between Bob and Scott because they were the same age, they were in the same school grade, and they lived next door to each other. By virtue of his age, Joe had sometimes been excluded from the rites of passage that Bob and Scott experienced a full year before he could. But, Bob and Scott always included Joe in the debriefings that followed each event. Joe learned of turn-about dances, proms, and homecomings one year before he was able to attend them. He enjoyed listening to the two older boys talk about their adventures. Bob and Scott always answered any questions Joe had, and they always told him he would see it all next year with them. The three boys shared everything they could share, and they had come to believe they would be together for a long time.

But "The Three Musketeers" were permanently broken up when Bob Popp was killed in the Middle East. A lump came to Joe's throat as he remembered that June 26th day. It was a Friday morning and Joe was having breakfast before he would leave to help his dad paint a garage. He had turned the television on to watch anything that would interject a human voice into the small kitchen. He could not recall what piece of television trash he had finally settled upon, but he clearly remembered pouring milk on cereal when a broadcaster cut off the regular programming with an announcement:

We interrupt this broadcast with breaking news from Saudi Arabia. A truck bomb has exploded outside a military housing complex in Dhahran, Saudi Arabia. It is being reported that hundreds of U.S. servicemen have been injured and at least nineteen are believed killed.

A cold shiver of fear engulfed Joe when he heard the television announcement. Somehow he knew at that moment that Bob was dead. The official notification of his death arrived the next day.

In response to Bob's death, Scott Miller drank the whole week. Joe allowed Scott to stay at his home every evening. In the morning, Scott would begin drinking again.

"You know I killed him, Joe. I sent Bob to his death," Scott would repeat over and over.

That's nonsense, Scott," Joe always replied. "You're not responsible for a terrorist attack in Saudi Arabia."

"Shit, I'm responsible for Bob being there," Scott would say in a voice filled with eternal despair. "You know I'm responsible. Everyone knows Bob wouldn't have been in the Marines if it hadn't been for me. I'm the one that should've been there. I'm the one that wanted to go. I should've been there looking out for Bob."

Of the three boys, Scott Miller had appeared to be the one most destined for success. Scott was strong and athletic and the most outgoing. He was a star in high school basketball, football, and track. Scott exercised at a feverish pace all year long, always pushing himself to do better in sports. He had drive, desire, and a plan.

"I'm going to join the Marines. Hooo Rahhh!" Scott began shouting during his senior year in high school. "I'm going to be a Marine officer. You guys can be in my company if you want."

"No thanks, Scott," Joe had replied. "I like it here in Kewanee."

Scott locked his arms around Bob's head and playfully rubbed Bob's hair.

"Well, Bob, I guess it is just you and me. We can join the Marines on the buddy plan. The few, the proud…that's gonna be us. We'll travel the world together. Whatta ya say, buddy? Are you with me?"

"Sounds like a plan to me, Scott," Bob laughed. "What the hell. We can always come back to Kewanee and visit Joe after we've seen the world. You're gonna miss out on a whole lotta fun, Joe."

Bob had always admired Scott and was his biggest fan. Although Scott was actually four months younger than he, Bob looked upon Scott as an older brother. He always wanted to be just like Scott. He also worked out all year long, but could never achieve the same results as Scott. He was always a step or more behind Scott, but he never lost sight of him and he was constantly trying to catch up with him. After their senior year, Scott and Bob enlisted in the Marine Corps and believed the recruiter's promise that they would never be separated. In the fall, they were to be sent to Paris Island, South Carolina for thirteen weeks of basic training.

Joe went to the train station in Kewanee to watch his two buddies depart for basic training.

"God, the Marines will kick my ass, Joe," Bob worriedly exclaimed.

"Hey, don't fret about it, Bob," Scott reassured. "I told you. I'll take care of everything. Anyone messes with you, they're messing with me. I'll take care of both of us."

Joe waved at Bob and Scott as their train pulled away from their boyhood town.

Bob's right, Joe thought, the Marines will kick his ass. He'll be back in Kewanee in few weeks, drummed out of the corps, and Scott will become a poster boy for the Marines. I was right to stay here, but I do miss them.

Joe's prediction of Bob's failure and Scott's success in the Marine Corps became the first paradox he had ever witnessed. Instead of success, Scott's plans were ruined in the fourth week of boot camp. During an obstacle course run, Scott fell while trying to rappel down a fifteen-foot log wall. He shattered his ankle and was honorably discharged from the Marine Corps. Bob went on to finish what the two had started; Bob became a Marine. After completing his advanced training at Camp Lejeune, he was sent to Dhahran, Saudi Arabia, along with 2,900 other American servicemen. Bob wrote letters to Scott and Joe explaining the reason he was in Dhahran was that the American military had established an airbase there to refuel and pull maintenance on the fighter planes that were enforcing the no-fly zone over Saddam Hussein's Iraq. He always ended his letters by writing *Hoo Rahhh!! Wish you were here!* Joe could tell from Bob's letters that he was lonely in Saudi Arabia.

On a June 25th evening, Bob was playing pool in the Khobar Tower apartment complex with three other servicemen when a 5000-pound truck bomb exploded outside of the building, killing all four of the men and fifteen others. Bob was nineteen years old when he died. His body was flown back to Kewanee where an elaborate funeral was held to honor the sacrifice he had made for his country. A detachment of Marines played taps and provided a twenty-one-gun salute while Scott and Joe helped place Bob's flag-draped coffin over his grave. Every Saturday for more than a year, Scott would visit Bob's grave and ask for his forgiveness. But, Scott found no cleansing grace in his efforts. He came to believe he was at fault for the death of his young friend, and Joe could not convince him that he was wrong.

Following Bob's death, Scott's life became one disappointment after another, and he met each new disappointment with more and more drinking. His success in high school had been tied to his athletic prowess, and all of that was stripped away when his shattered ankle made him limp. Scott was accustomed to success; unable to handle failure, and certain that he was being punished for the death of his best friend. He had tried to get an associate's degree at the local community college, but found it hard to concentrate and to stay focused. Instead, he wound up rotating through a number of minimum wage jobs, often being fired for missing work. If ninety percent of success in life is simply showing up, Scott only achieved a fifty percent success rate.

Scott's heavy drinking was an attempt to escape the pain that Bob's death had scratched across his soul and to escape a host of other disillusionments. Joe tried to take care of Scott and talked to him about moving on with his life, but instead, Scott's mental state became worse. Two years after Bob's funeral, Scott told Joe that he did not need anyone taking care of him any longer. He had learned how to live as a drunk.

"You can't take care of other people," Scott told Joe.

Joe's focus turned away from the huge oak tree and his thoughts returned to the present. Deputy Rogers is a prick, Joe thought as he sat alone in his house. But, he is right about one thing; years of drinking did change Scott. He did become bitter and resentful, and he was drinking harder all of the time…just trying to dull the pain and to forget, I guess. And, I know that lately his drinking made him mean spirited and caused a whole lot of ugly incidences. I've been bailing him out of trouble more often than before.

Joe slowly shook his head back and forth as he thought about his friend. He had to admit that drinking had changed Scott. He sat emotionally frozen on the sofa for fifteen minutes. He cried softly and tried to think of someone he could talk to. He looked at the empty tree and wished for happier days.

Scott and Bob are dead and I am alone, Joe realized. Maybe everything would've been different if I had pursued Katie harder. If I had tried more, maybe Katie and I would be together, and she never would have been murdered.

CHAPTER EIGHTEEN

T he murder of Katie Karver had sent shock waves through the county. The tourist bureau's slogan of *Where You Long To Be* and murder were diametrically opposed concepts. Murder by itself was bad enough, but Katie had not only been murdered, her body had been dismembered. There was a clamor in the community to settle the case. The culprit had to be found and made to pay for such a heinous crime.

Katie Karver had been reported missing by her husband, Larry, when she failed to return from a local shopping trip. The Kewanee Police Department treated Katie's disappearance as a missing person case until the bottom portion of a human leg turned up fifteen miles outside of the Kewanee city limits and in the Hennepin Canal. It did not take long for the state's forensic lab to identify the gruesome piece of evidence as proof that Katie Karver was dead. The mystery of her disappearance now became the jurisdiction of the Henry County Sheriff's Department. It was up to the sheriff' to find out how she had died, and there was little doubt in anyone's mind that her death was the result of foul play. Katie's death became a homicide investigation.

Katie's murder devastated the Karver family. The family was well known in Henry County and their ancestors were among the original settlers of the area. Larry Karver's great-grandfather, Vincent Karver, had owned a store in Andover when it was the county's only incorporated village. Vincent had taught his family how to prosper by working behind the store counter and by going out into the community to sell their wares. Larry Karver's father, Gerald Karver, had grown up working for Larry's great-grandfather. Young Gerald spent his afternoons and Saturdays making grocery deliveries in Andover. Gerald was a natural salesman who knew everyone in the village by their first name. But the small village of Andover lacked the market challenges that were required to meet the explosive nature of Gerald Karver's entrepreneurship. When he was twenty, he moved to Kewanee and opened a store specializing in hardware and appliances. He became a ruthless, shrewd businessman, and it was not long before his store laid waste to all competitors. His marketing techniques always kept stride with the latest developments in technology. Whenever a person was looking for a piece of hardware or the best deal on an appliance, the exemplary reputation of the Karver Hardware Store would prevail. *If you can't find it at Karver's, it doesn't exist* was the motto of the store, and that motto was repeated over and over again by satisfied Karver customers everywhere. Karver Hardware Stores were built throughout western Illinois and eastern Iowa. Under the tutelage of Gerald Karver, the hardware stores became a huge success, and the Karver family became extremely wealthy.

The tragic circumstances of Katie's death caused outrage to spew forth from the Karver clan. As patriarch of the family, Gerald Karver summoned Sheriff Armstrong and Deputy Lambert to an office he had in his Kewanee home. He wanted swift action from the sheriff and blood from the person who had killed his daughter-in-law.

Sheriff Armstrong respected Gerald Karver's clout in the county and so he agreed to meet with the Karvers in their home. It was a hot, July day when Sheriff Armstrong and Deputy Lambert pulled away in the sheriff's squad car from the Henry County Jailhouse in route to answer Gerald Karver's summons.

"Bet you and Scott spent a lotta your childhood in the Karver mansion," the sheriff said to Joe.

"Nah, not really," Joe answered. "Scott and I grew up together as friends, and Larry only butted in when we started drinking beer in high school. You know Larry…he's a user and he used us to get him beer. Larry's so goddamn rich, I should've charged him more for those beers," Joe chuckled.

"Well, from what the Kewanee guys tell me, Larry is still a drinker," the sheriff observed. "They've had to take him home a lotta times."

"That's Larry. Some things don't change. He always gets a pass."

When they reached the Cambridge city limits, Sheriff Armstrong jammed down on the squad car's gas pedal and raced east toward Kewanee.

"Hey, Mike, watch your speed," Joe joked. "You know I'm a duly sworn officer of the law. You either gotta slow down or kick the siren on."

Sheriff Armstrong eased the squad down to five miles over the limit.

"I gotta tell you, I'm a little pissed with this meeting," the sheriff explained. "I don't like being called over to the Karver mansion to explain what we're doing about this murder case. That son of a bitch should be coming over to see me if he has any questions. And, I don't like Karver telling me to bring you with me. Why'd he do that, you figure?"

Joe gazed out of the squad car's passenger window at farm fields packed with tall rows of green cornstalks.

"I think Larry probably asked him," Joe replied. "Damn, the corn has really gotten high, hasn't it?"

"Yeah, it's gonna be another bumper crop," the sheriff said. "We should've been farmers, not cops. Farmers got it made around here."

"Yeah, it's another bumper crop alright," Joe replied. "You know, Mike…I really don't want to go see the Karvers either. I mean, I had nothing to do with this. You know that, don't you?"

"Yeah, I know," the sheriff responded. "And, I know you and Katie were friends. That's probably why the Karvers asked to have you come along. I wasn't blaming you, Joe. I just don't like having Karver think he can tell me what to do."

"I can tell you this," Joe said. "I was only in that mansion maybe four times and I never did like it. Old man Karver's wife, she never let us touch anything, and she was always afraid we would break something. I don't think Larry's mom liked kids. And, old man Karver was just as bad. He's a control freak and everything has to be done his way. That old bastard would have skinned us alive if he knew we were supplying Larry with beer."

"From what I understand, old man Karver still tries to control everything in that mansion, especially his son," the sheriff replied. "Larry…now there's an acorn that fell far, far away from the tree. Larry's no Gerald Karver, and that's for sure."

"Yeah, its doubtful Larry will ever measure up to the Karver expectations," Joe laughed. "Everything the old man has touched turned to gold. Everything Larry touches turns to shit, or at least that's the old man's take on it. Probably the only good thing Larry ever did in his entire life was marrying Katie."

Anyone who knew the Karvers was aware that Gerald Karver had a knack for constantly making Larry feel useless. The father would not admit that Larry had a less than average intellect and had no interest in the hardware business. Gerald Karver constantly assigned business ventures to his son and hoped that Larry would successfully meet the challenges. Larry always failed to live up to his father's expectations.

The only thing Larry did that earned his father's respect was marrying Katie. Gerald Karver liked showing off his new daughter-in-law at social events. She was beautiful, and she knew how to work a crowd. Gerald's wife had died before Larry had graduated from high school, and old man Karver had made Katie his official escort at functions where he wanted the accompaniment of feminine charm. At every social event, Katie became the shining star of the Karver family. She was prolific in the art of small talk, and socially she became the success that Gerald Karver had hoped Larry would be.

"You're right there," the sheriff observed. "I guess that's the only thing Larry did get right was to marry Katie. I mean Larry's dad liked Katie, right?"

"Yeah, he liked Katie alright. But, the Karvers are all users, Mike. Hell, old man Karver wanted Katie to give him a grandson who could take over the Karver business. I bet that stupid bastard was upset when Katie delivered a girl."

"Bet he was," the sheriff agreed. "What's the grandkid's name?"

Joe stared out the window at the Karver complex as the sheriff turned off the highway and pulled his squad car onto a long, meandering driveway that led to the Karver mansion. The three-story Karver home sat on ten acres of land and had a large, two-story guest home built just to the east of it.

"Her name's Angie," Joe answered. "She's a beautiful child. She looks just like Katie."

The sheriff stopped the squad car in the circular drive near Karver's front door. He leaned his body over the steering wheel, looking through the squad car's windshield at the sprawling mansion and slowly shook his head.

"You know what I think, Joe?" the sheriff said. "I think wealth like this always ruins a man. You and I are better off than any of the Karvers. And when there is trouble, they need us more than we need them."

"You're right about that, Mike," Joe replied. "And, they sure as hell need us now."

CHAPTER NINETEEN

J oe climbed out of the sheriff's squad car and grabbed his hat to carry with him to the Karvers' front door. A feeling of apprehension engulfed him as he walked toward the expansive home. He detested the fact that Katie had married Larry, and he did not want to be in the house where she had lived as Mrs. Larry Karver. As the sheriff pulled on an antique doorbell, Joe's mind envisioned Katie walking within the grandeur of the Karver mansion.

A housemaid answered the door, welcomed the two law officers into the Karver home, and guided them to Gerald Karver's office. Joe felt Katie's presence in every room they walked past. Their short journey through the mansion was ripping him apart with feelings of jealousy and desire. His heart pounded as he looked up the stairs that led to the bedrooms. Joe hated knowing that Katie had been a vital part of the Karver family. He hated that she had lived here without him; that she had cooked meals that he never tasted; that she had walked amongst this wealth without him seeing her beauty overshadowing its splendor, and that she had laughed at elaborate parties without him seeing her warm smile.

Joe's desire for Katie was eternal and his mind became consumed with thoughts of the times they had made love. He wanted her to be alive again. He wanted her to run to his arms, smothering him with kisses and confessing her love for him. He wanted to hear Katie admit that she loved him more than anyone. In the home from which Katie had been ripped away by murder, a sense of her presence haunted Joe, filling him with apprehension.

I've got to concentrate and be professional, Joe told himself. I've got to get Katie out of my mind and do my job.

The swirling apparitions of Katie were soon dispelled from Joe's thoughts by the real presence of Gerald Karver, who met the two law officers in the doorway of his office.

"Sheriff. Deputy. Welcome to my home," Gerald Karver said as he shook hands with both men.

The two men were led into an office decorated in rich woods and soft, dark leather. The walls were adorned with congratulatory plaques and pictures of Gerald Karver standing beside dignitaries of state, national, and international importance. There were awards of appreciation from school districts, parks, libraries, chambers of commerce, Rotaries, Kiwanis, and numerous charities. Centered on the wall behind Gerald Karver's enormous desk was a prominent presidential award with a picture of him shaking hands with Ronald Reagan.

"May I offer you two gentlemen some refreshment?" Karver asked.

"No, thank you," Sheriff Armstrong replied. "Mr. Karver, we are all very sorry for your loss. I know this is a terrible tragedy for you."

The sheriff turned towards Larry Karver, who stood silent beside the huge desk. The sheriff knew that it was Larry's custom to remain quiet in the presence of his father.

"Larry, you have my sincere condolences for the loss you have suffered," the sheriff said.

"Thank you, sheriff. We appreciate your sympathy," Gerald Karver replied.

Deputy Lambert looked towards Larry Karver and made a slight, respectful nod, which was dutifully returned. It was obvious that at this meeting Joe and Larry would only be observers.

Joe noticed that Mr. Karver did not offer anyone a chair. Instead, they all gathered around Karver's desk. Mr. Karver moved behind the desk and assumed a pose that looked as if he was about to address a business meeting. He spoke as if he was a CEO and the police officers served on his board of directors.

"Sheriff, I'm going to get right down to the point," he said. "I asked you here to find out what you are doing about my daughter-in-law's death. You're the sheriff here, Armstrong. You're new to the office, but you're the law. This kind of thing is unimaginable for Henry County. This monstrous act has people afraid, and I want this killer caught. I want him brought to justice. I want this to be the top priority for your office."

The audiences Karver granted in his office resembled the court of an Egyptian pharaoh. Gerald Karver was accustomed to giving orders and having the orders followed. He was a force to reckon with in Henry County. Over many years, Karver had purchased a lot of political clout in the state and in the county, and he had the ability to ruin a politician's career. Sheriff Armstrong did not fear Karver, but he did respect the authority Karver had in the county.

"Mr. Karver, you have my word," Sheriff Armstrong said. "The animal that did this to Katie will be caught and punished. I will see to it personally."

The sheriff focused his eyes on Karver's face as he offered his solemn pledge. He knew how to handle Karver. He would promise fast results and deliver on his promise. He would keep his promise not because Karver asked for the results, but because he was the Sheriff of Henry County and the people of the county expected him to find the murderer.

"No one wants this animal caught more than I do," the sheriff continued. "My office is working on catching this guy, and we'll get him. Katie was a beautiful young woman and we all want justice for her and for your family. I understand how terrible this loss is for you…believe me, I do."

As he spoke to Gerald Karver, Sheriff Armstrong detected that the old man's demeanor was softening. He was sure Karver's facial expression had diminished from hard and business-like to that of a grieving father.

The sheriff was correct in his assessment. The murder of Katie had initially filled Gerald Karver with anger, and he was appalled by its brutality. But more than anything, the murder had thrust an ache into Gerald Karver's heart. Katie's presence in the Karver household had brought him a sense of new life. His wife had died three years before Larry had gotten married and Katie had taken her place in the family. The old man had connected with Katie immediately and openly reveled in her charm. She was the daughter that he never had. He intended her to become mother to a large number of his grandchildren. The death of his wife and Katie's murder were terrific losses for him. After years and years of successes, Gerald Karver had forgotten how to deal with losing.

Karver sat down in the massive chair that loomed behind his desk and his body slowly sank into the chairs' plush upholstery. He covered his face for a brief moment, and Sheriff Armstrong thought he heard a slight sob come from behind his hands. Then Gerald Karver stood up again and walked toward the sheriff. He put his hand on the sheriff's shoulder.

Armstrong noticed that Karver's eyes were misty. He felt sorry for Karver. The sheriff hated the brutal nature of the crime, too, and he recognized that Karver was out of his league in this terrible endeavor. Gerald Karver was a powerful man caught and confused in a situation in which he found himself powerless. He was a self-made man who was accustomed to solving problems on his own, and it was not easy for him to ask for help.

"Sheriff, you will have my undying gratitude when you get this killer," he promised. "I want to thank you for coming to see me. Please keep me advised concerning the investigation. And if you need anything…anything at all, just let me know."

Karver's hand slid from the sheriff's shoulder and he gripped the sheriff's hand. The two men shook hands firmly as if they were concluding a business deal.

"I'll keep in touch, Mr. Karver," the sheriff said. "Any time you want to call me, do so."

The brief meeting ended and the four men parted company to slip back into their respective layers of society.

As the sheriff pulled his car out of the Karver estate, he was struck with a feeling that he was a part of the old, Wild West. He was Wyatt Earp, heading out in pursuit of a desperate outlaw. He would solve this depraved crime, and by doing so, he would give relief to everyone in the county. In situations like these, the sheriff deeply believed that he was the law in Henry County. It was up to him to restore order and safety. Mike Armstrong lived for these moments. This was the reason he had to be the sheriff. He knew when he caught the thug who had committed this odious act, he would receive the undying gratitude of the entire county. And, he knew the first person to extend his gratitude would be the wealthy and powerful Gerald Karver.

"Joe," the sheriff said while accelerating to highway speed, "I know Katie was your friend. I imagine all of this is very hurtful for you."

"Yeah, it is," Joe confessed openly.

Deputy Lambert stared out of the squad car window, the countryside scenery slipped by unnoticed by him. He had not accepted that Katie was dead, and the visit to her home was tearing away at his ability to function as a police officer.

How could something that made up such a large part of my heart be cold and dead, Joe wondered to himself. God, Katie why wasn't I there for you?

Joe knew he was supposed to remain professional, but his state of mind was a wreck. One week before Katie's death, he had responded to an email she had sent him. He had hoped to see her again, but he had not heard back from her. Since her death, Joe had to fight the urge to cry uncontrollably. He often felt explosive rushes of energy surging through his body, and he found himself wanting to hurt someone badly. He wanted to get back at someone for the pain that constantly seethed within him. Often he blamed himself for Katie's death.

If I had fought harder for Katie, he thought. If she had come with me, she would be alive today...Katie.

"Joe, I want to tell you something before we get back to the jailhouse," the sheriff said. "I'm going to have you help me on this case...but I think Rogers will be my main man here. I really think you might be too close to all this. What with you being friends with Katie and Larry. Are you all right with that? Do you understand what I'm saying here?"

"Yeah, Mike, I understand. To be honest, I don't think I'll be very dependable on this. You're right in what you're saying. I don't know...I don't know how much help I'd be."

"We'll get him, Joe. We'll get the bastard that did this. You can count on me," the sheriff promised.

CHAPTER TWENTY

Deputy Rogers immediately began his investigation of the Karver murder. Rogers knew how important it was to solve the crime, and he knew how beneficial it would be to his career if he could apprehend the murderer quickly. Deputy Lambert's involvement was limited to questioning potential witnesses. Information Joe was able to obtain from Scott Miller became crucial in directing Deputy Rogers' hunt for the killer toward a man named Brad Stablein, a transient who had recently arrived in Henry County and had taken up residence in Kewanee. But, Deputy Lambert did not have to ferret out the information he received from Scott; instead, Scott voluntarily offered it.

"Hey, Joe," Miller said into a phone. "This is Scott."

It was 5:00 p.m., and Scott was calling Deputy Lambert from an old phone booth that stood in the corner of Hunter's Tavern in Kewanee.

"I know," Joe replied. "Did you think I wouldn't recognize your voice, Scott? What'd you need, guy?"

"I'm calling you about the murder," Scott said. "You know, Katie being missing and all that. I know something and it could be important. I don't wanna talk to anybody else about it, just you. Can I see you and tell you?"

"Is it really important, Scott? Do you really have something worth talking about?"

Yeah I do," Scott replied. "I really do. I wanna help. Can I see ya? But, I don't wanna come over to Cambridge. I don't wanna see Rogers or Armstrong. I just wanna talk with you. Can we do it that way?"

"Sure, Scott. I haven't seen you for a while. I liked to catch up on things. How about I buy you some lunch at Sweeny's tomorrow? You always liked the food there, right?"

"I'd like that," Scott said, "unless you want to meet here at Hunter's."

"Sorry, Scott, but we're not meeting at any bar. We're just gonna have a good lunch. If you've got some information, I want your head clear when you tell me about it. You understand?"

"Yeah, I understand," Scott said. "You want me sober. I can do that, but can it be a late lunch? You know I don't get up so early anymore. And, I don't want a lot of people around when we're talking."

"That's fine," Joe replied. "How about I meet you at Sweeny's around one in the afternoon? The lunch crowd should be thinned out by then, and they serve lunch up until 2:30. Would that work for you?"

"That'll be great, Joe. And you're gonna buy lunch, right?"

"That's right, Scott. Lunch is on me…so don't stand me up. And have something worthwhile to tell me. I'll see you tomorrow at one. Be there Scott, or I'll have to come looking for you."

"I'll be there, Joe," Scott promised. "See ya then."

Scott was ten minutes late in arriving at Sweeny's Restaurant, but Joe was happy to see his old friend. The two men sat at a booth in the back of the dining area, far away from the small number of patrons who were finishing their late lunches. Their plan to meet at one o'clock had worked. The noon crowds had already left, and Joe knew it was doubtful Scott could have arrived any earlier, unless he went to Scott's apartment and dragged him out of bed. They had both ordered the lunch special, and their table was crowded with two large platters covered with Swiss steak and potatoes, smothered in gravy. A basket of warm rolls and two cups of steaming, hot coffee completed the luncheon special. After a round of small talk, Deputy Lambert broached the reason for the two men having lunch together.

"So tell me," Joe began. "What's so important about the information you have for me? And remember…this isn't just any missing person we're talking about. This is Katie. We both knew her, so this is special and important for both of us. You understand that, right?"

"Yeah, of course I do. I liked Katie, too, you know. I mean, I know you were better friends with her, but I liked her, too. I wouldn't do anything to mess this up. You can trust me on this."

"Alright, Scott," Joe said. "But just know this…if you give me some information that screws things up, Sheriff Armstrong and Rogers are gonna be pissed. You know they're not real fans of yours anyway. You gotta be right about anything you tell me. So tell me right, understand?"

"I'm just gonna tell you what I know," Scott said. "That's why I wanted to meet with just you. You can hear what I have to say and then decide if it means anything. I don't want any trouble, Joe. I just wanna help."

"That's good. As long as we understand each other," Joe replied. "So what ya got?"

"Well, I saw a man following Katie the day she disappeared," Scott said in a hushed tone.

Joe stopped eating his food and stared at Scott. He felt his heart beating rapidly. He had tried not to think of what could have happened to Katie. He was glad he was not assigned to be the main investigator on the case. Now, the thought of someone stalking her and hurting her consumed his thoughts. His gut ached, and he felt blood rushing through his body.

"Who was it?" Joe said slowly. "Who did you see, Scott?"

"It was a guy that works at the grocery store," Scott answered. "Are you alright, Joe?"

"I'm fine," Joe answered. "I'm fine. I just want to find out what happened to Katie. I want the person who hurt her caught. If you can give me any information that will help with that, I know the sheriff will appreciate it. What's this guy's name?

"His name's Brad Stablein. Do you know him, Joe?"

"No. I don't know him. Do you know him?"

"I've had a few drinks with him before," Scott said. "He's mean, Joe. Real mean. He's not from here. He's mean. I'll tell ya that."

Deputy Lambert began to pull himself back from the adrenalin flow that was inhibiting his ability to think straight. I gotta think clearly here, he thought. Just get the info and turn it over to Rogers. Gotta pump everything I can from Scott about this. I gotta calm down or I'll scare him away.

"And you're sure you saw this Brad Stablein following Katie the night of her disappearance?"

"I'm absolutely positive. You know I wasn't drinking that night because I was going fishing with Foster early next morning. You know me, Joe. Fishing is my first love. I don't let anything interfere with my fishing."

Scott paused in his conversation to spread butter on a roll. Joe sat patiently and watched Scott wipe gravy from his plate with half of the buttered roll.

"And you saw this Stablein guy follow Katie to her car that very evening?" Joe asked again. "You gotta make sure you're right about this, Scott. This information could be real important."

Scott took a bite from his roll, chewed three times and swallowed the tasty morsel.

"I saw him," he replied. "I saw Brad Stablein. I thought he was gonna help Katie with her groceries, but he didn't have any bags with him. I was sitting on the bench in front of Karver's store. You know the bench I mean?"

Joe took a sip of coffee and smiled.

"Yeah I know, Scott," Joe said. "I guess the only fixture in this downtown area that is as old as that bench is you sitting on it."

"Well, yeah," Scott said laughing. "But I do see everything that happens down here. You know I sat there for a good twenty minutes that night and I never did see Stablein come back from the parking lot. I didn't think nothing of it until Katie came up missing."

Scott looked directly into Joe's eyes. His face became melancholy and his voice slightly trembled. "I'm sorry about Katie," he said. "Damn! Who'd have thought this would happen to her?"

Joe looked around the dining room, trying hard not to think of Katie.

"Yeah, who'd have thought."

"Hey, Joe, can we get pie, too?"

"Sure, Scott, you have a piece of pie."

Joe examined the boyish look that had come over Scott's face. He smiled at him and thought of a time long ago when Scott's mother would bake pies and have Joe over just so the two boys could eat pie together.

"We'll both have pie," he said. "And then I'll have Deputy Roger's check out this Stablein guy."

"I told you the information would be good," Scott said. "You have him checked out. You'll see there's something strange about him."

"You did good, Scott. Hell, maybe you should've become a cop."

"I would've been a good one. I know everybody. And, I know a lot about this town. You know what? I think I'll have cherry pie."

"Cherry pie sounds great," Joe agreed. "We'll both get that."

After leaving Scott, Deputy Lambert decided to do a little checking on Brad Stablein before taking any information to Deputy Rogers.

I don't want Rogers throwing anything back in my face, he thought. And the less I have to talk with him, the better my life will be.

By asking around, Joe discovered that Brad Stablein was a man in his mid-twenties and had been in Kewanee less than a year. Stablein had been eking out an existence working part-time at a grocery store, and Joe knew Katie often shopped at the same store. He did not believe that Stablein should be considered a prime suspect in the murder, but because Stablein must have run into Katie while she was shopping, he decided to turn Scott's statement over to Deputy Rogers. Rogers followed up by interviewing the other store employees. All of the them could remember Stablein making comments about Katie.

"Yeah, deputy, Stablein told me Katie liked it when he carried groceries for her," one of the baggers reported to Rogers. "He said he'd always look for her on Tuesday nights. Tuesday night was the time she usually did her shopping here. He'd look for her and make sure he was up at the cash register so he could bag her groceries. Once, he told me to 'get lost' when I was gonna bag up her stuff."

"Stablein told me Katie flirted with him and was always smiling at him," another recalled. "One time he bragged to me, saying that she came in here just to see him. What'd you think of that, huh? That guy doesn't live in the real world, does he?"

"Know what?" the produce manager said. "Stablein always fished in the same area where…the area of the canal where they found Katie's leg. I hope that you get the guy that done this. And I'll tell you this, that Stablein guy, he ain't right in the head."

CHAPTER TWENTY-ONE

Brad Stablein's existence in Kewanee was meager. He lived in an old two-story house that had been converted into apartments. A long time ago, the house must have been the proud home of a large family, but now the structure was occupied by poor tenets and owned by a landlord who took no responsibility for its appearance. The entire house was dingy and dirty, and Brad's apartment echoed that motif.

The landlord had converted the old home into three upstairs apartments and two downstairs apartments. Brad rented one of the upstairs apartments. His apartment consisted of two rooms. The largest room was a combination living room/bedroom and the other smaller room had been made into a kitchen. The kitchen was furnished with a refrigerator, a stove, a sink, a small table, and two kitchen chairs. The table and chairs were painted green to match the grease splatter green trim board that wound its way around the cracked and pealing linoleum floor. Both the refrigerator and the stove had once been brilliant white, but were now tarnished by age. A thin layer of grime covered both appliances.

A small entrance hallway separated the kitchen from the living room. In the living room, a foldout couch provided Brad with a bed. Brad never took the time to unfold the couch; instead, he always crashed onto it, covering himself with a blanket that he kept stuffed away on the top shelf of a small closet. The living room furniture was old and worn. A permanent layer of dust had settled over every object in the room and the whole apartment was heavy with the stench of stale tobacco smoke.

With the information he had from Deputy Lambert, Rogers obtained a warrant to enter Brad's apartment. He took Deputy Thomas with him to help conduct the search. Brad was not at home when the two police officers arrived at the residence. Deputy Rogers showed the warrant to a man who lived downstairs and who was considered the in-house caretaker of the apartment house.

"What the hell's he done wrong," the man asked as he looked at the warrant.

"Mr. Stablein isn't accused of anything," Rogers responded. "We just need to look around and this paper gives us the right to do so."

"Hell, I don't care what you do up there," the man replied. "I'll get ya a key and you can help yourself. Just so you know, Stablein shares a bathroom up there with the two other guys. It's only locked if someone's using it."

Rogers and Thomas made their way up an outside stairway that led to a second floor entrance. They entered the house and walked fourteen feet down a hallway to Brad's apartment. The hallway was dark and emitted a musty smell. When Rogers opened the door to Brad's apartment, the musty smell mingled with the heavy aroma of old cooking grease that emanated from the kitchen.

The two deputies took a quick right when they entered the apartment. Deputy Thomas moved to the center of the living room, put his hands on his hips and looked around.

"This shouldn't take long," he predicted. "There's not much here and I don't want to spend a lotta time in this flea trap.

"You look around," Rogers commanded as he and Thomas slipped plastic gloves over their hands. "I'm gonna go check out that bathroom at the end of the hallway. Make sure you look under everything."

"Christ, no telling what I'll find under this furniture," Thomas grumbled. "I doubt this place has ever seen a vacuum cleaner or a mop. It makes me itch just standing here."

"That may be, but I want this place turned upside down," Rogers said. "We're gonna look in every cupboard in that kitchen and in every bowl. I'll be back to help after I've had a look at that bathroom."

Shit, Thomas thought as he looked around the room. What a goddamn dump.

Thomas decided to begin his search by examining the couch. He bent down and pulled up on a handle that protruded from the lower middle of the couch. The couch sprung to life and easily unfolded, revealing a mattress that was covered with a ripped and dirty sheet. He pulled the mattress up and let it fall. A small cloud of dust bunnies scurried away from the mattress as it hit the floor. Thomas looked down through the bedspring and saw more dust and three coins lying on the floor. He pulled the unfolded couch away from the wall and walked behind it, padding the armrests and the back of the couch with his fingers as he moved.

"Find anything," Deputy Rogers said as he re-entered the apartment.

"Forty cents. I'll split it with ya if we can leave now."

"Just keep looking. I'll check out the kitchen."

Deputy Thomas left the couch and headed for a small closet that was on the opposite side of the room. He opened the door and pulled a large blanket off of a top shelve. The pungent smell of body odor rushed up into his nostrils as the blanket slipped by his face. Disgusted with his find, he was happy to hear his partner calling out from the kitchen.

"Thomas!"

Thomas gladly left the closet area and headed for the kitchen. As he walked into the small room, he saw Rogers had moved the refrigerator away from the wall

"Look back there," Rogers said as Thomas walked into the room.

Deputy Thomas squeezed passed Rogers and looked behind the refrigerator. The area behind the refrigerator was dark, but he could see that the floor tile was crumbled and wet. The back of the refrigerator was coated with thick layer of dusty grunge. Rogers handed him a small flashlight he had been using to conduct the search.

"Shine the light on the lower back part of the refrig," Rogers said. "Tell me what you see."

"Looks like something's taped back there. Looks like duct tape to me. Could be a gun."

"That's what I thought," Rogers responded. "Let's pull the refrig out a little more and you see if you can get to it."

Deputy Rogers pulled on the front of the refrigerator and Deputy Thomas pushed at the back corner, as the two men wrestled the appliance away from the wall.

"Jesus, what a mess," Thomas exclaimed as he looked fully behind the appliance. "But, that's a gun alright. Taped to the back with duct tape."

He pulled the tape away from the refrigerator and handed a small pistol to Deputy Rogers. Rogers held the pistol up with two fingers, sniffing the muzzle.

"Smells like its been fired recently," he said. "I think I'll have a talk with Mr. Stablein about this. You take the pistol to the lab. I'm gonna go pick this guy up and talk to the sheriff about all of this."

CHAPTER TWENTY-TWO

Deputy Rogers kept the sheriff up to speed on how the investigation was going. The sheriff always passed the information on to Gerald Karver. In the second week of the investigation, Rogers was certain he had the man in his sights who had killed Katie.

"We got our man," Rogers told Sheriff Armstrong. "I found an unregistered 22 pistol in Stablein's apartment. There are three bullets missing from the gun. And, I checked with the police chief down there in Wilton where Stablein grew up. Stablein's got a rap sheet with them. It's all petty stuff, but he has always been heading in the wrong direction. Been busted for drug use, too."

"Neil, you'd better have more than that!" Armstrong responded. "And, you'd better get moving on this. I want the son of a bitch who did this hanging on my door soon."

"Oh, I got a lot more than that," Neil replied. "I got a lot more."

"I'm listening. Make it good," Armstrong demanded.

"I took some dogs over to an empty yard behind Stablein's apartment. The dogs dug up part of a blouse that we think belonged to Katie…and there is blood on it. I sent it for lab work. I'll tell you, this guy's reeks. He's the one alright."

"What about Joe?" the sheriff asked. "Is he helping you with all of this?"

"Nah. It's like we agreed. I'm keeping him out of all of it."

"Good," the sheriff replied. "Joe's a good man, but sometimes a fellow can be too good. You know what I mean?"

"Yeah, I know, Mike. I'm keeping him at arm's length."

"And what about Larry Karver?" the sheriff asked. "I know you think you got the goods on this Stablein guy, but are you certain that we can exclude the husband in this?"

"I questioned him. He was playing poker the night Katie disappeared. Every two weeks he plays poker with six other guys. They play from seven until eleven. I checked with his poker buddies. Larry was with them."

"Yeah, but we don't know the time of death," the sheriff said.

"Katie always went shopping on the nights that Larry played poker. She went that night. She was seen by Scott Miller and Miller saw Stablein in the same area."

"Miller's a drunk," the sheriff observed.

"I tell you, Mike, Larry doesn't have the balls to do anything like this. I grilled him good. He's very distraught over the loss of his wife. Stablein…he's our man."

"And everything you've done has been on the up and up?" Armstrong asked. "You did it by the book? I don't want any of this stuff thrown out of court because some goddamn lawyer finds loopholes in your search warrant."

"Like always, Mike, I covered everything. You know me; I always make it neat and clean. And, there are no foul ups."

"That's what I want. I want it all neat and clean. That's why I chose you, Neil. I want you to make it stick, and I want this thing wrapped up. We can't have killers walking free in our county. You make it stick, and keep me informed on how it's going.

"Don't worry, Sheriff. I'll get it all done. Right now, I'm going over to talk with Larry Karver. I just want to tie up a few loose ends in my interview with him. Nothing serious. Do you want me to update him on the case?"

"No. Don't do that, Neil," the sheriff replied. "I will do all of the reporting and only to old man Karver. You go ahead and talk with Larry, but don't tell him anything. And, you get back to me right away if Larry Karver has anything important to say to you."

Neil Rogers did not tell the sheriff that it was Larry Karver who had contacted him and asked him to come to Kewanee for a talk. Deputy Rogers was ambitious, and he saw opportunity in being able to talk with anyone from the Karver family. Rogers had never been to the Karver mansion, and he was not invited to the mansion now. Instead, Larry arranged to meet him at one of the Karver warehouses at six o'clock in the evening. Rogers guessed that Larry did not want to talk in the presence of his father. When he pulled into the warehouse parking lot, Larry was there to greet him.

"Hey, Deputy," Larry called as Rogers stepped out of his squad car. "Glad you could come. I think I've got some important information for you."

Deputy Rogers shook hands with Larry and looked at the surroundings in a deliberate manner.

"This is kind of a strange place to meet. You don't work here do you Mr. Karver?"

"Call me Larry, Deputy. Nah, I don't work here. I've got a big office in the downtown store. But, I come here sometimes just to get away from everybody. I figured it would be a good place for us to talk. It's private and quiet. We've got four warehouses just like this one scattered all around the outskirts of Kewanee. Let's go inside and find some place where we can talk."

Larry Karver led Deputy Rogers to an office inside the warehouse. The office was small and furnished in a cheap, utilitarian manner.

"Can I get you a coke, Deputy?" Larry offered.

"That'd be great," Rogers replied.

Larry handed the deputy a can of soda that he had retrieved from a dented, mini-refrigerator and then sat down behind a desk that was stained with a variety of old spills and had a clutter of papers scattered across its top. He leaned back in a tattered chair and placed his right foot up on the half-opened, middle drawer of the desk. Rogers sat in a smaller, steel-framed office chair, which he had placed directly in front of the desk.

Larry took a swallow of coke and put the can down on the desktop.

"I'm glad that they've got you working this case, Neil," he said. "I want the animal who murdered my wife caught and put away. I know you're the man who can do that. I've always liked the way you handle yourself. You know, my family would be very grateful to the man who caught this killer."

"Can I ask you," Rogers queried. "Does your dad know about this meeting?"

"Nope, he doesn't. Does that matter?"

"Doesn't matter to me," the Deputy responded. "But, if there's anything to what you tell me here, he'll have to know. I'm just looking out for you. That's all."

"Yeah...my ole man, he has to know everything. You're right about that," Larry observed. "But, I'm my own man, Deputy. I don't have to clear everything with him. He doesn't know about this right now because it's none of his business. After all...we're talking about my wife. And besides, I wanted to let you know first. Hell, maybe what I'm gonna tell you won't matter. So, why bother him with it unless it's important."

"Like I said, Larry, I'm just looking out for you. I'm gonna get the guy that harmed your wife and I need all the evidence I can to do that. So...you said on the phone you have some information that might be important. Let's hear it, and then I'll tell you how important it is to the case."

"Great. But we're in agreement here...my ole man doesn't have to know about this unless it really goes some where, right?"

Deputy Rogers held his coke can in his hand, taking short sips from it while talking with Larry.

"Right," Rogers said. "There's no sense bothering anyone with what you got to say, unless I think it's important to the case. I'm handling everything, Larry."

"Well, I don't know if this will help or not, but this is what I want to tell you," Larry began. "I guess I should have mentioned it before...there was a phone call at the house a week before Katie disappeared and a man asked for her. When I asked for his name, he hung up on me. I hear you've got a suspect. Maybe if I could hear his voice...well, who knows...I might recognize it. Your suspect may be the man who called that night."

"Did you ask Katie about the call?" Rogers asked.

"Yeah, I did. She didn't know anything about it though. We both figured it was a telemarketer or something like that. But, now I wonder. I still remember the voice. I might be able to connect it to your suspect. You got a suspect, right?"

"Yeah, we've got a suspect," Rogers replied. "I can't say who it is, but I'll tell you what…I'll get him to speak into a recorder and, if you can identify his voice, it could make the case stronger. But Larry, you gotta be sure about this."

"Just let me know when you want me to listen," Larry replied. "We all want that murdering bastard nailed. He just needs to say, 'Is Katie there?' That's what the guy said when I answered the phone. The guy didn't sound very educated to me. That's what seemed strange to me…didn't seem right that a guy like that would be asking for Katie. So, you think this is important?"

"It's real important," Rogers answered. "But like you say, we should wait on telling anyone until you can listen to that tape. This is just gonna be between you and me."

"What about my dad?" Larry asked. "When will we have to tell him?"

"We'll have to tell him after you listen to the tape and make a positive ID on this guy," Rogers replied. "We'll work together on this, Larry….you and me. I'm not telling anyone. But, once you make that ID, we'll figure out how to tell your dad…and you know what I think? I think your dad will be proud of you."

"Yeah, well, maybe. Don't matter though," Larry shrugged. "What matters is you put that guy away. I loved Katie more than anybody."

"I'll get him," Rogers assured Larry.

The two men left the warehouse office. Larry walked Rogers to his squad car and added incentive for Rogers to be quick in apprehending the killer.

"It will be a feather in your cap if you can get this guy," he said. "You know, the police chief's job in Kewanee will be opening up in less than a year. People talk about you as a serious candidate for that position. I'd like to see you in charge of the law in our city, and I know my dad thinks the same."

Deputy Rogers ducked into the front seat of his squad car, held the door ajar, and looked up at Larry Karver.

"I'll get that tape to you, and we'll get the guy that hurt Katie," Rogers promised.

The next day, Rogers notified Larry Karver he had the tape for him. The two men agreed to meet at the same warehouse location so Larry could hear the suspect's voice.

"That's the guy! That's the guy I heard that night on the phone," Larry said. "I'm sure of it! He's the one."

"Alright Larry, this is good. This will help the case a lot. Now I'm going to tell the sheriff about this and you'd better tell your dad. You'd better tell him before the sheriff does. You understand?"

"I'll tell him," Larry agreed. "But, I'm gonna tell him I forgot about the phone call, and I remembered it when you came to see me at the warehouse. I remembered it because you were questioning me about Katie's whereabouts prior to her death. Right, Deputy? Isn't that how it all came about? You came to see me to question me, right?"

"That's it exactly, Larry," Rogers agreed. "I came to see you and while I was asking you some questions, you remembered the phone call. But, this is just between you and me. No one else needs to know any different."

CHAPTER TWENTY-THREE

With the evidence he needed in place, Deputy Rogers began an intense interrogation of Brad Stablein. The murder suspect was poor, illiterate and alone. Rogers used all of the evidence he had to confront and frighten him. At first Stablein objected to the charges against him, but over time, Rogers convinced Stablein that he was guilty.

"You've got no alibi for the night Katie disappeared. Your fingerprints have been found on her car. You're better off admitting everything to me, Brad," Rogers coaxed. "You'll be better off in jail than out on the street. People around here are pissed about what happened to Mrs. Karver, and they're gonna blame you."

"I didn't have anything to do with that," Stablein said. "All I done was work at the store where she shopped."

"You can forget about ever working at that grocery store, or any other place in Kewanee," Rogers replied. "Your life on the street is finished, but maybe you can tell me why you did it. Sometimes there are reasons for these things. I'm like you…a man of the world. We both know women can be a pain in the ass."

"I didn't kill her, but I can tell ya she deserved to be pushed around some," Brad admitted. "You know that bitch flirted with me all the time. You can ask some of the guys at the store. They seen her doing it. She was always smiling at me and then driving away in one of her big cars. It's not right that she flirted like that. She shouldn't of dressed that way neither. How's a man supposed to do his job with her dressed like that?"

"A man shouldn't have to take that, Brad," Rogers agreed. "You know all of us guys have had women do that. It isn't right. It makes a man angry, and it's so damn frustrating. Most men would understand your anger. I hate it when a bitch does that stuff."

"Yeah and those guys back at the store…they're always egging me on," Brad said. They were always telling me to make my move. They knew that she wanted it and they knew she liked having me help her. All I was doing was trying to fit in with those guys. Ya know…they liked hearing me talk about Katie…I know they did. They ain't no better than me."

Brad paused for a moment and frowned at Deputy Rogers. He fidgeted in his chair and ran his fingers through his long hair.

"Hey, shouldn't I have a lawyer here with me?" he asked.

"I can get you a lawyer…if you want one, Brad. But, we're just two guys talking about women right now. I mean what you've told me about her is a helluva a thing…the way she treated you. A man shouldn't have to take that from a woman. Is that why you followed her in the parking lot?" Rogers cajoled. "Is that when you showed her? Did you teach her a lesson that night? You can tell me. I'll understand, and I can help others to see what the problem was. What'd ya say, Brad…let's get this thing done."

Brad Stablein fidgeted again in his chair. He drummed his fingers against the top of the table that separated him from Deputy Rogers. His eyes darted up and down, looking hard at the deputy and then down at the table top.

"Well…she's dead, ain't she? I guess someone showed her," Brad said in a loud, agitated voice. "You think I'd let a woman treat me bad? I've knocked sense into plenty of women before. I've taught, em. I guess that one won't be messing with me any more."

"Tell me about that, Brad," Rogers coaxed. "I want to know how you put her in her place. You did a favor for a lot of guys around here."

"Yeah, well…like I said, she flirted with me. I could tell that she wanted me."

"You keep a gun on you, Brad? We found a gun in your room. There were only three bullets in it. You know how to use a gun, don't you?"

"Sure I do! I don't let nobody mess with me!" Brad arrogantly stated.

"I know you don't," Rogers agreed. "I saw your rap sheet from Wilton. One of the deputies down there told me that you're a tough dude."

"I know how to handle myself," Stablein said. "You can ask anybody down at the store. They know my rep. I built a rep with them, that's for sure."

"And you don't take crap from nobody, right Brad? The guys down at the store told me you can handle yourself. Tell me how you showed Katie that night. Tell me how you taught her a lesson."

"Hell, I don't remember a whole lot from that night…guess I was pretty high, I think," Brad mumbled. "I gotta problem with drugs. Maybe I seen her that night. Maybe…"

"You know, Brad…you don't really have to remember everything you did that night. I know you wanna make this right. You just have to admit that you did it. Hell, everyone knows a tough dude like you ain't gonna take crap from a woman."

"Maybe I did it. Shit…maybe I did," Stablein said. "I ain't saying I did, but she deserved what she got…I'll say that. Just remember she deserved what she got. It was her fault all of this happened."

"All you gotta do is talk to me about that night," Rogers advised.

Frightened, confused, and tired, Stablein agreed to be videotaped while Rogers asked him questions about the night of the murder. Deputy Rogers helped Stablein to remember what happened between him and Katie.

"I do remember…I remember asking her if she liked me," Stablein confessed. "I don't remember if it was that night though…could've been that night."

"What did Katie say to that," Rogers asked.

"The bitch laughed at me! That's what she did. She said, 'Get lost, jerk!' Hell…I got rights too, you know? I'm not rich like her…but I ain't no jerk. And it's like I said…she flirted with me, she came on to me. Ya know, I could take her any time I wanted…a woman shouldn't talk to a man like that."

"Did you hit her, Brad?" Rogers asked. "I wouldn't let any woman call me a jerk. What'd you do?"

"Like I said, I've hit women before," Stablein answered. "I've put them in their place. Yeah, I might've hit her. I ain't gonna let no woman talk to me like that."

"People tell me that Katie was a strong woman. It wouldn't be easy to hit her. I think she'd fight back and fight back hard."

"There ain't no woman who can handle me," Stablein bragged. "Yeah, she fought back, but I was tired of her crap, and I meant business. No woman's gonna treat me bad. She had it coming."

"How'd you do it? How'd you handle such a strong woman?" Rogers asked.

"You think a woman could stand up to a punch from me?" Brad boasted. "No way in hell! I'd punched her a good one if she fought back. I'm a street fighter and I can handle anyone. Christ knows…you get hit by me and ya know it. You get hit by me and you're going down."

"And then you shot her, didn't you, Brad? You shot her with that twenty-two we found in your apartment, right?"

"I don't remember shooting nobody," Stablein said. "I…I don't remember that. Ya found a gun in my apartment, huh?"

"Yeah we did, Brad. It's a twenty-two. You ever shot a twenty-two?"

"Yeah, I've shot a twenty-two. I've shot lots of guns…maybe I shot her…I don't remember anything like that. I told ya…I've got a drug problem. Sometimes I don't remember things. But…if she got shot, she earned it."

"She was hitting back at you, wasn't she?" Rogers asked. "I mean…a man's got a right to protect himself. And, I've seen this all the time. Things get out of hand. I mean she called you a jerk. It's hard for a man to control his temper. Do you have a temper, Brad?"

"Yeah I…I guess I do. But, that bitch shouldn't of called me a jerk though…that's not my fault…I mean, any man would've been mad at her."

"You bet, Brad. Let's get this all done," Rogers suggested. "I'm telling you, people will understand. Hell, every man will understand. I mean, you're right…she treated you badly, and you don't deserve that. Let's get this all out. You'll feel a lot better if you do."

Under the prodding of Deputy Rogers, Stablein confessed that he had shot Katie, put her body in the truck of her car, and drove out of town.

"We think Katie's body was all cut up," Deputy Rogers said. "You ever use a knife on anyone, Brad?"

"I've seen my share of knife fights," Stablein admitted. "And I cut a guy once. I ain't afraid to use a knife."

CHAPTER TWENTY-FOUR

Brad Stablein couldn't remember where he had dumped Katie's remains, but he remembered being out at his favorite fishing spot that night. A team of investigators searched the canal area again, but no more body parts were found. A butcher knife that had been missing from the grocery store was found near the canal, and Katie's blood was found on the knife. Katie's car with her personal belongings was found in an old, run-down garage, which was only two blocks away from Brad's apartment. The steering wheel and the door handles of the car had been wiped clean of any prints, but Brad's prints were found on the back window of the car.

Everyone thought Katie's body would eventually turn up. It never did.

Deputy Lambert stayed clear of the investigation fearing that his emotional state could interfere with a conviction. He wanted Katie's killer caught and punished, but he was unable to be objective about any of the investigation. He made it a point to leave and find something else to do whenever anyone brought up the case. He knew that Rogers was directing his efforts at finding Stablein guilty, and he doubted that would happen. He found it hard to believe that a man like Brad Stablein could get the best of Katie. He did not believe that she would make herself vulnerable to such a man. But, Deputy Lambert had underestimated the abilities of Deputy Rogers. In the end, Rogers got his man.

The evidence against Brad Stablein was not conclusive, but it was strong circumstantial. The judge allowed Stablein to enter an "Alfred Plea". Under the terms of the agreement, Stablein was able to profess being innocent of the murder, but admitted that the prosecution had enough evidence to convict him of the crime. The plea agreement put Stablein at the mercy of the court's sentencing.

The residents of Henry County wanted the murder resolved and they wanted the killer to pay. Brad Stablein was a misfit in Henry County, and there was no one to support his infrequent objections to the charges. There were times when Stablein seemed genuinely pleased with all of the attention showered upon him, and he acted as if he had solved the case by pleading out to the crime. At other times, he seemed confused and afraid. The public defender assigned to the case found Brad Stablein to be a difficult client.

"I'm going to jail," Brad told his attorney. "There ain't nothing you're gonna do for me. I got no friends here. I ain't guilty, but I'm going to jail. People like me always wind up in jail."

Brad Stablein was incarcerated for a month in the Henry County Jail while he awaited his sentencing. Deputy Rogers let Brad know that it was unsafe for him to come in contact with anyone, and Brad agreed to remain in protective custody inside of the jailhouse. Stablein was locked up in a single cell, ate alone, and was kept away from the jail's other inmates. In time, he became fearful of being outside of the county jailhouse. The longer he stayed in jail, the more comfort he found in being institutionalized. The sheriff stayed away from Stablein, and he made sure that Deputy Lambert was kept away from Stablein's cellblock. Neil Rogers was the contact man with Brad Stablein, and Rogers continually reassured Brad that he was better off in jail.

"I'm glad that we were able to work together on this case," Rogers said during a visit to Brad's jail cell. "You know, I think I am the one guy who understands why you hated Katie. I understand why you had to do it. I am glad we can talk."

Over time, Brad Stablein began to understand why he had hated Katie, too.

"I'll tell ya, Neil," he confessed, "I wish it hadn't turned out this way. I wish she'd treated me nicer."

A large crowd of curious onlookers and the news media attended Stablein's sentencing hearing. Judge Randy Hollenbeck accepted the plea and sentenced Stablein to serve sixty to eighty years of imprisonment. Those who attended the sentencing were interviewed outside of the courthouse. A self-appointed spokesman for the crowd happily volunteered to make a public comment.

"There was no way that guy was innocent," the spokesman said. "For God's sakes, I heard that he had confessed to the murder. And, he admitted hating Katie. But, just wait…soon this guy'll be shouting that he's innocent, but it's obvious that he's guilty, and he should rot in jail. No one should have to suffer like the Karvers have. The sheriff's office did a great job of getting this killer off our streets."

Sheriff Armstrong agreed that his office had done a great job in tracking down Katie's murderer. And, the Sheriff called a press conference to praise his deputies and himself.

"I made this case our top priority," the sheriff reported. "I assigned my best investigators to catching this killer. I want to especially congratulate Deputy Rogers for all the time and hard work he put in on this case. I know some people wanted to see Mr. Stablein sentenced to death. That didn't happen. But…it is not gonna be any picnic serving eighty years in Joliet State Prison with all those other harden criminals. Mr. Stablein will have to think about the terrible crime he committed for a long, long time."

Three days after the trial ended, Gerald Karver made an appointment to meet with the sheriff at the Henry County Courthouse. A private conference room was reserved for the meeting. The sheriff brought Deputy Rogers and Deputy Lambert with him to the meeting, and Mr. Karver brought his son, Larry. When he entered the conference room, Mr. Karver found the officers already seated behind a large conference table.

Sheriff Armstrong immediately moved from behind the table to welcome the Karvers, while Deputies Rogers and Lambert stood behind the conference table. Sheriff Armstrong shook Gerald Karver's hand.

"Gerald, I want to thank you for coming all the way over here," Armstrong said.

The sheriff nodded in the direction of Larry Karver.

"Larry, I hope you are well," he said. "Would you both like to sit down?"

"No, thank you, Sheriff," Gerald Karver said. "We won't be taking up a lot of your time. I know you are a busy man. I wanted to thank you and your men in person for putting that man in jail. I appreciate everything you did."

Gerald Karver then directed his attention towards the deputies, momentarily pointing in their direction.

"You've got two good men there, Sheriff," he said.

The sheriff glanced back at the two deputies and then placed his hand on Gerald Karver's shoulder.

"I know I do," he replied. "I made a promise to you, Gerald, and I kept it."

"It won't be forgotten, Sheriff," Karver replied.

The two men shook hands once again and then the Karvers left the courthouse, heading back to their world of business and wealth.

The following Monday, Brad Ernest Stablein was taken from the Henry County Jailhouse to the Illinois Joliet Correctional Institution to begin serving his sentence among the 2,773 other inmates who were locked up in the facility. Neil Rogers was one of the two deputies who transported Stablein to Joliet.

"You'll be a big man in Joliet," Rogers told Stablein. "A lot of the guys up there are gonna be afraid of you...you being a murderer and all."

When Rogers returned from Joliet, he reported to Sheriff Armstrong.

"You did a good job, Neil," the sheriff said. "This case was important. We needed to show the citizens that this office is here to protect them. No one likes murder, but solving murders is our business and, every once in awhile, it's good to have a situation where the public is reminded about how important this office is and why they need people like you and me."

"Thanks, Sheriff," Neil replied. "I worked hard on this case and I think the results speak highly for both of us."

Chapter Twenty-Five

After Mike Armstrong had become sheriff, he began to wear his uniform with added frequency. In fact, he wore his uniform more often than an army general. And like an army general, Armstrong looked out of character in his civvies; he preferred being in uniform. He liked the feeling of authority and power that came with donning the official garb of his office. He had come to believe that he even thought differently when he was ensconced in the formal attire of his office. Armstrong was certain he thought with more clarity and acted more efficiently in his police clothing. He knew other people would scoff at his thinking, but when he was in his uniform, the sheriff envisioned himself as a minor super hero whose costume bestowed special powers. He purposefully avoided being seen out of uniform because he had grown accustomed to the respect people gave him when he was in his dark brown shirt and his light tan pants. Armstrong knew people were less attentive to him without the badge, web belt, and Smokey the Bear hat he wore when taking on the role of sheriff. He had seen respect for authority decline over the last twenty years he had been a lawman, but a judge's robe and sheriff's uniform still commanded some esteem. The sheriff liked that, and he stayed in uniform as much as he could.

But there were some occasions when the sheriff had to go out in the community and leave his official uniform behind. Today was one of those days. This morning he was getting ready to help place political yard signs in the southern part of the county. He would only be out for two hours and, in order to avoid being seen by a large number of people, he made sure those two hours were before 8:00 a.m.

In preparation for his early morning activity, Armstrong pulled a light sweatshirt over his head and then ran a belt through the loops in his jeans. He looked in a mirror and shook his head at the image he saw there, but it wasn't his physical appearance that displeased him. The sheriff was generally pleased with his physical attributes. He believed his forty years of existence had been good to him. In fact, most people would consider him to be a handsome man who could be easily mistaken for a Marine drill sergeant. The sheriff kept his brown hair cropped short. His face was taut, with chiseled features. His eyes were dark brown and slightly sunken into his skull, a feature that allowed him to engage in a penetrating stare and to assume a steely expression of command. His body was sturdy and lean and, although he always wished he were a couple of inches taller, he was pleased that his height was just a fraction under six feet. No, it wasn't his physical appearance that displeased the sheriff. It was seeing his body wrapped in civilian clothing that upset him.

Damn I hate being out of uniform, he thought. It's lucky I only have to do this every four years. I feel naked running around the county without my sidearm. But I got to do this so I might as well get use to it. I know there are some bastards around here who think that I won't be able to hold onto this office, but I'll show them. I'll always get re-elected.

Armstrong exited his house through a back door after gulping down a piece of toast and having a cup of coffee. The sheriff never ate a full breakfast at home anymore. He had learned to eat his breakfast in shifts at an assortment of restaurants, fast food joints, and quick stops throughout the county. With his uniform on, he would parade among a large number of early morning voters, sharing coffee and donuts with them. Every morning he would intermingle with hundreds of farmers, truckers, teachers, retirees, cooks, waitresses, lawyers, and restaurant owners, keeping his eye on the pulse of the county and letting the county folk know he was on the job. The sheriff loved moving among the masses in his uniform.

When I get back from this chore and have changed out of these civvies, I'll stop by some places and hit the late breakfast crowd, Armstrong decided while heading for his garage.

There was an array of political signs in his garage. The vast numbers of the signs were dedicated to his own re-election. His re-election signs were clustered in rows of twenty, each standing three feel high off the concrete garage floor. The signs leaned against the west wall of the garage, waiting to be called up for duty. Armstrong collected forty of his campaign signs and hauled them to the trunk of his Crown Victoria. He made a mental note of the other signs in his garage that had been given to him by his political allies. His yard was nearly filled with a jumble of campaign signs, all announcing support for candidates who were running for judgeships, county offices, township supervisors, state legislators, and one congressman. He decided he would deal with the other signs in his garage at a later date.

The sheriff's yard signs were rectangular with a dark blue background and white letters announcing his re-election bid. *Sheriff Armstrong for Law and Order in Henry County* the signs proclaimed. The sheriff was proud of the re-election message. He could not remember where he had come up with the idea for the slogan, but he believed the slogan captured the essence of the way he wanted to be viewed by the people of Henry County.

"That's what I'm about," the sheriff had told his campaign workers. "Law and order. Let's put it on every campaign piece we can. After all, it's what the citizens of Henry County expect from me. It's what I promised them when I first ran for office. It's what I deliver."

A cadre of loyal political supporters were leaving their homes this very morning and descending upon the countryside and upon every hamlet in the county with the sheriff's campaign signs. By noon, a person would not be able to drive five miles in the county without knowing the sheriff was running for re-election.

Tonight I'll finish putting those other signs in my yard and try and get rid of the rest of my signs, the sheriff decided. Rogers must know contacts in his part of the county.

Armstrong threw two hammers, a sack of nails and a shovel into the car's trunk and hopped in behind the driver's seat. The Crown Vic had only eighteen thousand miles on the odometer. He rarely drove the car because it was his private civilian vehicle. He had the same feeling about vehicles as he did about clothing - -he preferred to drive around the county in his squad car. The Crown Vic made him feel ordinary, but during election years the car was his campaign vehicle, and he had it plastered with signs, all espousing the wisdom of re-electing Sheriff Armstrong.

Armstrong slowly backed the car out of his driveway and swung the back of the Crown Vic out onto the street, which ran along the eastern edge of his property. He then headed for the southern part of the county with his trunk full of signs.

I'll head down to Weller Township and then go over to Galva, Armstrong determined. Not many people there, but there are some new housing additions I should be visiting.

He stared at a wrinkled unfolded map that was lying stretched over the passenger seat of the car. Red spots on the map indicated favorable sites for erecting the campaign signs. The map was plastered with red markings, proclaiming the county's predominately Republican nature.

After driving for fifteen minutes, Armstrong arrived at a new housing addition that was being built just south of Galva. He pulled into the addition, parked his car in front of one of the new homes, grabbed a sign and a hammer from the trunk, and walked up the driveway of the new home, heading toward a loyal constituent.

"Robert Fisher! How are you this morning?" Sheriff Armstrong exclaimed. "I'd heard that you had built over here. Nice-looking house."

Robert Fisher gazed at his new home introspectively.

"Thanks, sheriff. I still got a lot of work to do," Robert replied. "Still got a lotta interior work that needs to be done. I haven't finished the basement yet and, of course, the yard still needs work. And, there're some damn moles out back. There's always something with a house. Damn moles are ruining my backyard."

"Yeah, they'll keep you busy alright. So, are you heading out to work now?" Armstrong noted pointing to the briefcase Robert held in his left hand.

"Gotta make a living, Mike," Robert responded. "What are you up to this morning?"

The sheriff noticed immediately that Robert had switched from addressing him as "sheriff" to calling him "Mike." The effect of his civvies had kicked in.

"Well. Robert," Armstrong said. "I would like to be able to put one of my signs in your yard. I am hoping I can count on your vote in November."

"Another election year, huh?" Robert said. "I understand you've got a guy running against you who's a pretty serious candidate. Is that right?"

"I never take any election for granted," Armstrong replied. "Every election is serious for me. I've been winning elections here in Henry County for two terms now, and I welcome competition. We all need someone lighting a fire under us. And, I need people like you to support me. So how about me putting one of my signs in your yard?"

"Yeah, of course...I was just razzing you, Mike," Robert said. "I voted for you in the last two elections...you know that. But, I am interested in something. What's your stand on the quarry expansion over on Wolf Road? My brother-in-law lives over there, and he is pretty upset about that deal."

"I'm concerned about it, too, Robert, and I'm looking into that situation. You know road safety will be an issue there for me."

"Yeah, you're right about the safety," Robert agreed. "My sister says those quarry trucks are huge. And, there's a lotta family vehicles that use Wolf Road. I hate to have them dodging those quarry trucks."

Armstrong held his campaign sign up next to his chest.

"Well now...I haven't finished my study of the situation yet, but it looks to me like it would be better off for everyone if the quarry just stayed down below that ridge," the sheriff said. "I'll be making a statement about it as soon as I complete the report."

"Tell you what, sheriff," Robert responded, "go ahead and put a sign in my yard. I'll tell my sister what you said and we'll all be waiting to hear what you have to say about the quarry."

"We'll get it all straightened out," the sheriff promised. "Thanks for letting me put up one of my signs in your yard."

Robert Fisher slipped into the front seat of his car, shut the door and opened the driver-side window.

"Have a great day, Mike," Robert called out while backing down the driveway.

Armstrong selected a location in the middle of Fisher's lawn to place his sign. While pounding the yard sign down into the ground, the sheriff heard a voice calling out to him. He turned in the direction of the noise and saw a man across the street waving and smiling at him.

"Hey, Sheriff! Over here," the man yelled. "Over here."

The sheriff tapped the yard sign one more time with his hammer and then walked across the street to the talk with the man who had been hailing him.

The man reached out to shake Armstrong's hand.

"How you doing, Sheriff?" the man exclaimed. "I'm new in the county. Name's George Borne. I just moved in about a month ago, but I know you. I saw one of your ads on television last night. Good ad, Sheriff."

Sheriff Armstrong pumped the man's hand with an energetic, election-year handshake.

"Glad to meet you, George," he said. "Welcome to the county and thanks for the compliment. We all want it safe out here, and that's why I'm running for re-election. If there's anything my office can do for you, let me know."

"I appreciate that," George said. "And, thanks for the welcome. We're glad to be living out here. It's great to get away from the cities and be out in the country."

"You got any kids, George. This is a great place to raise kids."

"Sure, Sherri and me, we've got two kids, a boy and a girl," George answered. "We hear there're great schools out here, and I've heard about you, Sheriff. I'd be proud to have a sign in my yard. I'm a long time Republican. I was an auxiliary deputy over in Rock Island County. You know the sheriff over there, right?"

"I sure do. I work with Sheriff Ryan all the time. Very good man! Glad to hear you were able to help him out. You know, we've got one of the best auxiliary units in the state right here. I'd like to have you working with us. I could use your help."

"Well, that sounds good...real good," George replied. "I'm interested in being part of your auxiliary. You know, I like to help out. Just let me get settled in, and I'll give your office a call. I've got a lotta work to do what with the move and a new home...always a lotta work to do with a home, you know. But give me one of your yard signs, and I'll be happy to put one up."

"Great. I'll get one from my car. Be right back," the sheriff said.

Armstrong hurried away in the direction of his campaign vehicle. He pulled a fresh yard sign out the trunk and turned to head back to George's yard, pondering this stroke of good fortune.

Got to be two new votes in that house, Armstrong calculated. And, it always helps to have a sign on both sides of the street. Makes people think the whole neighborhood's behind me.

Walking back up the driveway, Armstrong saw George coming out of his garage with a hammer and holding up a large sign for him to read.

"I got to get this sign up, too, Sheriff," George said.

Stop the Quarry! the sign in George's hand declared. The sign was cut in the shape of a stop sign and had a bright red background with white letters. Armstrong noticed that the quarry sign was larger than his sign.

"Hey, where do you stand on this issue, Sheriff?" George questioned.

"Well, just like I was telling Robert over there," the sheriff replied, "I am real concerned about what impact the quarry expansion will have on Wolf Road. I gotta study it further, but it looks like there is a safety issue there. You know some of those quarry trucks can be huge."

George Borne gathered up Armstrong's re-election sign into his arms.

"Yeah, you bet they are," George agreed. "You know I drive by there every day on my way to the cities. I work at John Deere and car pool with a fellow who lives over in Hazelwood. It's a pretty drive now, but I know the quarry will change all of that."

"Well, George...keep in mind...that expansion request can't happen without the county board's approval," Armstrong said. "There are a lot of good Republicans sitting on that board. You should contact them. It is an election year, you know."

"I will contact them," George said. "And, you think about it, too, Sheriff. It would help lots to know where your office stood on an issue like that. I mean, traffic control, that's right up your alley. I am new here, but I hear you're a man of action. People say you got moxy."

"Lot of good folks in this county," Armstrong replied. "I've enjoyed their support for eight years. And, I'm always glad to see more good folks moving out this way."

"Its quiet and peaceful out here, Sheriff. My wife and me, we want that for our kids."

Mike Armstrong gave George a small pat on the shoulder.

"You'll like it here, George. Sorry that I have to rush off, but I gotta get going to get some more yard signs up. It's nice to meet you. Say hello to your wife for me and give my office a call about being a part of the auxiliary."

"You'll be hearing from me," George shouted out at the departing sheriff.

That goddamn quarry expansion and that damn Scott Miller are both a pain in the ass, Armstrong fumed to himself as he walked toward his car. Nothing's ever simple. You'd think all of this crap could've waited until after the election.

Armstrong hopped back in his car to continue his search for more partisan ground on which he could stake out his re-election decree. Many of the places where Armstrong pushed or pounded his campaign message into the earth were already filled with other Republican signs. It was a busy year for local politicians. And, it was a busy time for the homeowners who were concerned about the quarry's special use permit. Wherever he drove, the sheriff noticed the eye-catching red stop signs sticking up high out of the ground, asserting opposition to the quarry expansion.

Keeping his left hand on the steering wheel, Armstrong rubbed the top of his head with the fingers of his right hand while gazing in wonder at another the anti-expansion sign. Jesus! The whole county's up in arms about the quarry expansion, he conjectured. I gotta take this issue and make hay out of it. I wonder what Taylor's been saying about it?

Armstrong drove the last of his yard signs into two small hills that bordered a rural intersection. Thankful this job was finished, the sheriff hopped in his car and headed for home. He could not wait to get out of his civvies and get back into his uniform.

CHAPTER TWENTY-SIX

After he had planted the last re-election sign, Sheriff Armstrong promised himself he would forget about Scott Miller and concentrate on beating Taylor in the race for County Sheriff. But with his morning work accomplished and while driving home through the countryside, Scott Miller's confession crept back into the sheriff's head.

Maybe Scott was telling the truth. God damn it! If Miller *was* telling the truth and info like that got out before the election, I'll be screwed. That bastard Taylor could sink me with a story like that. Son of a bitch!

Armstrong pushed down heavily on the gas pedal of his Crown Vic. Thousands of tall, autumn cornstalks loomed along each side of the road. The dense, jam-packed foliage made him feel as if he were passing through a deep gully. With no radios to distract him and completely alone in his car, Armstrong's mind began to rehash his jailhouse interrogation of Scott Miller.

After sending Deputy Lambert home, Sheriff Armstrong had gone to the jail cell where Scott Miller was being held. He relieved the cellblock guard, telling him he would have to substitute for two hours of night patrol. The cellblock was quiet, and the prisoners were sleeping. Armstrong had entered Scott's cell silently. He stood over Miller's bed and nudged him awake with a nightstick. Scott turned over in the bed slowly. He looked up into the darkness and saw the silhouette of a police officer standing over him. He rose up slightly on one elbow and stared into the darkness.

"Who's there?"

Miller's eyes adjusted to the dark, and he saw the muscular silhouette of the sheriff. His head fell back onto a pillow while he rubbed his face with both hands.

"What do you want Armstrong? I should've been out of here by now," Scott said in a muffled tone.

Sheriff Armstrong used his nightstick to poke at Scott again.

"Sit up in bed, Scott. You and me…we're going to have a talk."

"I don't have nothing to say to you," Scott replied. "I just want out of here."

Out of a fearful respect for the sheriff's nightstick, Scott sat up and crunched his body back toward the corner of the cell.

"You'll be out soon," the sheriff said. "But first, we have to talk about what you said to Deputy Lambert. You have to tell me everything you know about Katie's death."

"Hey, I didn't tell him nothing," Scott protested. "And, I ain't telling you nothing. I done enough for you when I helped get Katie's killer. And, what did I get for that? You didn't help me when I asked you for a job, and I ain't gonna help you now. Just let me out of here."

"Scott... think back," the sheriff said. "When you came and asked me for a job, what reason did I give for turning you down? Why didn't I hire you?"

"You said I was a coward," Scott answered. "But, I ain't no coward. I'm as good as any of the men you hire."

Although it was dark in the cell, the sheriff's vision had adjusted to the surroundings. Armstrong sat down on the edge of the bed and looked directly into Scott's face.

"Can you see me, Scott? It's dark in here, but I can see you. Can you see me alright?"

Scott felt dryness in his mouth as he tried to swallow in preparation for his reply.

"Yeah, I can see you," he said, "and, I ain't afraid of you."

"Then listen carefully to me," the sheriff said. "You're a coward, Scott. Just like I told you before."

The sheriff spoke quietly, but in a firm manner.

"You are going to talk to me, and I am going to tell you why you're gonna talk," he said.

"You can't do nothing to me."

The sheriff detected a noticeable quiver in Scott's voice.

"Oh yes I can," the sheriff replied. "I need to know what you know. And, here is what I am going to do, Scott. If you don't talk, I am going to beat you. When I am done with you, you'll have just enough life left in you to piss your pants, but that's all you'll be able to do. You're a coward, Scott, but don't feel bad about it...most people are cowards. The difference is you're in here with me. So, you gotta make up your mind. Talk or take a beating."

The sheriff watched as Scott's face dropped into his folded arms. He heard Scott softly sobbing, and knew he would not have to use any force to get Scott to talk. He had played a thousand games like this in the past. The sheriff had no intention of beating Scott, but twenty years of dealing with criminals and misfits had taught him how to read people. He knew Scott was a broken-down man who drank because he could not face life's hardships, and he knew he had to know what Scott knew. When the sheriff played these kinds of games, he did like winning. He was certain he was winning now.

"It's alright, Scott," the sheriff consoled. "Just tell me what you know, and you can go back to being a drunk again. No one expects more than that from you. When you're done telling me, I'll let you out of this cell, and you can head home."

Scott Miller broke down that night and told the sheriff everything, and Armstrong found himself torn apart by Scott's revelations. If Scott's jailhouse story was right, the whole department had screwed up badly. Armstrong knew he could be brought down by this information. He knew his re-election was in jeopardy. Even if he did win the election, the disclosure of this information would produce a deadly sting of abject humiliation that would become his constant companion. Armstrong would be the laughing stock of the county, probably of the entire state. He might be forced to resign his office. These were consequences the sheriff found impossible to accept. Somehow he needed to gain control over the situation.

Now only five miles away from home, dressed in civilian clothing and driving an ordinary car through the countryside, Mike Armstrong became more convinced that Scott's confession was a powder keg that could blow up in his face and steal away his dream of becoming a life-long, successful sheriff.

That goddamn Rogers, the sheriff thought. He's always been an overzealous kiss ass. He promised me Stablein was our guy. I wonder who he was trying to impress more, the Karvers or me. I know he's thought about applying for the Kewanee chief's job. The son of a bitch probably thinks about being sheriff, too. Well, no one likes a kiss ass...maybe I could blame all of this on sloppy detective work. I know a lotta people don't like Rogers. He could be my fall guy if this blows up before the election.

As his mind searched to find an answer that would expunge him from the charge of malfeasance and protect his re-election bid, Armstrong saw a car flash by him on the opposite side of the road.

"That damn guy's speeding," Armstrong mumbled to himself. "And me out of uniform and without my squad car. That son of a bitch wouldn't be driving like that if he saw me approaching in my squad. When I'm out of uniform, I'm just another prick driving through the countryside."

Armstrong looked in his rearview mirror and watched the speeding vehicle disappear over a hill. With the speeder out of his sight and out of his reach, his mind turned again to the trouble Scott's confession could cause him. He felt as if a plague was bearing down on him, a plague that had been inflicted upon him by other people.

And what about my good Deputy Lambert, Armstrong thought. Joe's a nice guy, but he got Scott's testimony on this case. Scott lied to Joe big time, and Joe brought that damn lie to my office. He should know you really can't trust a drunk. I don't care if Scott was his friend...that's just more reason to be suspicious of the guy. Every good cop knows you can't trust your friends in a murder case. Joe screwed up on this one. I'm not the only one at fault here. My best men let me down. I can't be expected to do everything. I wonder how much Joe knows about all of this?

Armstrong's car finally broke away from the tall cornfields. The road he was traveling was now defined by rolling pasturelands. He paused at a stop sign and then turned west onto Illinois 82.

That pompous, rich-ass Karver, Armstrong thought. He's the major player in all of this. He thinks he owns the goddamn county. He pushed for a quick conviction on this thing…everything had to be done yesterday for him. I know one thing…if I had a daughter-in-law, she wouldn't have gotten murdered. The man can't even protect his own family. People around here call him the Emperor of Hardware. What kind of "emperor" is that? If what Scott said is right, this is Karver's mess, not mine. Of course, a rich bastard like that never really takes the fall. He'll find some way to wiggle out of it, the son of a bitch. That bastard doesn't have to stand for election, not like me. Everybody's going to be pointing fingers at me when they should be blaming him. Damn, all of those people really have screwed me over.

Fuming with disappointment over those who had let him down, the sheriff decided to get his mind off his worries by counting the number of Armstrong signs along the highway. Counting the signs would calm him and help him to think straight again. But, his attempt to acquire tranquility was immediately shattered as he approached the southern edge of Cambridge. Standing high in an empty field and placed just thirty feet from the side of the highway was a gigantic red sign that read "Stop the Quarry!"

"Christ, look at that sign," Armstrong groaned out loud to himself. "The damn thing as big as a barn!"

Armstrong slowed his car down and scrutinized the monstrous sign. He rubbed the side of his face in exasperation.

Well by God, maybe I can kill two birds with one stone, he thought. Maybe I can make this quarry thing work for me. If Scott was right, the only evidence that can ruin me is buried somewhere in those fifty-nine acres River Bend wants to revamp for their expansion. Taylor can't beat me on a level playing field. If I stop the expansion, my re-election will be guaranteed. Hell, I really wouldn't even have to stop the expansion completely…all I've got to do is slow it down until after the election. I mean, maybe all those homeowners are right. Why should they have to put up with a quarry sitting right next to Wolf Road and a housing addition? It's a noble cause to help all those people out. That quarry should be stopped. I've always been a man of the people. Maybe I can make this all work for me.

As he drove into Cambridge, the sheriff began to piece together a strategy that would guarantee him access to the two things he wanted most, re-election and continued respect. He knew the strategies racing through his mind were excessive and perilous, but he was desperate. He felt boxed in and trapped. Although he was popular in the county, he had made enemies, too. He knew those enemies were always waiting like vultures for an opportunity to pounce on him and pick apart his carcass. There was no way he could face such mortification; he would not have his career irrevocably scarred by scandal. He needed time to slow down the events that could ruin his life, and he decided upon a plan that would give him that time. The sheriff decided he would put his reputation and the full weight of his office behind the movement to stop the quarry expansion.

I can do this, the sheriff decided. I can delay the goddamn quarry expansion and then control the spin concerning that body…I just need more time. If I just take my time…maybe figure out when to find the body, and then take credit for solving the murder. If I can do those things, I can become unbeatable. I just need to have the events timed right. First I'll slow that quarry expansion down, then I'll win the election, and then I'll handle the spin on the murder. I'll come out ahead on all of this. I'll beat them all. I'll become the longest serving sheriff this county has ever seen.

CHAPTER TWENTY-SEVEN

"**I**'m taking the rest of the day off, Al," Deputy Lambert called out to one of the clerks who worked in the sheriff's office. "When you see the sheriff, tell him that it's personal leave."

"Sure Joe," Al replied. "Hey, I was sorry to hear about Scott. Anything I can do just let me know."

"Thanks, Al. Just let the sheriff know," Joe repeated as he walked out of the office door.

This is the smart move, Joe thought. I don't want to be in the office today, and I have the next two days off. I really don't want to see Armstrong or Rogers for a while and this will clear the air for me. It's better if I don't see them. And, I want to talk with Robin about all of this before she reads about Scott's death in some obit column.

Driving home, Joe had to admit to himself that he was more than just a little upset with Sheriff Armstrong. He knew the sheriff had a difficult time connecting with people on a one-to-one personal basis, but he believed the sheriff should have been the one to tell him about Scott.

Armstrong prefers to play the role of sheriff all the time, and that puts a wall between him and everyone else, Joe thought to himself. He likes to be in charge, and you lose control when you get too close to someone. But I thought that he had more respect for me than to send his hatchet man out to my house. Christ, he should know better than to have that dickhead Rogers tell me about Scott. What the hell was he thinking? I guess I have misjudged everything…well, the hell with it. I've gotta talk to someone I can trust. I've gotta see Robin.

It took Joe an hour to get up enough courage to call Robin. Calling her at this time of the year was out of the ordinary, and they had already had their two summer season get-togethers.

Robin's probably busy anyway, Joe speculated. And, what if Frank answers the phone? It's always awkward talking to him. What am I gonna do if he answers? I really don't want to talk to him, and I sure as hell don't want to explain why I'm calling. Frank didn't even know Scott.

When Joe did sit down to dial Robin's number, he hung up twice before he finished punching the last two digits into the phone.

"This is nuts," Joe said to himself. "I'm almost thirty years old, and I'm a cop for god's sakes. I'll let it ring four times, and if no one answers, I'll call it quits."

"Hello! Is that you, Joe?" Robin's voice called out after just two rings.

"Yeah, it is," Joe laughed. "How did you know it was me?"

"We have caller ID," Robin answered. "And, I don't get many calls from Kewanee. Besides, I could feel your vibes. I'm psychic, you know?"

"Oh, you're psychic, huh?" Joe replied. "So then you can tell me why I am calling?"

"I can't imagine, but I am glad that you are," came Robin's cheery response.

"It's good to hear your voice, Robin. I'm glad I called too."

"Are you coming over this way some time soon?"

"I want to. I need to see you, Robin. It's important. That's why I'm calling. I know this is inconvenient, and I don't want you to go to any bother, but I really do need to talk with you."

"You've got great timing, Deputy Lambert," Robin replied. "Frank's out of town for three days at a conference in Chicago, and I'm here sitting home alone in this brand new house. Hey, I know what…why don't you come here? I'll fix you supper, you can see the house, and we can talk."

"You sure that's OK?"

"Of course it is. I want you to see the house and I'll be hurt if you turn down my offer for supper. I'm a great cook, but it is no fun making a meal just for me. Besides, we're getting too old to be carousing in bars."

"Alright," Joe agreed. "I could use a good home cooked meal, and I don't want to hurt your feelings. After all, you're my buddy. What time do you want me there?"

"Come around seven," Robin replied. "I'll make something special for us."

"Seven will be great. And, tell you what, I'll bring a bottle of wine and get a dessert."

"You don't have to do that," Robin protested. "Some beer would be fine. But, you bring whatever you want. Just be here or you'll be in a lot of trouble with me," Robin joked.

"I'll see you at seven," Joe promised.

Joe hung up the phone and walked down the narrow hallway of his house heading for the bathroom. The phone call took him back eight years to his phone conversation with Katie.

Robin could be dangerous, too, he thought. She is beautiful and one of the few women that I can talk to. Maybe it's stupid for me to go see her.

Standing inside his small bathroom, he looked into the vanity mirror and wondered if he should shave again. Instead, he gave his face a slight slap.

Stop it you dumb ass, he admonished himself. It's silly for me to even be thinking this way. I'm just going to see Robin's new home and tell her about Scott. I just need to talk with her, that's all. Robin and I have always had an understanding. We're good buddies…we're just good buddies. But, I gotta admit there are times when I wish she wasn't so damn attractive. Very few times though, Joe thought. Very, very few times.

Absentmindedly, he pulled a can of shaving cream out from under the bathroom vanity, wet his face with hot water, and began to spread the rich, white foam over his cheeks and his chin. He looked at himself in the mirror and frowned at what he was doing. Bending over the basin, he washed the cream off his face and dried himself off with a towel.

No shave, he decided. I'll just take a shower. I'll work out a little first, shower, and then be on my way.

On his drive west toward Rock Island, Joe decided that he would get a special bottle of wine for his supper with Robin. He knew a wine cellar in Moline, which specialized in fine wines.

I know Frank thinks that I'm some rube from the sticks who only drinks beer, but Robin deserves the best, he thought. I'll stop in at Gendler's and get us some great wine.

I'll never understand what Robin sees in Frank. All I see is a pompous ass. I know I should try harder to get along with Frank, but every time I make an effort the guy goes right into his 'let's talk about how wonderful I am' routine. Robin could have done a lot better than that guy.

Joe knew he was out of his league when he stepped inside of Gendler's wine store and found himself surrounded by hundreds of bottles of wine. He quickly decided to consult with the owner of the store, telling him he was looking for a fine wine and a rich dessert. The owner suggested a bottle of Cabernet Sauvignon to compliment the meal and a bottle of Black Muscat-Gallagher Ranch for dessert. Joe bought the recommended bottles of wine and carried the costly packages to his car.

Joe opened the passenger side door of his car and nestled the two bottles down on the seat. The bottles were enclosed in two separate, slender white, monogrammed bags, which made them look like gifts. He shut the door and leaned against the side of his car, looking up at the beautiful, autumn sky. The Midwest was still operating under daylight savings time. The sky was bright blue, and the late summer sun blazed a fiery red as it hung above the horizon.

I suppose I'm overdoing this, he thought. But it is a housewarming gift and I would like Robin to think I have a refined side. I really miss those days in college when we'd hit the bars. I really miss being with Robin…she's such a great person.

God, I'm such a romantic fool, he concluded. This is the type of evening I always wanted to share with Katie. Katie was so beautiful…and Robin…God, she's beautiful, too.

In his mind and in his heart, Joe could feel the two women morphing into one. He knew it wasn't fair to Robin, but his heart was turning toward her. He got into his car and headed out to find her new home.

"Seeing Robin on a night like this could be dangerous," he said to himself. "I'll be extra careful tonight."

CHAPTER TWENTY-EIGHT

J oe pulled into Robin's driveway just a little before seven p.m. The home was brand new and built in a housing addition located on the southern edge of a large metropolitan area called "The Quad-Cities". The houses surrounding Robin's home stood in various stages of completion. Only eight of the twenty lots in the addition had been purchased. Robin's home was bordered by two lots with looming, skeletal wood structures, each structure waiting on construction workers to install sheets of plywood, insulation, siding, and roofing in order to make them whole. Fresh, dark green sod covered Robin's lawn. The new grass butted up against the brown, clay yards of her future neighbors. The home was a two-story, French Colonial brick house and it looked massive compared to the small house Joe had purchased from his parents after they had retired.

A small stone patio wrapped around the front entrance to the new home, and Robin was sitting there in a cushioned white chair, waiting for Joe to arrive.

"Hey, Deputy!" she called out.

Robin walked quickly to the driveway and was standing next to Joe's car when he got out of it. She greeted him with a warm hug. She was wearing beige shorts, a white cotton top, and sandals. Joe admired a casual look on women, and Robin looked beautiful to him.

She smiled brightly and rested her hands on his shoulders.

"Hey, how come you didn't bring your squad car?" Robin asked. "We could use some excitement out here."

Joe pulled Robin to him, returning her hug.

"Can't carry alcohol in the squad," Joe replied. "Wow, you smell great. Like peaches."

Robin laughed and held her wrist up to Joe's face.

"Very good, Detective Lambert," she said. "Do you like it?"

The peach fragrance promptly dominated Joe's senses. He smiled broadly.

"I like it a lot. What is it?"

"Jean Patou," Robin replied. "It's called 'Joy for Women.' I just got it yesterday. You're the first to experience it."

Joe took Robin's arm in his hand, pressed her delicate wrist closer to his face, and inhaled deeply.

"I think it is a joy for men, too," he said.

Robin smiled again and batted her eyes flirtatiously at Joe.

"Did you bring wine or beer?"

"I got wine. Let me get it out of the car."

Joe reluctantly let loose of Robin's arm, walked around to the passenger side of his car, and pulled out the wine. He held the two bags up for Robin to see.

"Very nicely packaged, Joe," Robin said. "Looks special and expensive. I hope you didn't pay too much for it."

"No, no," Joe replied. "But, I have to confess...I had help picking out the wine. It's not beer, but I think we'll like it. I got a dinner wine and a dessert wine. They're housewarming gifts."

Robin hooked onto Joe's arm and walked him toward the front door.

"I know we'll enjoy the wine," Robin said. "Now come and see the house. I'll give you the tour and then we have to eat. I don't want the supper to spoil. I made you an extra special meal for our evening together. I hope you like spicy chicken and pasta. Even if you don't, you better rave about it."

"And you better rave about the wine," Joe teased.

Robin laughed and patted Joe on his ass.

"Two bottles," she exclaimed. "Our drinking skills will be tested tonight. I promise, I will enjoy the wine and I'll try to not take advantage of you."

"You're right about our drinking skills. Maybe we should ease into this and have a glass of Cabernet before supper. What do you think?"

"That's a great idea," Robin replied. "I'll get us some glasses and we can sip wine while I take you on the tour."

Robin and Joe spent the next twenty minutes touring the new house. Robin was proud of how she had decorated her new home, and Joe let Robin know he was impressed with what she had done with all of the rooms.

"You have a beautiful home," he complimented.

"Yes...it is lovely, but it's too big for me. Maybe I'll feel less dwarfed by all this if Frank and I have children."

"You're planning on children, right?" Joe asked. "I mean you always said you wanted children."

"Yes, but Frank's not ready right now. You know, he's caught up in pursuing his doctorate. Let's forget about all that. Supper is ready and I want to talk about you...and I'm dying to know why you had to see me. But, I know you, Joe...I'll wait until you are good and ready to tell me. Though I warn you, you'd better tell me soon!"

Joe decided to wait until the end of the meal to broach the subject of Scott's death. The two friends ate their supper in a large alcove, which had been built adjacent to the kitchen and served as an informal dining area. A series of windows wrapped around the room, allowing its occupants to view the wooded area directly behind Robin's home. The meal was served on a small, dark cherry table that could expand to comfortably seat six. In its current retracted state, the table provided an intimate, cozy atmosphere. Joe was seated at the head of the table and Robin sat near the kitchen to his right.

Robin poured Joe a third glass of wine.

"I hope you are enjoying the chicken, Joe. I really like the wine. The store owner made an excellent choice, and you were wise to shop there."

"It is excellent," Joe agreed. "But, the real toast is to your culinary skills."

Joe lifted his glass and carefully clinked it against Robin's. They both smiled and took a sip of the wine. For a brief moment, they looked into each other's eyes.

"You've got a great house here, Robin."

"You already said that, Joe. But, I accept your appreciation of the house."

She set her wine glass on the table and slowly guided her index finger in a circle over the rim of the glass.

"Joe," she said hesitantly, "did you ever see Katie again before…before her death? I mean did you ever see her alone? It's none of my business, but I always wondered."

"I don't mind you asking," Joe responded. "No, I didn't see her. But she did email me."

"Really? Katie emailed you? What did she write?" When did she email you?"

"She emailed me a week before her death. It was nothing really. I mean…I don't know, Robin. I know what the words were, but I don't know what she meant by the words. I suppose I read more into them than I should have."

Robin's facial expression became intent. She stared at Joe and felt sorry for the confusion and the anguish she saw on his face.

"What were the words, Joe? Do you remember?" Robin asked.

"Yes…I know the words. I still have the message in my email account. I've never deleted it…and I know the words by heart."

"Tell me the words," she said. "Maybe I can help."

"Robin, I've always wanted to ask you about the email. I know Katie talked to you. Maybe you can figure it out. This is what she wrote, 'Hi, Joe. Thanks for taking me water skiing!' I think if we work together, we can water ski again.' That's it. Christ, what does that mean?"

Joe started to get up from his chair and then sat back down again.

"Robin…I took Katie water skiing seven years ago!" he said. "Why would she write those words to me now?"

"Did you email back to her?"

"Yeah, I did email her," Joe replied. "I didn't know what to say. I just wrote, 'Hi, Katie. You're welcome. I miss summer very much.' That's what I wrote. Stupid, huh? Robin...do you know what she meant by her email?"

"She loved you, Joe. She told me so. I think she wanted to get back with you," Robin said softly.

Joe shook his head.

"I know she loved me," he said. "She told me she loved me. But, that was a long time ago. I thought she was over that. I didn't think she even thought about me anymore."

"I know she thought about you. I know she thought about you a lot. She told me she did. She missed you, but she was afraid to say so. She was afraid to admit it to herself."

"Tell me this. Was she happy with Larry?"

"No," Robin replied. "Katie was happy with life, but not with Larry. Larry...He didn't know how to make her happy. I'm sure that's why she emailed you. She was lonely."

Joe looked exasperated.

"She didn't seem lonely," he said. "I mean, she was always the center of attention."

"She was lonely in bed, Joe," Robin said. "That's the worst kind of loneliness. You still miss her, don't you?"

"I miss what we had. I miss the closeness. I miss making love with her. I bet all of this sounds silly to you. I mean, hell, it's been seven years ago!"

"No. It doesn't sound silly. You're right; Katie and I did talk. She told me about you, about the two of you. It was a real struggle for her to marry Larry."

"Then why?" Joe asked. "Why did she marry Larry? Was it his money?"

"It wasn't just money. I don't know if I can make you understand. You're not like Katie and me. You're not like anyone I know."

"Robin," Joe said. "I didn't come here to talk about Katie. But, I want to hear what you have to say. You and I...we've talked about most everything. But, we've always circled around the question of Katie and me. I want you to tell me about her now. Tell me what you know. Tell me what you think...I need to know."

Robin could feel a special bond being built between her and Joe. They had always been close friends, but now they were being drawn together in a very unique way by the memory of Katie. She felt as if Katie was in the room with them, urging her to tell him everything. She felt a shiver run down her back. Robin knew Katie's story mirrored her own, and she wanted Joe to hear it. She wanted someone to understand the ache she felt in her own heart. She folded her hands together on the table and looked directly at Joe.

"Joe, Katie was afraid. She was afraid of being alone."

Joe looked at Robin. His frustration spilled forth in an exasperated sigh. He stood up and walked to the bay window. He looked out the window, shaking his head slowly. Robin wanted to rush to him, but she let him be by himself. Soon he turned around and looked at her again. He seemed angry, but when he spoke, the tone of his voice was full of frustration.

"You're right, Robin…I don't get it," he said. "Look out this window. We're never alone. We're part of life. We're surrounded by life. It swarms around us, and it circles above us in the stars. How can a person be alone with all of that happening? Everywhere we go we are accompanied by life."

"Is that where you get your courage from, Joe? Is that it? I always wondered," Robin said.

"Why didn't she come with me?" he asked, ignoring Robin's observation. "I would have made her happy."

"Joe, Katie was surrounded by life, too. She enjoyed life. But, she was afraid of falling in love. She was afraid of heartbreak. She was in love with you, but she was afraid of losing you…afraid that you would leave her. Don't you see? She knew she could control Larry. Larry would never leave her."

"I wouldn't have left her," Joe said sternly. "She should've known that."

Tears welled up in Robin's eyes.

"She didn't know that, Joe," she said. "I mean, she couldn't be certain of it. She loved you so much. She was sure of Larry…sure that he couldn't hurt her."

"But she's dead," Joe said. "I wouldn't have let anyone hurt her. All Larry got her was dead."

Joe saw tears spill from Robin's eyes. He realized he had said too much. He was angry, and he had spoken like a cop in an interrogation room. He moved quickly into the kitchen and returned with a wad of tissues in his hand. He sat down across from Robin and handed her the tissues.

"Robin, I'm sorry. I didn't mean to make you cry."

Robin wiped her eyes with the tissue Joe had given her.

"I'm alright," she replied.

"Robin, maybe I'm the one who messed this all up."

"What do you mean?"

"I don't think I tried hard enough," Joe said. "I mean, I should've called Katie or seen her somehow. I should've talked with her. Maybe she'd be alive today if only I had tried to talk with her."

"Don't blame yourself, Joe. Katie could be difficult sometimes…she was insecure, and she surrounded her heart with walls to protect herself. She thought she always had to be in control. I know she seemed cold to you sometimes, but she was afraid of getting hurt. That's all it was. That's not your fault."

Robin saw moisture glistening in Joe's eyes.

"You know what it is, Robin?" he said. "It's this damn job…it's this god-damn job! Katie built walls and so have I. Mine are different kinds of wall, but walls just the same."

"Joe. Listen to me. You're a sweet guy. Katie knew that. And Joe, you've always talked with me."

"You're special, Robin. You do talk, you communicate and share. God…I feel so alone sometimes. That stuff I said about being surrounded by life…well, that only goes so far. You know what happens…you know what this job does to me?"

"It can't be easy being a cop," she said. "I know that."

"You get so you just don't trust anyone," Joe confessed. "You get it in your head that everyone's hiding something or has a hidden agenda. Some-times I would stop thinking about Katie because…because I would become suspicious of her. I mean I'd start wondering if she was just using me to make Larry jealous. God, I hated thinking that way about her. It's this damn job. It makes you lonely. And, I used to think I was doing something noble, some-thing good. But, I don't know anymore…Katie's dead, and I'm not even sure we got the right guy locked up for her murder."

"Really, Joe? I never knew you doubted that."

"I don't like to think about it," he answered. "I've never told anyone about my doubts."

Robin forced a smile onto her face and squeezed Joe's hand.

"You still miss her a lot don't you? I miss her too."

"Listen, Robin," Joe continued. "It doesn't matter anymore. It's all over now…I know that. And, Robin, I'm not as courageous as you think. I shouldn't have said those things."

He smiled back at her.

"And yeah, I do miss her…and I know you do too," he said softly. "Thank you for telling me about Katie. I understand more now. I'll never really understand all of it, but I'm dealing with it. I know it wasn't easy for you to tell me all of that. You're a good friend."

Joe took Robin's right hand in his, lifted her hand slowly and kissed her fingers. He pressed her hand against his cheek.

"You OK?" he asked.

"Yeah," Robin replied with a genuine smile. "I'm fine, Joe. But, I have to ask you a question. If you didn't come here to talk about Katie, why did you come? I mean, what's the big secret? Why did you need to see me? Did Frank tell you that I was a great cook?" she teased.

"No. I haven't seen Frank since the memorial service for Katie. I don't think he and I ever hit it off. You know, I was always hoping that you would marry someone who would like me," Joe said, laughing.

"Frank's not very friendly sometimes. I don't think that he is jealous of you though. He never seems to be jealous of anyone. You know all of Frank's friends are...well, I don't see them much at all. I know what you mean about feeling lonely, Joe," she slowly confessed. "I should be careful what I say. I've already had too much wine. But, I can say this with absolute clarity...I'm glad you are here. I miss seeing you."

Joe reached for Robin and held her hand again.

"I miss you, too," he said. "That's why I am here. It seems like all my old friends are gone now. I needed to talk with an buddy, and you're it."

Robin clasped Joe's hand affectionately. She saw pain reflected in his eyes.

"What's wrong, Joey," she said in a sympathetic tone.

"Scott's been killed," Joe blurted out.

The desperate words tumbled from Joe's lips as he vocalized Scott's death aloud for the first time. He stared at the table in an effort to control his emotions. Tears welled up in his eyes and spilled down his face. Robin was immediately at his side. She put her arm around his shoulder and bent down to kiss the side of his face.

"I'm your buddy, Joe. I'm here," she comforted. "Come on, let's go sit somewhere where we can talk more comfortably. Let's get away from all these dishes. We'll try that other wine. Dessert will make us both feel better."

Joe nuzzled his face against Robin's cheek. He closed his eyes and enjoyed the touch of her hands, the softness of her lips, and the smell of her hair. He felt immediate comfort in her presence.

"Yeah," he said softly, "that's a good idea...let's try the other wine."

CHAPTER TWENTY-NINE

Robin led Joe to a four seasons room that was attached to the back of the house. The room was carpeted, beautifully decorated, and had a large sofa running along the back wall. She had filled two new wine glasses with the dessert wine, and she sat them on an end table next to the couch.

"I like this room," Joe commented. "I've always wanted a four seasons room."

"I told Frank I want a hot tub out here," Robin replied, laughing.

Robin dimmed the lights in the room, moved towards Joe and hugged him again. Then she kicked off her sandals and sat down on the couch.

"Lie down, Joe," she said patting her lap. "Lie down with your head on my lap."

Robin stroked Joe's face and played with his hair. She assured him that everything was all right and gently kissed his forehead every time he expressed grief or doubt. They shared in sipping the dessert wine, emptying first one goblet and then the other. Robin felt good being able to talk with a man, and she knew that she was helping Joe feel better. She moved to lie alongside of him and held him in her arms. She ended up lying on top of Joe and talking to him, using his chest for a pillow while he put his arms around her. They were friends, and they had always cared deeply about each other, but now they were expressing tenderness toward each other that they had never exhibited before. Joe did not know it, but Robin was as much in need of kindness as he. She needed the type of understanding and warmth that can only be expressed through close physical contact. She needed to be loved by a man.

The darkness of the evening and the warmth of the wine surrounded them, and they fell asleep in each other's arms. It was after midnight when Joe woke up and sensed the lateness of the hour.

"Robin," Joe whispered. "I think it's very late. I should go."

Robin lifted her head and smiled at Joe. She snuggled up against Joe's warm body.

"I think you should stay," she replied. "I think you should stay, Joe," she repeated. "Let's just camp out here on the carpet. We've camped out before."

"Robin...it's very late."

Robin pushed her head down firmly on his chest.

"You're a cop, Joe," she said. "You of all people should know you can't be driving with all the wine we've been drinking in you. Think of me as your designated mother."

"You're right about the wine," Joe admitted. "Why don't I sleep here on the couch, and you can sleep upstairs in your bed?"

"Forget it," she said softly. "I'm sleeping with you. You're a guest, and you have to do what I tell you. Besides, I have an obligation to comfort you. We're buddies, remember?"

"I know better than to argue with you," Joe admitted. "That's an argument I'll only lose. Just tell me what I need to do."

Robin sat up, straddling Joe's body and pushed a finger against his forehead.

"Wait right here," she said. "I'll be back in a few seconds, and then we'll make camp. It'll be like old times. Remember that time I stayed over at your apartment after we had closed every bar in Rock Island?"

"I remember everything," Joe said. "The one thing I've got going for me is a precise memory."

"I stole a kiss from you that night," Robin confessed. "A pretty good one, too. Remember that?"

"What I remember is me kissing you, and then you passed out...not very flattering," Joe laughed.

"Well, smart guy," Robin said smiling. "Just so you know...and this is for the record, Deputy Lambert...I didn't pass out that night. I just pretended to pass out because I liked that kiss way too much. You frightened me that night."

"We gotta drink wine more often. I'm learning a lot tonight," Joe said, laughing.

"So am I," Robin said. "I'll be right back. You can think of more things to tell me while you wait."

Joe sat on the couch and waited for Robin to return. He smiled to himself as he thought about what she had said.

I do remember that kiss, he thought. I gotta admit that kiss kind of scared me, too. Robin's a great kisser. God...she's a wonderful woman. And, she looks so good tonight. I know this is dangerous, but it's great being here with her and not having to share her with anyone. Maybe this is wrong, but I don't give a damn. I want to stay with her.

Robin came back into the room, her arms loaded with bedding.

"We'll move some of this furniture around and spread the comforter out on the carpet," she said. "It'll be just like camping. Aren't the woods pretty, Joe?"

"They're beautiful," he said staring at her.

"Hey, after all that wine, I bet you need to use a bathroom," Robin said. "I know I do. You use the one down the hall, and I'll go upstairs."

Joe went to the bathroom and stood over the toilet relieving myself.

God, how many times did I go to the bathroom and empty my bladder like this while out drinking with Robin? And, how many times did I go back to our table to find some guy hitting on her? She would always point to me walking her way and the guy would disappear. Robin...she's great. We weren't together then and she could've easily talked with any of those guys. She was under no obligation to me. But she never did that. She always stayed with me. Robin never plays any games. God, she's great.

When he came back from the bathroom, Robin had changed her clothes. She was wearing blue sweatpants and a light gray t-shirt. Robin smiled and stretched her arms out wide, giving him a full view of her sleeping apparel.

"Hope you don't mind me wearing these old sweatpants," she said. "I know they're not very flattering, but they are comfy."

"Robin, you'd look good in a sack," Joe blurted out.

"Why, Joe, I didn't know that you were such an admirer," she said winking. "You get comfortable, too. I brought a pair of sweatpants for you."

Robin reached down on the couch, lifted up a pair of navy blue sweat pants and handed them to Joe.

"These are Frank's," she said. "They'll be a little loose around the waist for you, but they'll do. You'll be comfortable and warm in them. It might get a little chilly out here at night."

Joe left the room again and changed into the borrowed nightwear. He returned in the baggy sweatpants and his own white t-shirt.

"You'd look good in a sack too, Joe," Robin laughed. "In fact, those pants are as close to a sack as you could get."

The two friends smiled, and moved toward each other. Joe put his arms around Robin's waist and pulled her to him. She wrapped her arms around his broad shoulders.

"I'm going to steal another kiss from you, Deputy Lambert," she said softly.

Their lips met, and the two kissed fully. Joe's right hand dropped below Robin's waist, and he pulled her body close to him. When they stopped kissing, Robin rested her head against his chest. She could feel his heart beating. They hugged each other tightly and their bodies firmly pressed together. Robin moved her fingers gently up and down the back of his neck.

"You're not frightened now are you," Joe whispered.

"I'm not frightened," she replied. "I'm happy. I'm glad you're here, Joe."

The two friends dropped slowly down to the comforter. Robin pulled a light cover over them as they maneuvered to discover their sleeping positions. Robin turned on her side with her back facing Joe and scooted her body up against him.

"Hold me, Joe," she whispered. "Hold me close."

Joe's arm wrapped around her, and he pulled her close. He laid his head on Robin's pillow and took pleasure in the smell of her hair. He kissed her on top of her head. She moved his hand up to her chest. She sighed as his hand touched her breasts. She felt Joe's desire pressing against her body. The feel of his hard passion made her head swim. She longed for love. She turned onto her back, and Joe's lips found hers. They devoured each other's mouth, tasting each other's lips in a wild frenzy of delight. Robin's body arched with pleasure when she felt Joe's fingers moving up inside her t-shirt, gently touching her breasts. She trembled with joy while Joe's lips kissed her eyes, her nose, and her neck. He rose up and knelt beside her. His fingers pulled at her nightwear, peeling off her sweatpants as she pulled off her t-shirt. Joe's fingers ran slowly up and down her naked body, and she watched as he looked in wonder at her charms. He paused for a moment to pull off his t-shirt and the borrowed sweatpants. Robin watched Joe undress; his eyes were filled with yearning for her. Her fingers trembled as she reached to touch his bare legs. The two friends stared at one another; their gaze roamed and then became fixed, as they looked deep into each other's eyes. Although both of their hearts raced with desire, the world seemed peaceful and right. Robin smiled, rose up halfway, and pulled Joe's powerful body to her. The two lovers intertwined and coupled as one.

There was little sleep for Joe and Robin that night. Joe's appetite seemed insatiable, and Robin's hunger matched his. The night air was crisp and cool, but the nest they had built was warm and inviting. Feeling the warmth of Joe next to her, and feeling his strong arms wrapped around her made Robin feel safe and secure.

CHAPTER THIRTY

J anelle Cannon was preparing to do what she always did on an early, warm
Sunday morning. She had just arrived at the Great River Road Mississippi
Bike Path, and she was pulling her twenty-speed mountain bike out of the
back of a green Dodge van. Holding her bike at chest level, she gazed appre-
ciatively at the half mile-wide girth of the Mississippi River and then slowly
lowered her bike to the ground, propping it up on its kickstand. Soon she
would ride twenty miles upriver on the bike path, make a loop through Port
Byron, and then head back to her car, a forty-mile mental and physical health
excursion.

Janelle enjoyed exercising outdoors and was disciplined in her routine,
which accounted for her slim, athletic appearance and her vibrant nature. It
was a beautiful, sunny autumn day, and she looked forward to a long ride in
the hot sun. She knew days like this were precious and that it would not be
long before cold midwestern air would bring a seven-month hiatus to her bike
riding.

As Janelle tightened the strap on a small pack that hung from the back of
the bicycle seat, her cell phone sounded to the tune of *Bohemienne.* Annoyed
by the interruption, she thought about disregarding the call and leaving her
cell phone in the van to avoid any further distractions.

"Damn phone", she said to herself.

Reluctantly, Janelle flipped open her cell phone, glanced at the caller ID,
and saw the call was from Robin Karlson.

"Hey, Robin, what's up," Janelle said into her cell phone.

"Hi, Jan. Listen, I'm really sorry to bother you, but I need to talk to
someone. I know this is your private time, but that's why I'm calling you
now. I need to talk and I don't want Frank or Andy to know. Is this alright?"

"My, such intrigue. This must be important," Janelle said.

"It is. Believe me, it is," Robin replied.

"Hey, you know you can always talk to me, even on Sunday mornings.
But, you're gonna owe me for taking away my biking time…you know that,
don't you?" Janelle joked. "It's an awfully beautiful day, and I already have
my bike out of the van."

Robin's voice took on a desperate tone.

"I know, but I got big problems, and I can't hold them in any longer. I
need to talk with you."

"Hey, listen, it's alright, Robin," she replied. "Andy's away most of the day, so you can have my full attention. Where do you want to meet? I'm parked by the Channel Cat landing on the Illinois side of the river."

"How about I meet you on the Iowa side of the river? You know that little park just down river from the Bettendorf Bridge?"

"Yeah, you mean the one with the statues of kids skimming rocks into the river. Am I right?"

"That's it," Robin replied. "We can sit in the sun and talk. I'll bring some coffees. Can you be there in twenty minutes?"

"I'll be there," Janelle said. "Hey, bring two muffins. If you're going to spoil my day, you might as well make it complete."

"I really appreciate this, Jan. I'll see you in about twenty minutes."

Janelle and Robin had only known each other for three years, but they had clicked as friends when they first met at a softball game. Janelle was new to the area, and Katie's death had created a void in Robin's life. The two young women quickly became good friends and confidants. Both had been married for less than four years, and they had much in common. Janelle and Robin were becoming good buddies, and whenever they got together their conversation was filled with laughter. They both understood it was better to laugh at life than to let it get you down. Andy Cannon was Janelle's husband, and the Karlsons and the Cannons had gone out together on a number of occasions. The husbands got along well enough, but it was the wives who kept the contact between the couples alive and who planned all of the social outings.

Janelle arrived first at the park in Bettendorf. She was happy to find the park area deserted. She pulled off her t-shirt and sat down on a bench, wearing shorts and a sports bra. Since she was no longer going to ride her bike, she had changed her gym shoes for a pair of sandals she had in the van. She sat facing east, basking in the sun with her eyes closed, waiting for Robin's arrival.

"I should've brought my bike," Janelle heard Robin say. "We could've both gotten some exercise."

Janelle opened her eyes to see Robin walking toward her holding a white bag in each of her hands, one bag contained coffee and the other contained muffins. She handed the bag with coffee in it to Janelle as she sat down.

Janelle pulled the two coffees out of the bag and looked up at Robin.

"You OK?" she said. "You sounded so worried on the phone."

"I'm OK," Robin replied, smiling. "I just gotta get some things off my chest. Hope you don't mind. I probably shouldn't have bothered your biking."

"Hey, don't talk like that," Janelle said. "I'm always here for you. Someday I'll have a problem, and you can help me and then I'll bring the muffins. So, tell me…what is all this?"

"You remember me telling you about Joe?" Robin began.

Janelle took a sip of coffee, reflected briefly on conversations she has had with Robin about Joe, and then smiled.

"Sure," Janelle said. "The hunk cop, right? How could I forget Mr. Wonderful? When do I get to meet him anyway?"

"Joe came over for dinner last night, and I slept with him," Robin blurted out.

"You slept with Joe? Oh my God, this is big," Janelle responded. "Are you alright? And where was Frank? Are you still with Frank?"

"Frank's out of town. Do you hate me for it?" Robin asked.

Janelle put her coffee cup down on the concrete that surrounded the park bench and reached for Robin's hand.

"Don't say that! I don't hate you. Are you OK, Hon?" Janelle asked again.

"I'm fine. I've just got a lotta issues here."

"We'll talk, Robin. It'll be all right. Can you smile a little?" Janelle asked.

"Yeah, I can smile. I just need to talk with you. Maybe you can make me laugh about some of this?"

Janelle affectionately squeezed Robin's hand and smiled brightly at her.

"OK, I'll start the ball rolling," Janelle said. "Tell me this. Was he good?"

Robin smiled back at Janelle.

"I should've known you'd ask me that," she said, laughing.

"Sooooooo. Was he? "Janelle asked again.

"OK, we'll get this out of the way first, but then you have to promise to listen and give me some good advice. Do you promise?"

"I promise," Janelle answered.

"I'm going to hold you that promise," Robin said. "Here it goes. You remember me talking about my friend Katie, don't you?"

"Yeah, what about her? I mean, how does she fit into all this?"

"Katie had a fling with Joe before she got married. I never told you, but I'm telling you now."

"God, this is big," Janelle said sipping more coffee. "So, was he good?"

"I'm getting to that. But first tell me...do you think badly of me?" Robin asked.

"That depends on how good he was," Janelle said, smiling.

She poked her finger lightly against Robin's shoulder.

"Hey forgive me. I'm just trying to make you laugh, but you know I don't cast stones, Robin. Besides I know you...you're a good person, and I am here for you."

"You're a good friend, Jan."

"Yeah, I am a good friend. You got that right. So tell me...was he good?"

Robin took a sip of coffee and then put her cup down on the concrete slab. She looked out toward the river and exhaled deeply while her eyes glided along the huge steel beams that make up the undercarriage of the I-74 Memorial Bridge.

"Well…you know Katie always told me that Joe was insatiable," Robin said. "I'll say this…Joe hasn't changed. He was insatiable and very good."

Janelle poked Robin's arm again.

"Hmmm, insatiable, huh? So, how many times did you do it?"

"Are you ever gonna listen to my problem? Or are you just interested in the bedroom part of it?" Robin teased back.

"I'm gonna listen, but I need some bedroom details. Besides, I can see that Joe is still very much on your mind. So, how many times?

"Three. OK? Three! Now you know," Robin said. "Can we move on?"

"Three! Three in one night!" Janelle exclaimed. "OK we can move on now but I gotta tell you I'm envious. Andy couldn't do three. Could Frank? But wait…wait! Three in how many hours?"

"I think around three hours," Robin said. "You know…we were sleeping. I'd fall asleep and wake up to him touching me and then…and, no, Frank couldn't do three. Frank couldn't do three in five days," Robin said with a slight laugh.

Janelle looked down into her coffee cup.

"OK. OK," she said. "Just let me get focused. But, three times in three hours…God, the guy is insatiable. And it was early morning… jeez…just think what he could do during normal waking hours. Better give me a muffin."

Robin reached into the second bag, pulled out a blueberry muffin and a large napkin and handed both of them to Janelle.

"I've got a lot to tell you, Jan, if this is making you hungry, I should've brought more muffins."

"Hey, Robin I'm sorry. I'm not being very good here. But, I do want to help. I'm just a little shocked. I'm not condemning though. You've never really been overly enthusiastic about Frank. I mean…and don't get me wrong…I've never said anything to anybody or even drawn any conclusions…but I always wondered. You don't seem happy with Frank. I hope I'm not way off base saying those things."

"No," Robin replied. "You're right on base. That's why I need to talk to someone. I'm hurting, Janelle. I gotta make some real important decisions. But I hope I'm not just dumping all my problems on you."

Janelle placed the napkin and her muffin down on the bench. She put her arm around Robin's shoulders.

"Dump away, Hon," she said. "I don't mind at all, really. You know I want to help. It can suck being a woman. We both know that."

"OK…here it goes," Robin said with a sigh. "Frank's gay."

Janelle's eyes opened wide and she instinctively moved closer to Robin, hugging her tightly as Robin leaned towards her.

"You alright, kid?"

Janelle heard Robin softly crying as she held her.

Soon, Robin pulled away, straightened her back, and smiled briefly at Janelle.

"I'm OK." she replied. "Really...I'm OK. I don't blame Frank, but I don't love him anymore...I mean I don't love him like a wife loves a husband."

"Did he tell you he's gay?"

"Yeah, he told me two weeks ago. This is terrible, Jan but I was happy to hear him tell me. He's been such a jerk ever since we got married. I'm not mad at him for being gay; he can't help that. And, I understand him trying to cover up. I really do. He was hiding his sexuality as much from himself as he was from me. I understand that, too. I just don't want to be married to a jerk. Does that make any sense at all?"

"It's all crazy, but it does make sense," Janelle answered. "I always thought Frank was a jerk too...and so does Andy. It doesn't bother me that he's gay. Really it doesn't. Like you say, that's nobody's fault. But, being a jerk...that's his fault. God, what a mess for you! Does Joe know?

Joe knows Frank's a jerk," Robin said. "He doesn't know he's gay. I gotta tell Joe about all of this."

"What are you planning on doing?" Janelle asked. "What does Frank want to do?"

"Frank wants out. I do, too," Robin answered.

"Does Frank...does he see anyone?"

"He's been seeing someone for four months now. We haven't made love for over six months. Frank doesn't come home much anymore...not after he told me. Janelle, I know he's a jerk, but it broke his heart to tell me. I've been begging him to talk with me for over a year now. When he finally talked to me, he cried and cried. He sobbed. I felt so bad for him. I just feel so good now that we've got everything out in the open. And, I feel bad for Joe. I think I took advantage of him."

Janelle smiled and massaged her friend's back.

"Three times, Robin," she said. "I don't think you took advantage of him. I think he saw something he wanted."

"Do you really? I hope so," Robin said. "I really do. Joe and I...we've always been good friends. I've always liked him a lot. I don't want to hurt him.

"Three times, Robin. I think he likes you a lot, too. And I think he came along at the right time for you. You deserve happiness, hon. I think you should call Joe and talk to him."

"What'd you think he'd say about me being married to a gay man?"

Janelle dropped her arm away from Robin's neck and put both of her hands on her on own legs. She looked out at the river and sighed.

141

"Ya got me there," she said. "Men can be such idiots when it comes to issues about gays. Is Joe an idiot?"

"I don't think so," Robin replied. "I mean, no....no, Joe's not an idiot! He's a sensitive, good man. I think he'll understand."

"You gotta give it some time, Robin," Janelle advised. It's nobody's business why you and Frank are getting a divorce, but you can't hide it from Joe. At some point he has to know. I mean, I think he has a right to know. But, what's most important is this...none of this is any reflection on you. You know the truth is...I'd probably have married Frank myself. I mean...he's a good-looking guy and he was a great catch. You can't let any of this get you down. Marriage is always risky business. Always. You're a beautiful woman, and you deserve to be happy...to hell with anyone who condemns you or Frank. Let Frank find his happiness, but you find yours, too. See Joe again...that's my advice. I mean, three times, Robin!"

Robin smiled and laughed.

"You know, there's more to a relationship than that," she said. "But, it was awful nice. It's been a long time and Joe...well, Joe's a good-looking guy...and so sweet. And, like you say, three times. That's a good thing."

"Do you love him?" Janelle asked.

"I do love him," Robin answered, "and, I think Joe loves me. We've always said we were just friends, but there's always been something between us...something more than just friendship. I know I always wanted him. I mean, wait until you see him...he's a hunk."

"I'd like to meet him sometime," Janelle said.

You know...it's strange...Katie was my friend, and Joe loved her," Robin continued. "And, somehow Katie brought Joe and me together. It's strange, but wonderful. I know Joe feels it too...and, somehow I think Katie would like us to be lovers. I mean, now that she's gone."

Janelle put her arms around Robin's shoulders again.

"I didn't know Katie, Robin. But, I think you're right. She would want you and Joe to be happy. And, I want you to be happy, too. You've got a good thing here. You've got the chance to be happy and to make Joe happy. Take it. Don't you worry about what other people think. You find happiness, and make Joe happy, too."

"I knew you'd understand. That's why I wanted to talk to you. You're a good friend."

"That's true, but even I want more trash here," Janelle said, smiling. "Tell me how Frank told you about being gay. That must've been some evening, huh?"

"It was. I don't think I've ever had such an emotional roller coaster ride as that," Robin admitted. "Do you really want to hear about it?"

"It's none of my business, Robin. I do want to hear about it, but it's none of my business. If you think it will help you to tell someone, I'm here. If it's too painful to tell now…then tell me whenever you want."

"I'll tell you now," Robin said. "The pain's over, but I think it'd be good to get it out, too. You sure you want to hear?"

"I think you should tell someone. I think you need to tell someone before you have to tell Joe. I'll tell you what…I'll change back into my gym shoes, and we can walk down the path and talk. That'll be good for both of us."

CHAPTER THIRTY-ONE

Janelle went to her car and changed her shoes while Robin sat on the park bench looking out at the river. When Janelle returned, the two friends began walking on the bike path. To their immediate left, the Mississippi River flowed rapidly along the banks of the Iowa border, and to their right, beautiful, 19th century mansions loomed on gentle hills overlooking the expansive river scenery. The sun's morning rays felt warm on their backs as Robin and Janelle headed toward the city of Davenport.

During their walk, they encountered a few early morning joggers, two bicyclists, and a small flock of Canadian geese. But for most of the walk, they had the path to themselves and Robin was able to talk openly about the night Frank told her he was gay.

"I already told you Frank was very upset that night," Robin explained. "He wanted to be honest with me, but he was afraid of hurting me. I know Frank's a jerk, Janelle…but you know…I've got this theory about jerks. I think they're all afraid of life. I think they hide behind all that insensitivity because they don't know how to communicate with people. I think Frank's afraid…not just afraid of being gay…that's a whole other issue. He's just afraid of letting people know him. He's afraid that he'll have to let his guard down, and afraid that he'll get hurt. I think Frank's a coward…you know, he's like a bully. I think most bullies are really cowards. Am I making any sense? Do you know what I mean?"

"Yeah, I do," Janelle answered. "That's what I like about you, Robin…you don't hide anything or play games. So many people play games. I guess Frank was one of them, right? Or, maybe he's just a jerk. I'm not arguing with you…but who knows? There are so many complexities when you try to analyze people. Could be he's just a jerk."

"Yeah, you're right, Jan. Who does know? I've never said this to anyone, but my friend, Katie…she played a lot of games, too. I always felt so sorry for her, but I understood. Katie was always afraid of being hurt. And, she always thought she had to project some kind of image…always thought she had to protect her heart. In a lotta ways Katie was like Frank. I mean, she was kinda afraid of life. God, I'm really bearing my soul to you!"

"It's OK, Robin," Janelle consoled. "Really…I understand. You're not doing anything wrong. I know you loved Katie."

"I do love Katie," Robin said. "I always hoped she would grow out of all that foolishness. But, I know she treated Joe badly when she broke it off with him, and she always ran roughshod over Larry. Katie had a venomous tongue, and she used her words like heavy boots. You see…Katie and I…well, we were really foolish in high school. But, she kind've stayed in high school after we graduated. She could never get over it. I mean…she couldn't get over all of that shallow popularity stuff and hanging with the cool kids."

"Why would Joe put up with that?"

"I don't think he did. Remember, Joe's time with her was limited and devoted to passion. I'm not sure he ever really knew her. She was always afraid of being hurt. I know she was afraid of Joe's love for her. Oh God, so many games. Do you see that in other people? I mean do you know people who are afraid all of the time?"

"Yeah, I do," Janelle answered. "They just don't grow up. I don't know why."

Robin stopped walking and slowly shook her head back and forth.

"Me either," she said. "I know I'm going in circles here, but I've got so much on my mind…I was supposed to be talking about Frank."

Janelle put her arm around Robin's waist, pulled her close, and smiled.

"I know you've got a lot on your mind," she said. "It's alright. Just say what you want to say."

Robin tenderly squeezed Janelle's hand in an expression of sincere gratitude.

"Thanks."

The two women continued walking on the path.

"OK, let's talk about Frank. Frank didn't even know he was gay," Robin continued. "God, the world is strange. Anyone who says they can sort it all out is just kidding themselves."

"What do you mean when you say he didn't know he was gay?"

"I mean he didn't know what it means to be gay," Robin replied. "Listen to this…Frank told me that he never was attracted to females, but he grew up in a traditional, conservative surroundings, and he was taught…I mean through example…that a man marries a woman and has kids. That's what he thought was supposed to happen, and what he was supposed to do. He lived in a small town all his life, and he never knew anything different than that. God, it is all so strange."

"How did he come to find out that he was gay then?" Janelle asked.

"Well, he told me about that, too," Robin answered. "I know I was a big part of that discovery process for Frank. Our sex life was dismal and when anything ever did happen, there was not much to it."

Robin paused momentarily again on the path. She placed her hands on her hips, exhaled deeply, and looked up briefly at the sky. Her eyes were misty.

"I suppose Frank began to wonder more about his sexuality each time he had an encounter with me," she said. "The poor guy."

Janelle turned and faced Robin. She placed her hands on Robin's shoulders and looked directly into her eyes.

"Hey, Robin…you just keep something in mind. You just keep in mind what happened last night with you and Joe…three times in three hours. You're a hot woman when you're playing in the right ballpark. But, you gotta be in the right ballpark," Janelle laughed.

"Yeah, I admit I am glad for last night for a number of reasons," Robin confessed. "And, one of those reasons is I was beginning to doubt my sex appeal. Joe's helped me in that area…that's for sure!"

"You bet he has," Janelle responded. "So forget this nonsense about you not being attractive, alright?

Janelle saw tears in Robin's eyes.

"Promise me," she said.

Robin wiped away her tears and smiled.

"I promise.

Janelle smiled back.

"But, I'm not letting you off the hook," she said. "I want to hear more about what Frank told you. I've got a lotta questions. What was Frank's other source of enlightenment for his discovery? What was that all about?"

"Well…keep in mind…he must've known something was wrong when he was growing up," Robin continued. "And this is where it gets strange, but interesting too…I mean interesting like in a study of human nature. Frank told me that he thought his gay desires were just normal behavior. He thought the feelings he had happened to everyone, and that you just got over them when you got married."

"You've lost me," Janelle said. "How can that be?"

"Here's what happened to Frank," Robin explained. "All of his adolescent life he had feelings for other men, but he never acted on them because he was always taught that such behavior was a sin. Then, when he was seventeen, he went to visit his aunt…she lived somewhere in Des Moines then…she's deceased now. When Frank went to see her he had to stay overnight in a motel. That's where he had his first gay experience."

"Hold it, "Janelle said. She pointed in the direction of a park bench that was ten yards north of the path.

"I want to hear this without you having to be interrupted," she said. "This is interesting. Let's go sit on that bench and talk. You know, Robin…you really should've brought more muffins."

Robin laughed and walked off the path with Janelle, heading for the bench.

The two women sat down facing the river. They both remained quiet for a moment while they drank in the grandeur of the Mississippi River. At the location where they were sitting, a huge slice of land called Arsenal Island divides the river's water, causing the main channel to travel along the Iowa border and a smaller channel to make its way around the island along the Illinois border. The U.S. government owns the island and keeps the grounds immaculately landscaped. Massive, old sandstone buildings with red tile roofs protrude between the huge oak trees that dominate the island's scenery. The walls of the government buildings glistened in the morning sun and, in between the island and the bike path, the steady, timeless flow of the Mississippi River rushed by the two women, its swift current indifferent to the problems they were discussing.

"Ever wonder how many life-altering stories have been played out in front of this old river?" Janelle asked. "I always wondered that when I'm riding my bike. How many stories has this river seen? It must be millions."

"Joe and Katie first made love on this river," Robin said.

"Holy Cow! And I thought your phone call this morning was gonna take me away from an interesting ride on the river," Janelle laughed. "I may give up bike riding and just sit on this bench with you from now on."

"Well, this is another story for the river," Robin said. "You wanna hear about Frank's first gay experience, right?"

"I'm all ears," Janelle replied. "Let's hear it."

"This is what happened," Robin began. "Remember I told you Frank was seventeen, and he registered at this motel. He went out to eat supper right after registering and then decided to take a swim in the motel pool."

"I can see what's coming," Janelle sighed. "There must be something about water."

"You're right," Robin laughed. "It's all in the water. While Frank was swimming around in the pool, another guy gets in the pool and strikes up a conversation. Frank told me he thought the other guy was in his twenties. Then one thing leads to another…he didn't really tell me the details…and Frank winds up in the guys room having his first gay experience."

Robin stopped talking, stared out at the river, and the expression on her face became reflective. Soon, she turned her head toward Janelle, and reached for Janelle's wrist.

"Hmmm…you know what? Frank did tell me they did it twice that night."

"See what I mean? Wrong ballpark," Janelle said laughing loudly. "You gotta be in the right ballpark."

The two women laughed uncontrollably for more than thirty seconds. Each time they tried to control themselves, they would look at each other and start laughing again.

"OK…OK," Janelle said. "Let's get a hold of ourselves here. So he has his first sexual experience. Why doesn't he get it after that? Why doesn't he understand he's gay?"

"I think he did know," Robin replied. "But, remember we live in a different age now, and Frank is nine years older than we are. Frank grew up in a small, very conservative town in the Midwest. He wasn't gonna announce his gayness. Instead, Frank came up with his theory, this rationale. He figured what he was feeling and what he had done at the motel was just sowing his wild oats."

"Sowing his wild oats!? Do you believe that?" Janelle asked.

"Yeah, I do," Robin replied. "I believe Frank was being honest with me that night. He poured his guts out to me. He really did believe that. He thought that's what sowing your wild oats meant. You have a few flings before you get married, and then you put all of that behind you. He really thought that's what would happen. That's what I mean, Jan...anyone who thinks they've got this world figured out just doesn't know what they're talking about. I bet that old river would agree with me."

Janelle shook her head back and forth.

"Wow! I wish we could ask the river to rate that story," she said. "It's gotta be in the top ten. Gotta be top ten."

"So, what do you think?" Robin asked. "Have I led an interesting life or what?"

"Ya got me beat," Janelle said. "Poor Frank. His timing was way off...and his bad timing became your bad timing. But, then there's Joe. You know, if it weren't for Joe, I'd be crying my eyes out for you."

"Yeah," Robin replied. "Joe and me, we've always been there for each other. And now he means more to me than anyone. I need him, and I'm gonna make him happy. Three's a good number, right?"

Janelle stood up, reached out for Robin's hands, and pulled her friend up off of the bench. She wrapped her arms around Robin and the two women hugged each other warmly.

"Three's a great number, Robin," she said. "Everything's gonna be great for you and Joe. I can feel it."

Later that day, Robin went home and emailed the following message to Joe:

Hi Joe! Thanks for bringing the wine last night, and thanks for staying with me. I know we may have acted prematurely last night, but I want you to know I loved being with you, and I want to see you again. Frank will be coming home Monday, and I need to talk with him, but don't worry – I am not going to say anything about you. Frank and I have not been getting along and we both know we need to do something. I am NOT asking you for any commitment, and my talking with Frank is NOT because of what happened last night. I do miss seeing and talking with you. Joe – I hope you share some of the feelings I am having right now. I want to see you again, but I need some time so I can talk with Frank. More than a buddy – Love, Robin

CHAPTER THIRTY-TWO

Sheriff Armstrong stood in front of a five-foot by four-foot map of Henry County. The map was attached to the south wall of the sheriff's briefing room. The room was large enough to accommodate fifteen deputies seated at three conference-style tables. Today, five newspaper reporters and three television crews were sharing the room with Sheriff Armstrong and Deputy Lambert.

"Now, the place I want you all to look at is right here," the sheriff said.

Sheriff Armstrong leaned toward the wall and pushed his finger onto the surface of the map.

"Me and my deputies have done some checking…we've been, measuring the road and counting cars…and the way I see it, the quarry expansion will cause a significant increase in truck traffic at the junction of Billy Wolf Road and Cleveland Road," he said.

"You know, this office has always been concerned with road safety," the sheriff continued. "There was a time when traffic on Wolf Road was just a dribble. Of course now with all the home additions…traffic there has increased quite a bit. I mean, there are two other places in the county where I am concerned with the increase in traffic, too, but Billy Wolf Road has become one of our most heavily traveled roads, and I can see where we have to make it wider in the future…I'm talking maybe five years from now. But, for right now, Billy Wolf Road cannot handle an increase in truck traffic at that junction. This is not the time for the quarry to be expanding up on the ridge. As sheriff, I am announcing today that my office opposes the River Bend quarry expansion plans."

During his two terms in office, Sheriff Armstrong had acquired a knack for being able to appear in the local news. He had developed a network of reporters who could be counted on to deliver him print and airtime. Today, he was conducting a news conference to state his official position concerning the quarry issue. He had called media representatives from Henry County and from adjoining Rock Island County to attend the conference. The sheriff wanted all the voters in the county to know he opposed the quarry expansion, and he was pleased with the media crowd that had showed up. But, there was another reason why a large number of media people were present, and that reason went beyond the sheriff's influence. The issue of the quarry was considered good ink in the large Quad City region because any disruptions in the tranquil County of Henry were always jumped on by the neighboring metro-politan news agencies. In the Quad-Cities, trouble in paradise was always welcome news.

The sheriff turned away from the map and looked directly into the television cameras.

"Now, let's get my media friends involved. I'll take any questions you have," he said.

"Sheriff, will you be addressing the County Board on the issue of safety?" a reporter questioned. "It is my understanding the Planning and Development Committee is going to approve River Bend's special use permit."

"River Bend has a long way to go before they can move any dirt along Billy Wolf Road," the sheriff began. "Change isn't something that should happen overnight, you know. I've seen a lot of good changes happen here in the county and the best ones took time. You know, the procedure to grant a special use permit is complicated, and all parties must have a say concerning its impact. My office and a large number of citizens will be contacting every county board member about this issue. Our voices will be heard."

A woman with a mike in her hand and a television camera shooting over her shoulder moved closer to the sheriff.

"How many votes do you need to stop the expansion, Sheriff?" the woman asked.

The sheriff looked directly into the camera's lens and pointed a finger in the air.

"Well, you know we have to follow the law, and the law states that if twenty percent of the adjoining property owners object in writing to the expansion, then the special use permit can be stopped with only nine of the twenty-four board members voting no. It is my understanding that all of the neighboring property owners have objected. I've talked with a number of them about this issue and I can tell you they are mad. One of them bent my ear for over a half hour the other day about this. She was plenty mad. You know, I think we can easily get nine board members to see this expansion is not what the people of Henry County want. To be honest, I think we'll get more than nine board members to vote with us."

"Sheriff," another reporter called out. "I understand that the Cleveland Village Board is going to come out in opposition to the expansion. Have you talked with anyone over there?"

"Yes, I have," the sheriff responded. "I was just out there the other day checking with some of my auxiliary officers. There are a lot of good folks in Cleveland, and you know Cleveland's had a lot of trouble with flood waters. A lot of those folks just recently got federal buyout money to move away from the river. The village leaders want the town to grow by developing up on the ridge just west of the area where the quarry wants to expand. They know nobody's gonna build a new home that has a rock quarry next to it, and I don't want those people moving out of the county. We need to keep the county attractive for homeowners. The County Board needs to give those homeowners in that area some help."

"Sheriff," another reporter said. "The County Board's controlled by the Democrats. You're a Republican. Is this a partisan issue?"

"Partisan politics isn't an issue here," the sheriff responded. "I'm talking about road safety and the value of homes. I know it's not easy to stand up to a big company like River Bend, but I believe a lot of board members, both Republicans and Democrats, will be with me on this issue."

After the news conference had ended and the media people had left the briefing room, the sheriff turned to Deputy Lambert and smiled broadly.

"I think we got their attention, huh Joe?" the sheriff said. "We should get good press on this."

Deputy Lambert shrugged his shoulders slightly.

"You always get good press, Sheriff," Joe replied. "But, I don't understand why you are getting so involved in this. This issue isn't a clear winner. There's division in the county over what to do at the quarry. I mean...I know some people are putting up signs and writing editorials, but there are a lot of other people in the county who depend on the quarry for rock and jobs."

"What are you saying, Joe?" Armstrong replied. "Don't you think I know a winner when I see it?"

"Of course you do, Mike," Joe answered. "And, I'm just wondering out loud here...I mean... zoning...that's a County Board issue. I don't know if those guys on the County Board are gonna take kindly to you getting so involved in a zoning issue."

"Screw them. I've been police officer here longer than they've served on the County Board. What the hell do they know anyway? You're not questioning my political judgment, are you, Joe?"

"No, Sheriff," Joe replied. "I'm not doing that at all. You're the political expert around here. But, I just don't understand why you're getting so involved in such an issue. You don't need this on your plate to get elected. Why not just leave the quarry expansion alone and let the County Board take any heat for the zoning issue?"

"You need to understand something," the sheriff shot back. "This office is opposed to that quarry expansion plan, period! More importantly...I'm opposed to it. I want my men with me on this and that includes you. I've already talked with Rogers about this, and he's with me. Are you?"

"Sure, Mike," Joe said. "Sure I am."

"Good," the sheriff replied. "I'm going to go and start lobbying some of our illustrious board members. I'll get those nine votes. A lot of those guys owe me and it's time they paid up. Why don't you straighten this room up a little, and I'll see you later today."

OK, Mike," Joe said. "I'll see you later."

When Armstrong left the room, Joe sat down on the edge of one of the conference tables and wondered about what the sheriff was doing.

Something doesn't feel right about all of this, he thought. I don't see any real safety issue with the new quarry traffic. The truck pattern really shouldn't change that much. At least not enough to deny River Bend the zoning change they want. I understand people in the housing additions being mad about the change in scenery, but why is Mike so riled up about an issue like this? It can't be because of votes. Hell, nobody's gonna hold a sheriff responsible for a zoning change. Of course, it could be that Mike's just posturing for the voters. All politicians tend to overdo it when they're up for election. But still...I don't get it. It just seems to me Mike could lose votes on an issue like this. And, I know for sure that this is gonna piss off a lot of county board members. There must be something I'm missing, but then I'm not an elected official. One thing I do know for sure...the sheriff's made it clear that I just work here.

Joe looked around the briefing room and made mental notes on what he would have to do to put the room back in order. He shook his head slowly when he thought of what the sheriff had just said to him.

"So, Mike asked Rogers about all this, huh?" Joe said quietly to himself. "Well, fuck Rogers and fuck Armstrong, too!"

Joe moved away from the table, looked around the briefing room one more time, and then left without touching any of the furniture. He strolled through the main room of the sheriff's office complex and called out to a clerk who was working at her desk.

"Hey, Sheila!" he said. "When Rogers comes in today, tell him the sheriff wants him to straighten out the briefing room."

"OK, Joe. I'll tell him," Sheila called back.

Fuck 'em both! Joe thought as he walked out of the office door.

CHAPTER THIRTY-THREE

Deputy Lambert did not see Sheriff Armstrong for the rest of that day. Instead of looking for the sheriff, he made a commitment to steer clear of his boss for as long as he could. Joe decided he needed to work out a number of problems in his mind. He was coming to the realization that his relationship with the sheriff had either changed or was never what he had imagined it to be.

I wonder who has changed, Joe thought. Has the sheriff changed or have I changed? Maybe Mike is right...maybe I was never meant for this line of work. I know I'm an idealist, and I'm not tough enough sometimes, but...God...I do think there's a place for someone like me in law enforcement. I've got a lotta things to think over...and then there's Robin. I really enjoyed being with her, but I hope I didn't hurt her. I miss her right now.

That evening Joe went home and checked his email messages. There were three new unread messages displayed in his inbox. One message was from someone named Carmen, whose attached subject line promised kinky sex on demand. A second message was from his union, the FOP, with an attached subject line about the need to buy inexpensive term life insurance. And the third message was from Robin Karlson with a subject line of 'Hi Deputy!' typed in it. Joe was overjoyed to see he had an email from Robin. He moved quickly to open it, read it twice, and then immediately called her on the phone.

"Hi, Deputy Lambert," Robin responded when she answered the phone.

"Hi, Robin!" Joe replied. "Are you still psychic? Do you know why I'm calling you today?"

"Let me guess. Either you left something at my house, or you read my email, or you wanted to call and tell me what a terrific time you had visiting with me. I'm hoping the answer is number three."

"The answer is both two and three," he said. "I just read your email. I loved being with you, and I miss you, too. I want to see you again, but I need to know something. Are you all right? I mean...have I messed up your marriage with Frank?"

"No, Joe you haven't done anything wrong, and I'm fine," Robin replied. "Frank and I have been having troubles for a long time. What's happening between Frank and me has nothing to do with you, but there are a lot of things

I want to tell you. So many things I want to say to you. I do want to see you again, and I'm glad you want to see me…I just don't want you to be in the middle of what's happening between Frank and me. I loved being with you. I just wish we could be together like that…well…after I have worked things out with Frank. Do you understand what I'm saying?"

"I understand this…I loved being with you, too," Joe replied. "And I want to see you again and talk with you. I want to share with you. I have wanted to call you and tell you how much I miss you. I have been thinking about you all day.

"I'm glad you called," Robin said. "I've been thinking of you all day too. I haven't hurt you in any way, have I?"

"No," he said. "Robin…I've felt disconnected for a long time. The other night with you made me feel whole. I loved waking up and finding you next to me. I don't want to be the cause of breaking up your marriage, but I have to say these things to you."

"My marriage with Frank is over. It's been over for quite some time. I need to talk with Frank and then I really want to talk with you. Joe…you know this will take some time. I mean…it will take awhile for me to be able to see you. I don't want to be sneaking around to see you. Do you understand that?"

"Yes…absolutely," Joe replied. "I don't want you to have to do that either. I want us together in the open and publicly. I want people to know we're together."

"But, I do want to see you again," Robin blurted out. "I want to see you so we can talk. I don't want to just talk with you on the phone or email you. I want to see you face-to-face, Deputy Lambert. I need to see you when I talk with you."

"I want that too, Robin. And, we can do that. We can meet somewhere in public…just like we always have when we were buddies. We need to talk."

"I'm wondering something, Joe."

"What's that?"

"I'm wondering if we can pull this off. I mean…do you really think we could meet and just talk?"

"No," Joe answered. "I doubt it very much. I love you and I want you. I'm excited just talking to you on the phone."

"So am I, Joe," Robin confessed softly.

"But, I don't care if we do fail," Joe said. "I want to be with you…that's what I know. But, what I don't want to do is upset the process you will have to go through with Frank. Tell me about that…what does Frank want to do?"

"Frank doesn't want to be married any longer," Robin answered. "I don't want to get into the details of all of that right now over the phone, but Frank wants out of the marriage just as much as I do."

"I'm sorry about your marriage, Robin. I never did like Frank, and I think he's a fool to give you up...but I'm glad he's a fool."

"I'm glad we made love, Joe. We should've done that earlier in our lives."

"The past doesn't matter anymore," Joe replied. "All that matters is we have found each other and we need to protect that. I love you. I want to be with you."

"I love you too, Joe. When are we going to see each other again?"

"I want to see you right now. But, tell me this, when will you talk with Frank?"

"This week sometime," Robin replied. "I can't say for sure when. I want to talk with him as soon as possible, but the timing has to be right. Frank will be anxious about his work when he gets back from the seminar. It'll take a little time for him to settle down...so I think I'll talk with him on Wednesday or Thursday."

"I understand," Joe said. "You have to make the call as to when it is right, and I know that it will take some time for everything to sink in. No matter what he's been feeling about you, it will be a blow to him to hear the words spoken out loud. You need to give it some time...but, I'll be here, and we can talk anytime you need to. I just really think we should wait to see each other until after you have talked with Frank. I really do want to see you right now, but it would be better for you if we waited. Do you understand?"

"I understand," Robin answered.

"Do you agree?

"Yeah...I agree," Robin said sadly. "I really do agree, but right now I want you to hold me, and I want to kiss you."

"I want that, too, Robin. And, soon we will talk, face-to face, just like you said. Hey...did I ever tell you that you have a nice ass?"

"Yessssssss...you did," Robin said, laughing. "And, you'd better tell me again...soon! Thanks for saying that, Joe."

I love you, Robin. Email me to let me know how things are going, OK?"

"Alright, but you email me, too."

"I will," Joe promised. "I want to hear from you every day and I'll email you every day."

"You're sweet, Joe."

"I love you, Robin," Joe said again.

CHAPTER THIRTY-FOUR

Sheriff Armstrong was a skilled politician. When he made up his mind on an issue, he enthusiastically attacked it in full force. He knew that there were many arguments against granting the special use permits for River Bend's expansion plans: aesthetics, property values, traffic safety, water run-off, environmental factors, and loss of farmland. All of those things were on his side. He would employ all arguments to get the nine votes he needed.

The sheriff wanted to remain confident in his plan to stop the quarry expansion, but he also knew his strategy was a long shot. He knew his effort to stop the expansion could become folly as the issue of rezoning the land headed toward the process of county board consideration. He was painfully aware that some of his strongest opponents sat on the Henry County Board.

The board member who most frequently questioned the practices of the sheriff was Ted Chapman. Ted was the Vice-Chairman of the County Board, a member of the County Finance Committee, and a member of the County Administration Committee. He was also a township road commissioner. For his livelihood, Ted had worked as an electrician for Montgomery Elevator and had been a labor leader in the local IBEW. Ted had been educated through life's experiences, and he had graduated magna cum laude. He was a unique combination of proletarian experience and superior managerial skills. Ted had recently retired and was giving Henry County the benefit of his enormous abilities. He was articulate, precise and bold. And, Ted Chapman's name was written at the top of the list of the sheriff's political enemies.

Ted Chapman and the sheriff were oil and water. Ted was a Democrat, and Sheriff Armstrong was a Republican. The elected responsibilities that Ted had assumed in county government were broad, giving him responsibility to oversee the operations of eleven county departments, whereas the sheriff's focus was narrowed by his fervent interest in law enforcement. Ted Chapman was frugal and was always looking for ways to reduce county expenses, while the sheriff's departmental needs constantly required additional funds. Ted always examined the fine print of every county plan or contract to make sure the authority for implementing the agreement was properly placed; whereas the sheriff glossed over documents, looking only at those words that would be most beneficial in promoting the goals he had set for his department. Chapman rarely spoke in public and was thrifty and unassuming with his words. When Sheriff Armstrong spoke, he favored an audience and was voluminous in his discourse. Even the attire of the two men was diametrically opposite. Ted's clothing style was working class casual. He often attended county functions in jeans and a plaid shirt. The sheriff was always spit-shined, polished, and decked out in his official uniform. There was a place for both of these types of men in county politics, but whenever the sheriff and Ted crossed paths, the roadway was never wide enough to accommodate the two.

During his sixteen-year tenure as an elected county board member, Ted had sparred numerous times with the sheriff's department over issues involving finance and jurisdiction. The accounts of his battles with Armstrong's predecessor had been logged in newspaper stories and told hundreds of times at gatherings around restaurant tables and in bars. When Mike Armstrong was elected sheriff, Ted Chapman's careful scrutiny of the sheriff's department continued and his disagreements with the new sheriff were unrelenting. Now, both Chapman and Armstrong were taking stands concerning the matter of the quarry expansion. There was no way that they would be on the same side of the issue.

"Hey, Ted, did you read about the sheriff's press conference on the quarry?" Doug Weaver asked.

Doug had seen Ted walking in the main hall of the county courthouse and had hurried to catch up with him. Ted was marching toward a conference room where the Administration Committee was about to meet.

"Yeah, I read it." Ted replied.

"So…what did you think?"

Doug Weaver was the Chairman of the Administration Committee, and he knew Ted leaned in favor of the quarry expansion, but he also knew Ted would weigh all of the consequences before making a decision. Ted always chose his words carefully when asked about any issue. Doug on the other hand was a rascal, and he often spoke out of turn using humor and guile to prod information from a conversation. Doug was enjoying being able to egg Ted on by inserting the sheriff's stance into the equation concerning the rock quarry.

"Are you with the sheriff on this one, Ted?" Doug asked.

Ted stopped walking and turned to face Doug. He pointed a finger at Doug's chest.

"Will you do me a favor, Doug?" he said. "If you ever see me standing with the sheriff on an issue that I have not thoroughly examined, walk around behind me, and kick me in the ass, OK?"

"Ted," Doug replied, "whenever you need someone to kick you in the ass, you can count on me. But seriously, what do you think about all of this?"

"What do I think about the quarry expansion? Or what do I think about Sheriff Armstrong butting in on the zoning issue?" Ted replied.

"Hell, Ted, I know what you think about the sheriff butting in," Doug said. "That's a given. I mean, who wants him meddling around with zoning? That's our turf. What I'd like to know is what do you think about the expansion plans? After all, that's your district out there, and you've got sort of a conflict on this issue."

"Now what conflict do I have?" Ted asked.

"OK...we're going to play games, right?" Doug replied, smiling. "Then let's play games."

Doug held his right hand up and extended his four fingers.

"Let's pretend like you don't know the conflicts, and I'm here to explain them to you," he said. "Here we go."

Doug used his left hand to separately pull back on each of his extended four fingers, one by one, as he explained the conflicts to Ted.

"One...you've got voters in that housing addition mad as hell because River Bend wants to pile a mountain of rock next to them and build an asphalt plant there. Two...you're a township road commissioner who needs crushed rock for roads. Three...that proposed asphalt plant would help your township responsibilities. And four...you've got voters in your district who depend on that quarry for jobs. Those seem like conflicts to me. Am I spelling it out clearly for you, Ted?"

"Well, you certainly know how to count. I'll give you that," Ted said. "But I'm not saying your numbers add up to anything that bothers me."

"You don't feel like you're in the middle on this one?" Doug asked.

"I like being in the middle," Ted answered. "When a guy is in the middle, he can see both sides of the issue...and, that's what I intend to do. I'm gonna look at both sides of the issue before I make up my mind. I suggest we all do that."

"Do you think the sheriff's done that?" Doug asked, smiling at Ted.

Ted scowled.

"That's doubtful," he answered. "Seriously though, I really don't know what the hell the sheriff's doing with this. I do know he's all about being re-elected. So somehow he's tied stopping the quarry expansion to him winning the election. But, I don't see it. Do you?"

"Well, there are a lot of those 'Stop the Quarry' signs up," Doug observed. "They seem to be all over the county. But still, I think this issue is one of those hot button things. I suspect the heat for this is being generated by a small number of people in the housing additions. Seems to me the issue will explode for a while and then go away. I can't imagine the quarry being a vote-getting issue. It doesn't make any sense to me."

"Me either," Ted said. "I can't see a majority of voters really giving a damn about it. I'll bet a lot of those signs are just sympathy gestures. I know half the voters in my district want the expansion, and the vast majority of them don't want River Bend leaving here. The bigger the quarry, the more jobs there are. And, hell, what if River Bend did leave this area? Where would we get rock then?"

"I seems like you've already made up your mind, Ted."

"No. No, I have not!" Ted replied. "I'm just weighing all of the possibilities. I need more information, and I'm willing to listen to all sides. A man should listen before he acts. But for right now, we'd better get to the committee meeting."

The two men continued down the hallway to the room where the Administration Committee meeting would be held, walked in the room, and greeted those who had gathered to conduct business.

Five county board members who served on the committee were already in the room. In addition, the County Administrator was there, along with three contractors. The agenda for the meeting was short and the committee concluded its business in just over an hour. When the meeting adjourned, Doug Weaver watched as people hovered around Ted Chapman like hummingbirds floating around flowers. Everyone was anxious to know where Ted stood on the quarry issue and, as usual, Ted was elusive. But his disagreement with the sheriff's judgment was clear.

"Let's just say I think the sheriff is premature in his decision concerning road safety," Ted stated. "That doesn't mean he's wrong, but we've been looking at Wolf Road for some time now. The Transportation Department has a request in with the state to get funds to widen that road. The quarry expansion plan may work in our favor there."

"What about the homeowners?" one of the contractors asked. "Won't the expansion hurt them?"

"The county board will be looking at how the expansion impacts everyone," Ted replied. "I want to make sure everyone's voice is heard on this issue before I vote one way or the other."

"But would you vote against the expansion request?" another contractor asked.

"Like I said, I want to make sure everyone's voice is heard first," Ted replied. "And we have to keep in mind there is more here than just River Bend making a rezoning request. There's a larger issue here...an issue that has already been decided by the Supreme Court. The Supreme Court protects what a private landowner can do with his property. River Bend has rights too, you know. I'm not in favor of involving this county in an expensive lawsuit that we could easily lose. In the end, I want us all to be good neighbors, and I think River Bend wants that, too."

Although Ted Chapman had not definitively announced his stand on the quarry expansion issue, it was obvious that a major obstacle was rising to the sheriff's attempts to stop the expansion of the River Bend quarry. If the sheriff wanted to stop the expansion, he would have to out-maneuver Ted Chapman's influence on the Henry County Board.

CHAPTER THIRTY-FIVE

Because Ted Chapman was a Democrat, he had an advantage over Sheriff Armstrong when it came to the quarry expansion issue. His advantage was that Democrats outnumber Republicans on the county board and, therefore, they exercise majority control of the board.

In addition, two other traits of the county board members favored Chapman in his repeated disagreements with the sheriff. Those two traits are: frugality with public funds and protection of the limited authority the local board members are granted by the Illinois State Statues. Universally in Illinois, county boards and sheriff departments butt heads when trying to define how these traits should be applied to their relationships. The Henry County Board and the Henry County Sheriff's Department are no exceptions to this conflict of wills.

In Henry County, the county board members' concern with spending public revenue was always being tested by Sheriff Armstrong's desire to expand and improve upon the functions of his department, and a number of the county board members had become aggravated with the sheriff when it came to the issue of spending county revenues. Armstrong was a strong advocate for his office and he was always asking for increases in his spending authority. He believed that the sheriff's department was the most important department in the county, and that he should get the lion's share of any revenues that rolled into the county's coffers.

Each year, Ted Chapman found himself listening to what he believed were unjustified requests for funds from the sheriff. Each year, the Finance Committee would ask the sheriff for further information concerning his budget requests. And, every time Armstrong was asked for more information, he would return to the Finance Committee with additional arguments that addressed his need for expanding the services of the sheriff's department.

Annually, Armstrong sang the same song when he submitted his proposed budget to the Henry County Finance Committee. "My department should get top priority," he would declare. "My department is in charge of peace and security. Without us, there would be no safety for the citizens."

The struggle between the county board and the sheriff over expenditure of funds reached its highest plateau when the board considered a tentative budget that refused the sheriff's request for additional deputies. In his response to the proposed budget, Armstrong offended all of the board members by immediately taking the issue to the press.

"I want the citizens of Henry County to know the county board is playing games with public safety by denying my request," the sheriff announced to a gathering of reporters.

"But Sheriff," a reporter asked, "didn't the board make cutbacks in all of the county departments?"

"My department needs three additional deputies," the sheriff responded. "The people in my department protect public safety. Without the three deputies, the safety of everyone in Henry County is threatened."

"The budget has been laid over for thirty days, so the board members can review it...right, Sheriff?" a reporter asked.

"That's right," he answered. "And during that time, I want the citizens of Henry County to contact their board members and tell them they want our county to be safe. I need that budget amended to include my requests. The board needs to know the harm this budget will cause. The operations of my department are essential for the welfare of all citizens. And, everyone needs to know that the Henry County Sheriff's Department is a money maker for this county."

"What do you mean by that, Sheriff?" another reporter asked.

"I'll tell you what I mean," the sheriff replied. "My department takes in out-of-county prisoners and houses them in the county jail. Our department has been doing this for many years, and the county gets money from the federal government for me to do that. Why this year alone I have brought in almost one million dollars for the county with that program, and that money should be used for public safety. This budget is actually taking money from my department to give funds to other departments. That's not right, and it is the board's responsibility to provide the funds I need to protect the citizens of Henry County. I expect them to amend this proposed budget to get me the men I need to do my job. As law enforcement officers, we do our jobs, now the board needs to do the right thing and pass a budget that allows for the extra deputies I have requested."

At the next county board meeting, the County Finance Chairman submitted the proposed budget. A lone supporter of the sheriff's request for additional deputies attempted to change the budget.

"Mr. Chairman," county board member White called out. "I move that the budget be amended as follows: in the upcoming fiscal year, the county budget will reflect a reduction of two employees in the Circuit Clerk's office, one in the County Treasurer's office, and two employees in Probation. These layoffs will provide the funds the sheriff needs in order for him to hire three more deputies."

"Is there a second to the motion?" the County Chairman asked.

Parliamentary procedure required the County Chairman to make three requests for a second to the motion.

An uncomfortable silence reigned in the room among the Republican board members as the Chairman waited for a second to the motion. The silence was pleasant chamber music for the Democrats. Ted Chapman sat with a smirk on his face as the silence continued.

"Is there a second?" the Chairman asked once more.

Again, there was no response.

"Is there a second to the motion?" the Chairman asked a third time.

Quiet prevailed in the room. The long silence was broken by the fall of the county chairman's gavel.

"Hearing none, the motion dies," the Chairman declared.

CHAPTER THIRTY-SIX

S heriff Armstrong was mad at the county board for not supporting his budget amendment, but what he failed to comprehend was that the board members were incensed with him because he went public over the budget. And, many of the board members resented Armstrong's use of the press to lecture them.

Now, Sheriff Armstrong upset the board members again by holding a press conference over the quarry expansion issue. He was using the quarry expansion issue to interfere in an area that was clearly the county board's jurisdiction. According to the law, the authority to grant or reject River Bend's expansion and special use requests belonged exclusively to the county board. When informed of the sheriff's meddling in the issue of rezoning, board members on both sides of the political spectrum chanted the same mantra: No interference in the board's authority to act upon zoning requests.

"I'm not going to take any advice from the sheriff on this issue, "a Republican board member said. "Every time we ask him to justify the revenue his office wants, he launches into an explanation about the need to upgrade his department. He's always talking about us undermining his authority. Why should we let him dabble in our jurisdiction?"

"I agree that the sheriff has the authority to issue a road safety report," another Republican board member declared. "But, that report should have been filed with the Planning and Development Committee, period! He had no right to go to the press with that information. And, he shouldn't be lobbying us on this issue. Zoning is our business!"

The more the sheriff pushed for county board support for his position on the quarry, the better River Bend's chances of procuring the rezoning and the special permits became.

Ted Chapman was pleased to hear the discord that the sheriff's actions caused among all of the board members, and he attacked the sheriff's opposition to the quarry on every front.

"That quarry provides jobs for a number of the county's citizens," Chapman told county board members. "Talk to any of the township supervisors and you'll find out they depend on the quarry for inexpensive crushed rock for the township roads. And, why hell, that's where the County Highway Department gets all of its rock too."

When talking with the ten county board members who were farmers, Ted informed them that twenty percent of the quarry's rock production was geared toward agricultural needs.

"And, the county gets a lot of tax revenue from the operation of that quarry," he reminded them. "I know a lot of people are concerned about what the expansion will look like, but I've been talking to the guys over at River Bend…they're very concerned about that issue. Bill Stevens is the main man over at the quarry, and he has shown me the landscaping plans they have for hiding the rock deposits. They're going to build a berm and landscape that whole area. They'll make the area look better than it ever did."

When a local reporter called Ted's home to ask about the noise and the smell of the asphalt plant, he was ready with an orchestrated reply.

"I've asked River Bend to find a comparable asphalt plant that is currently in operation so we can go take a look at it. Mr. Johnson, the CEO of River Bend, contacted me this morning and told me River Bend just built a new asphalt plant in Michigan. River Bend is willing to pay the cost of a shuttle bus up there and back for anyone interested in looking at the new plant. It's the same type of plant that they want to build here. I'm going to make the trip and so are several members of the Cleveland Village Council. If that plant is noisy and smells, I'll be the first to vote 'no' on the quarry's plans."

"What about the homeowners' fear of declining property value?" the reporter asked.

"I've seen the facts. Appraisers are divided on the question of potential property value loss," Ted answered. "Even the appraisers who project a drop in property values can't put a dollar amount on the impact. Their information is subjective and wouldn't hold up in court."

"Doesn't voter opposition to the quarry issue concern you?" the reporter continued.

"Of course I am concerned about what the voters think, but they need to have all of the information," Ted replied. "It's a common reaction for people to oppose such a huge change. As a county board we've done what we are elected to do. We have slowed down the process so all of the facts can be discussed. The Planning and Developing Committee sent River Bend's request back to the Zoning Board of Appeals just so everyone could have their say about this. We're listening, and we're taking into consideration all of the facts. Any attempt by us to stop the quarry expansion based on popular whim would be met in court by an army of corporate attorneys. In order for any objections to be valid, they must be proven. Do you think the sheriff can prove that truck traffic on Billy Wolf Road will be more dangerous as a result of this expansion? In fact, River Bend has shown me a new truck entrance they will be using, which will address all of the sheriff's concerns about increased traffic on Wolf Road."

When asked why the sheriff was so vehemently opposed to the expansion, Ted Chapman would just scratch his head.

"Sheriff Armstrong and I don't see eye to eye on a lot of things", he said. "I'll say this…Armstrong is one hell of a good law enforcement officer, but, and don't quote me on this…on this quarry issue, Armstrong's driveway just doesn't meet the road. Do you understand a quarry's profit is made within a fifty-mile radius of the pit? What if River Bend shuts down over this issue? What would we do for gravel?"

Ted Chapman did enjoy the challenge of political debate, and he loved defending his principles when he believed he was operating in the best interests of the county citizens. But, the quarry issue took on a new dimension for him when the sheriff interfered in the rezoning process. He could not understand why the sheriff was taking such a stance, but in private circles he did speculate on the sheriff's motives and on the Armstrong's frame of mind.

"You know the sheriff is shrewd," Ted noted. "He has recruited a large number of auxiliary deputies into his department. That auxiliary unit is a tight-knit group, and they have been the core of his support during election years. I wonder how many of them live on the Billy Wolf corridor. Maybe that's why he is opposed to the expansion. Of course, I could be wrong…there could be other reasons, too."

In order to make sure his support for the quarry's request was sound, Ted Chapman did go to examine a modern asphalt plant. A contingent of village officials, County Board members and concerned citizens also rode the shuttle bus to Traverse City, Michigan. In viewing the plant, the curious observers were shown a sophisticated network of silencers that had been placed in the plant. With the silencers installed, the noise levels produced by the plant were found to be comparable to the noise produced by a household air conditioner. The observers were also shown that any threat of odor had been eliminated by the way in which the plant had been designed. When they returned from examining the plant, the Cleveland village officials announced that, due to the new technologies they had seen and River Bend's willingness to landscape the area, Cleveland would be dropping their opposition to the expansion of the quarry and would be working with River Bend in an attempt to make the expansion aesthetically acceptable. The Cleveland Mayor, Tom Robinson, announced that the quarry expansion was now being viewed as positive for the small Village of Cleveland.

"We have been talking with River Bend about annexing the quarry land into the village," Robinson told reporters. "River Bend has indicated to me that they will not oppose such a move. We're hopeful the expansion will be economically beneficial to both River Bend and Cleveland. We will be asking the county board to approve River Bend's requests."

169

A part of Armstrong's success as the sheriff was attributable to the fact that he fulfilled his responsibilities as the county's chief law enforcement officer and, as much as possible, he had stayed away from county issues, which were unrelated to his department. But now, Armstrong was trespassing on county board territory, and the continuation of his success as sheriff was about to be tested by the board's actions on the quarry issue.

The sheriff attended the county board meeting on the night in which the quarry decision was to be made. He stood in the back of the room, nervously pacing back and forth prior to the vote.

When the Planning and Development Committee Chairperson reported on River Bend's request, she informed the board members that River Bend had satisfactorily answered all of the previous concerns over environmental issues.

"The Village of Cleveland has withdrawn their objections to the expansion plans and to the special use permits for the asphalt plant," the committee chairwoman reported. "Mr. Chairman, I move that the River Bend's requests be approved by the Henry County Board."

"I second the motion," Doug Weaver declared.

"We do have registered complaints from a majority of the adjoining property owners," the County Board Chairman announced. "In order to pass, this motion will require sixteen affirmative votes. Will the clerk please call the roll?"

The sheriff appeared anxious, as he mentally tracked the 'no' vote count to seven.

Two more no votes, the sheriff mentally noted. I just need two more votes and I'll prevail.

But there was to be no other 'no' vote. Of the seven votes cast against the quarry expansion, board members who had been allies of the sheriff cast four of them. The other three 'no' votes were cast merely for public consumption. County board members had decided in advance that the four board members who lived in the quarry district should vote 'no' so as not to offend their constituents in the housing additions. Ted Chapman was the only county board member from the quarry district who declined the opportunity to vote 'no'.

The sheriff's anguish intensified as each remaining vote was cast as a 'yes'.

"The vote has been taken," The County Board Chairman declared. "On this issue there are seventeen 'yes' votes and seven 'no' votes. The land is now deemed as commercial and the special use permits are granted."

As the County Board Chairman's gavel banged down, officially proclaiming the vote tally, Sheriff Armstrong hurried out of the boardroom. Armstrong knew the bang of the County Chairman's gavel was also affirming the worst of his fears. The fall of the chairman's gavel was a devastating blow to the sheriff's re-election chances. It was now possible his career would end after only serving two terms as sheriff. Time was no longer on his side.

A newspaper reporter watched the sheriff rush out of the county board-room. The reporter turned to a colleague and whispered in her ear.

"The sheriff looks sick. Hope he's OK."

CHAPTER THIRTY-SEVEN

R iver Bend wasted no time beginning the expansion of the quarry. Heavy construction equipment, workers, and an on-site construction office quickly appeared upon the fifty-nine acres of rezoned land.

In order to convert the area into an expanded rock storage location, the workers would have to bulldoze a tree line, level the fields, and rearrange the rich soil into the promised landscaped berm.

Bill Stevens was the coordinating engineer for the quarry expansion project and was the man who spent the most time in the on-site construction office. The second full day of work was nearing an end, and Bill was in the office leaning over blueprints that described in detail how the new section of the rock quarry would be constructed. He had examined the blueprints more than a hundred times. He wanted the construction to be done right because he was painfully aware that the good citizens who lived in the nearby Barker Housing Addition viewed the quarry expansion as impending doom. He was anxious to complete the groundwork for the expansion, begin the work of building the berm, and then landscape the areas that bordered Billy Wolf Road and the Barker Housing Addition. He hoped that getting the berm built and landscaped would take the edge off some of the homeowners' fears.

Bill studied the blueprints as the rumble of diesel engines droned heavily through the office walls of the trailer. He felt the office trailer tremble from the power emitted by the machines that were working on transforming the acres of farmland into a future depository for ten enormous heaps of crushed rock. When he visualized the piles of rock, Bill did sympathize with the residential neighbors. After all, he would not want to look out his house windows and see those mountains of crushed rock. The landscape for the adjacent homeowners was going to change significantly no matter what Bill did.

The job would be a challenge. The workers had to make the new quarry section attractive from the outside and functionally profitable on the inside. Bill took the challenge seriously. He was a life-long resident of Henry County, and he knew many of the people who lived in the nearby housing addition. He also knew there were a lot of people in all four corners of Henry County who were watching the development of the quarry. It was important to replace the farmland that had been there for over a century and a half with a new, appealing landscape. The berm would be the proverbial fence that makes for good neighbors.

While he was contemplating the southeast corner berm, Bill's concentration was interrupted by an abrupt commotion outside the trailer door of his office. The door opened violently and a young construction worker, Dan Lawrence, leaped inside.

"Bill! Bill! Come outside. We got trouble," Dan shouted.

"Slow up, Dan," Bill advised. "Get your breath and tell me what's happened. No one's hurt, are they?"

"No, not one of our guys. Someone else. You gotta come and look, Bill," Dan pleaded.

Bill noticed that the sounds coming from the construction equipment were the sounds of machinery at an idle. He could tell that the construction work had been halted. He moved quickly out of the trailer to assess the situation, hurrying to catch up with Dan who was moving at a fast pace toward the equipment that had been working on clearing a tree line. All of the bulldozers were standing still, and there were eight men gathered in a semi-circle looking at something by the trees.

"Christ! Look at that!" Bill heard one of the men say.

He pushed his way through the men and caught his first glimpse of what had halted the construction.

"Oh my God!" Bill exclaimed loudly.

He stood in front of the men and looked at a slice of earth that had just been exposed by a bulldozer. The Cats had been leveling the earth by scraping away five feet of dirt close to the trees. All of the men stood and stared at a large, black plastic bag hanging suspended in the middle of a newly created hill. The bag had been buried three feet down in the earth, and a Cat had uncovered it. Part of the plastic was torn open and the skeletal remains of a human skull were protruding out of the bag.

"Dan. You go back to the trailer and call the cops," Bill commanded.

Bill's eyes were still fixed on the skull. No one moved. The grisly sight mesmerized all of the men.

"Dan! Go now. Call the county cops," Bill commanded again.

Dan broke away from the group and ran back to the trailer.

"OK guys, let's step back away from all of this," Bill ordered. "The police are going to make this a crime scene. Let's not screw it up for them. Everyone go, and meet me at the trailer."

The men turned and walked slowly toward the trailer. Bill took one more look at the skull and then turned to follow his men.

"Shit!" Bill heard one of the men say.

Yeah, shit is right! Bill thought.

Bill knew the gruesome discovery would halt the work they were doing, but that was not what was upsetting him or his men. It was the sight of the skull that upset them. They knew they had stumbled upon a murder. A chill ran down Bill's back as he wondered who was in the bag and what had brought the person to this field.

"God rest the soul," he heard one of the men say quietly.

Yeah, God rest the soul, Bill repeated in his mind. And, God help the family of whoever that is. This is not a good day.

Bill made the sign of the cross as he walked behind his men.

In the trailer, Dan found the sheriff's office number posted on a wall along with several other emergency phone numbers. A dispatcher answered his call.

"This is Dan Lawrence. I'm a worker over at the quarry site on Wolf Road. We need a cop over here quick."

"What's the problem, Dan," the dispatcher asked.

"We found some remains over here," Dan said. "A skeleton. My boss, Bill Stevens, told me to call you."

"Dan, you tell Bill I'll have someone there in just a few minutes," the dispatcher replied. "And, tell Bill not to touch anything, OK?"

When the dispatcher sent out a radio call for assistance, Deputy Lambert answered.

"I'm north of Geneseo on 84," Joe informed the dispatcher. "Let them know I'll be there in under ten. And find the sheriff to get him out there, too."

"Roger that, Joe," the dispatcher responded. "We are trying to locate the sheriff now. Thomas is heading that way, too, but he's out on 80 at marker 36, so he'll take longer.

The first thing Deputy Lambert saw when he pulled onto the construction site was Bill Stevens walking briskly toward his squad car. Joe pulled up near Bill and quickly got out of his squad.

"What's happening here, Bill?" Joe asked.

Bill Stevens pointed toward the tree line where the remains had been uncovered.

"We got real trouble here, Joe. I think we've uncovered a body. It is in a plastic bag over by the tree line."

"OK, Bill, you show me. But I want your men to stay back here at the trailer. We're going to have to ask some questions of all of them."

"Joe wants you guys to stay here and wait. I'll be right back," Bill shouted to his men.

It seemed to him that the men were happy to stay back at the trailer. It took Bill and Joe just two minutes to reach the area where the plastic bag was.

"There it is," Bill said. "That's what we found."

Bill pointed to the plastic bag with his right hand and then put the palm of his left hand on top of his head.

"God help, there it is…I've never had anything like this happen to me before," he said slowly. "I suppose you are used to this stuff?"

"You don't get used to it. It makes me just as sick as you," Joe replied.

Joe's eyes swept back and forth along the freshly cut hill and then came to focus on the plastic bag.

"Why don't you go on back with your men? I'm gonna look around a little and then call for some help. We've got another squad heading this way. Maybe you will want your men to take a break, and I can ask them some questions later. This is going to take some time. I think your workers are done for the day."

"Sure, Joe. I'll tell them. Do you want me to call for more help?"

"No. Not yet. I'll call in little bit. Thanks though. If Thomas shows up, send him out this way. And Bill, don't let your men call anyone about this. We don't need a bunch of reporters out here right now. Let me check it all out first, OK?"

"Sure, Joe. We don't want that either. Who do you think it is?"

"Can't tell right now," Joe answered. "It'll take some time to find that out."

"Yeah…I bet that's so," Bill said quietly. "I'm going back to the trailer."

Bill turned and started walking back to the trailer.

I'm glad that I'm not a cop, he thought on his walk back to the trailer. They don't pay those guys enough money. God damn it, I don't like this! I don't like being around anything like this.

CHAPTER THIRTY-EIGHT

J oe stood and looked at the bag from a distance. There was definitely a human skull protruding from it. He thought about Katie, but quickly dismissed the thought.

This quarry site is more than two miles north of the canal and it's a good twenty-four miles west of where they found…No, that's not Katie, he thought. It couldn't be. Thank God for that. I'll just take a quick look around and then I'll get a CI unit out here.

Joe walked back and forth in front of the hill making sure that he did not get too close to anything.

I'll just make a visual exam, he thought. That's best.

Walking west ten yards away from the freshly dug hill, Joe spotted what looked like a wallet. It lay completely exposed on the ground, and looked like the type a woman would carry in her purse. Apparently, the wallet had been uncovered and dragged for a short distance by one of the Cats. He walked to the wallet making a mental note of how it was laying on the ground so he could put it back just as he had found it. He pulled plastic gloves on his hands, picked the wallet up and carefully loosened a snap, causing it to spread open. Dirt fell out, and a thin layer of dust covered the plastic window of an inside pocket. Joe brushed the dust away from the plastic and saw a driver's license. The picture was dirty, but he immediately recognized the smile and the blond hair.

Katie's name exploded in Joe's mind. His body was immediately awash in pain. He felt his stomach tighten and waves of torment stabbing at him. His mind reeled with anguish. His knees felt as if they would buckle.

Oh God! Oh God! Oh God! Joe repeated over and over in his mind.

His head pounded with pain, and tears began to streak down his face. His vision became blurred as his eyes welled up with tears. He wanted to fight the internal pain by causing physical harm to himself. He wanted to slam his body into something. He wanted to hit something with his fists, but he was standing alone in an open field. He tried to say Katie's name, but could only utter a guttural sound. The weight of his grief drove him down to the ground. As he fell to his knees, the wallet dropped out of his hand, and he cried out in a thunderous sob.

"KATIE!!"

The men at the trailer had been watching Deputy Lambert. They saw his body wretch, and they watched him fall to his knees. They heard his cry of agony.

"Oh my God, it's Katie," Bill Stevens said. "Dan, call for more help."

Bill turned to the small crowd of construction workers.

"Bob, Nick, Ron," Bill called out. "You men come with me. Let's go help Joe."

The other workers watched the four men moving rapidly towards Joe.

"Who's Katie," one of the men asked.

"Katie Karver was a young woman who was murdered over in Kewanee a year ago," a second worker answered. "They never found her body. That must be her."

"Is she related to the deputy?" the first worker questioned.

"No, not related. I went to high school in Kewanee with her and Joe," the second worker explained. "They were seniors when I was a freshman. I think that they were real good friends, or they might have dated. I can't remember. But, that's a hell of a way to find a friend…that's a hell of a thing."

The first worker nodded in agreement.

"Yeah, a hell of a thing," he said.

Bill Stevens reached Joe first and saw him struggling to get back up on his feet. He reached for Joe's right arm and lifted him up.

Joe turned away from the men and fought to compose himself.

"You OK, Joe?" Bill asked quietly.

The moment was awkward for all the men. They watched Joe's back expand as he breathed in air. Bill put his hand on Joe's shoulder.

"It's Katie isn't it, Joe. We're sorry, " he said. "What'd want us to do?"

"I'm alright," Joe replied.

Joe was fighting to get back in control and trying to methodically analyze the situation, but thoughts of the past raced through his mind and collided with the reality of the present. He stood facing away from the grim crime scene and tried to focus on the need to be professional. His vision was still a blur, but his mind was beginning to clear.

"I'm alright," he said again.

He turned and faced the men who had come to help him.

"Katie was a good friend of mine," he explained. "I didn't expect this."

Deputy Lambert purposefully straightened up to his full height. He squared his shoulders and tried to adopt the demeanor of a man in charge, but he knew he had to get away from the ghastly spectacle extending out of the newly overturned earth. He wanted to run away from it all, but he found himself caught between his own personal loss and the obligations of being a law officer. He hated finding Katie like this, but he had to know what brought her to this location.

She needs me now, he said to himself. This time I won't let her down.

"I'd like all of you men to go back to the trailer...stay there until we get a chance to talk with you," Joe said. "I'm gonna call for more help."

Deputy Thomas' squad car pulled into the quarry site just as Joe was headed toward his own car; he promptly changed directions and moved swiftly to meet Thomas and inform him of the situation.

"Ken, they've uncovered the remains of a body over by that Cat."

Deputy Lambert pointed north where the Cat sat.

"I think its Katie Karver".

"Katie!" Thomas exclaimed. "Katie Karver here? That don't make any sense, Joe. This is too far away from the canal, and we're over thirty miles out of Kewanee. Can't be Katie. You sure?"

Joe's gaze remained fixed in the direction of the remains.

"Yeah...I know," he said. "It doesn't make any sense...I thought that too, but there's a wallet out there. It's Katie's wallet. You start taping off the scene. Ask Bill Stevens for some help and give the scene a wide berth. And, keep those other guys back at the trailer. I'm gonna call for more help."

Deputy Thomas grabbed a bag of material from the trunk of his squad and moved toward the crowd of construction workers. Joe climbed into Thomas' squad car and used the radio to call in to the sheriff's department.

"Dispatch. This is Deputy Lambert. Copy?"

"Roger, Joe," came the dispatcher's reply.

"I'm at the quarry expansion site on Wolf Road," Joe said. "There are remains of a body that have been uncovered here. I'll need assistance. Send a CI squad and radio for help from all available units in the area. I wanna shut this area off to any gawkers or the news media. Is the sheriff headed this way?"

"That's a negative on the sheriff, Joe," the dispatcher responded. "I'll send a call out to all available units to report to the quarry. The sheriff's aware of the situation there. I notified him when I sent the call out to you. The sheriff called in. He wants you to meet him at the Karver warehouse. He wants you there right away."

The tone of Joe's response was filled with disbelief and frustration.

"Kewanee!" Joe said loudly. "He wants me to go to Kewanee now? Confirm Kewanee dispatch."

"Roger, Joe," the dispatcher repeated. "He wants you there ASAP. I'm supposed to find Rogers too and have him go there. I just got the call from the sheriff a few minutes ago."

"Dispatch," Joe questioned. "Which Karver warehouse?

"It's the warehouse the Karvers have at the west edge of town," the dispatcher replied.

"Dispatch," Joe responded angrily. "Does Sheriff Armstrong know that this may be Katie Karver here?"

There was a pause in radio conversation.

"You sure of that, Joe?" the dispatcher asked. "You sure it's Katie Karver?"

"It's Katie," Joe responded. "Let the sheriff know it's Katie."

"Roger, Joe," the dispatcher confirmed. "I'll tell him that, but the sheriff was real direct about you meeting him in Kewanee. I think he's gonna still want you there. He said to get you and Rogers out to that warehouse. He said to have Thomas handle things there. You copy all of that Joe?"

Silence prevailed on the radio.

"Joe? Did you copy that?" the dispatcher asked again.

"Roger that, dispatch," Joe shot back. "I got it. Karver warehouse. West side of town."

Joe put the mike back onto the dash.

God damn it! Joe thought. This had better be good. Report to a fucking hardware warehouse. What the hell for? This had better be goddamn good."

Joe sat motionless in the police squad car. He looked out across the field and watched Deputy Thomas and Bill Stevens stringing yellow crime scene tape along a line of four-foot poles they had erected forty yards out from the perimeter of the hill.

It was a beautiful day. A deep, blue sky stretched overhead, and a late afternoon sun was shining down on the construction site. He shook his head and looked down at the ground.

Katie! What the hell you are doing here, he thought. What the hell are you doing here?

Joe's thoughts were soon distracted by the sound of sirens and police vehicles rushing toward the quarry area. It appeared as if his painful cry had resonated throughout the county. Within minutes the construction site was swarming with squad cars from the state police, the sheriff's department, the Colona city police department, and the Geneseo city police department.

Joe made his way to the group of police officers that were assembling at the trailer. The officers all began to gather around him.

"What we got here, Joe?" a Colona cop asked. "We heard something about Katie Karver being found here."

"I can't say that for sure," Joe replied.

He scanned the faces of his fellow police officers. By their expressions, he could tell they knew what had happened just a few minutes ago. He knew they understood how hard this was for him.

"I found a wallet out there," Joe said. ""I'm sure it's Katie's wallet, but we'll have to wait for verification on the remains."

"Joe," one of the county deputies said. "Why don't you let us handle this? Go back to the office or take the rest of the day off."

Without mentioning the dispatcher's call, Joe agreed to leave the scene.

"Yeah, that's probably best," he said. "Katie was a good friend of mine, and I don't want to jeopardize the crime scene. I'll leave everything to you guys. Thomas will be in charge."

The expression on Joe's face turned cold and stoic as he pointed toward the freshly dug hill.

"The wallet's out there on the ground about ten yards west of the remains," he said. "I...I dropped the wallet when I saw Katie's license."

"We'll get it, Joe," one of the deputies said. "You go on back now. We'll keep you informed of what happens here. Is the sheriff coming?"

"I don't know," Joe replied. "He should."

CHAPTER THIRTY-NINE

Joe pulled out of the construction site in his squad car. He turned left onto Billy Wolf Road, turned on his emergency lights, and punched down on the gas pedal. Looking north toward the quarry site, he saw a phalanx of police officers cordoning off the scene with more yellow tape. He noticed two police officers with trained dogs were scouring the area, moving toward the hill where Katie's remains had been uncovered.

Christ Katie, Joe desperately thought. What are you doing here? It just doesn't make any sense. Goddamn it, somebody's really screwed this up. I know one thing for sure...I've let you down. Goddamn it, I should've been on top of this all along. That bastard Rogers and his stupid ass investigation. None of this fits into what he came up with. That son of a bitch was kissing old man Karver's ass. Goddamn it, I let all that happen. I won't let Katie down again.

As Joe's squad car sped east on Wolf Road, 20 police officers began to methodically comb the crime scene. Using the remains as a center point, they fanned out in a manner that formed an ever-widening circle.

"I don't get it," one of the state troopers said to his partner. "They're saying there aren't any bullet holes in the skull. Wasn't Katie shot three times in the head? Isn't that what the killer said he did?"

"That's how I remember it," his partner commented. "She was killed by that drifter in Kewanee. The guy confessed to the crime. And, the thought was he dismembered Katie and dumped the remains in the canal. But we're a long ways from Kewanee and a long ways from the canal."

The two men walked slowly through a field of low grass that stretched one hundred yards northeast of Katie's remains, searching for anything that would help explain the death of Katie Karver.

"Yeah we're a long ways from Kewanee," the first trooper replied.

The trooper stopped and glanced back at the men working in the center of the circle.

"And, it looks to me like they are digging a complete skeleton out of that hill. That body hasn't been totally dismembered. There is something really wrong here."

The second trooper paused and turned to look back toward the hill.

"Yeah it does look like more than just a skull there," the second trooper agreed. "I know the prosecution claimed the killer had cut up the body. I wonder where Sheriff Armstrong is. Shouldn't he be here?"

"It'd seem like he'd wanna be here. He certainly was always on the scene when we looked up and down the canal last year," the first trooper replied. "But, I didn't see him today. Maybe he's with Joe. I guess Joe took all of this kinda hard. I hear he and Katie had been real good friends."

"Well, I like Joe, but I'll tell you, none of this looks right," the second trooper said. "Something's fucked up here."

"What'd you mean? You don't think Joe had anything to do with this, do you?"

"Hell no! I'm not saying that," the second trooper answered defensively. "I'm just saying that something is really wrong here. None of this squares with the case. What the hell is the body doing all the way over here? And, that body is not the body we were looking for last year. Like you said, the guy they convicted of killing Katie said he chopped her up. If that's Katie Karver's remains, then the case was all screwed up, and that guy's confession isn't worth a tinker's damn."

"I know this," the first trooper said. "I wouldn't want to be Sheriff Armstrong right now and have this dumped into my lap. I mean this is real bad timing for him. This is gonna be a lot to explain during an election year. Christ, Jim Taylor will eat him alive with this."

"Yeah, you're right there. You know, I do remember that drifter guy who got convicted...Stablein was his name...I remember he kept going back and forth on his confession," the second trooper said. "You know, one minute he was saying that he was guilty and the next time he was saying that he was framed. Maybe he was framed? Guy like that's got no one around here to help him. But, who would frame him? Something's wrong, alright."

"Hey, I don't know who would frame him, but I do know this...if that's Katie's skeleton, then there's been a whole lot of screw-ups on this case."

"What the hell was the name of the attorney who defended Stablein?" the second trooper asked. "That guy didn't stay around here long. I don't know if he even practices law any more. You remember his name? You know, he was kind of a dumbass, dufus guy."

"Erickson," the first trooper answered. "Corey Erickson. He lived in Atkinson. I know I wouldn't have taken any legal advice from that guy. I think he drank a little, too."

"Yeah, that's right," the second trooper agreed. "Erickson. Corey Erickson, attorney at law. Hell, that guy couldn't litigate his way off a one-way street."

"Well, this will be good news for Stablein. You watch. There'll be a new trial over this," the first trooper predicted.

184

"If that's Katie, there'll be more than just a new trial," the second trooper said. "Heads are gonna roll over this. And, I do mean headsssss. More than one person's gonna take some serious heat for this. And, imagine how pissed old man Karver's gonna be."

"Oh hell, yes," the first trooper agreed. "Karver will be pissed and just wait until the press gets a hold of this. They'll have more questions for Armstrong than my three-year-old boy can ask in a year."

"Yeah. Old man Karver isn't accustomed to getting stiffed," the second trooper said. "He'll be mad as hell, and he's sure to raise a stink all the way to Springfield."

"That's true," the first trooper concurred. "I'll tell you someone else who will be mad, too. He's probably mad right now. And, that's Joe. I wouldn't want Joe pissed at me. And think of it, it was his department that must've screwed up the case. You remember who handled the case?"

"I'm pretty sure it was Neil Rogers," the second trooper answered. "Yeah, I'm right about that. It was Neil Rogers. Hell, he wants to be the Kewanee Chief of Police."

"Neil does?"

"That's what I hear," the second trooper said. "He's been sucking up to all of the big wigs in Kewanee."

"Well, he can kiss that job goodbye. He'll be lucky to keep his deputy job."

"I can't say that makes me sad," the second trooper stated. "I never cared for Rogers."

"Rogers is a prick. Everyone knows that," the first trooper agreed.

"It would be dangerous to give that guy authority," the second trooper observed. "Give him authority and everyone's life will be miserable."

"From what I hear, Joe didn't care much for Rogers either," the first trooper said.

"Well...now Joe has more reasons to dislike the guy," the second trooper said. "Hell, I wouldn't want to be in Rogers' shoes right now. Joe's quiet, and he's always polite, but he's one strong man. Who knows what will happen when he meets up with Rogers. I'll tell you something else too...I always thought Stablein's conviction came about a little too quick."

"Yeah, me too," the first trooper agreed. "And, no body? That's always trouble. I don't care if you do have a confession. No body is always trouble."

The second trooper stopped walking and scanned the land in front of them.

"Well, we got a body now," he said. "Hey, we've gone far enough out on this, don't you think? There's nothing out here."

"Yeah, let's head back. Maybe they've found something more at the crime scene. The evening news is going to be interesting tonight. You can count on that."

CHAPTER FORTY

It took Joe thirty-five minutes to reach the Karver warehouse. He pulled on to a large gravel parking lot that surrounded a metal-framed building. Driving slowly toward the building, he noticed Sheriff Armstrong's empty squad car parked along the backside of the building. Joe listened to the crunch of the loose gravel grumbling underneath the tires of his squad car as he maneuvered slowly toward the building and scoped out the situation. Deputy Rogers' squad car was nowhere in sight.

Maybe Rogers and the sheriff rode over here together, but I doubt that, Joe thought. It's probably just Mike and me for right now. That's good though. I can ask him some questions before I confront Rogers.

The sun was beginning to descend on the horizon and the Karver warehouse sat empty of any human activity; the employees had long ago abandoned their work and headed home. The only light inside the building shone through two small office windows that were positioned to the left of the rear entrance door. It was obvious to Joe that the sheriff was waiting for him inside the building. He pulled his squad car next to the sheriff's car, exited his vehicle, and moved briskly toward the warehouse door. While driving from the quarry, he had filed a multitude of questions in his head concerning the gruesome discovery made there. He was anxious to confront Armstrong with the questions that plagued him, and he was anxious to know why he had to meet the sheriff and Deputy Rogers at the Karver warehouse.

Joe entered the building through the rear door, heading quickly in the direction of the lights. He passed through an open interior door and found the sheriff standing beside a small table in the warehouse office. Armstrong looked haggard and nervous as he stared at Joe. Joe paused and glared defiantly at him. A threatening silence hung in the air and filled the room with tension.

The sheriff was first to break the silence as he desperately attempted to connect with his deputy.

"Joe," he blurted out.

Joe could not contain his anger. He quickly moved toward the sheriff.

"What the hell is Katie doing out there at the quarry?" he demanded. "How could her remains be there?"

"Joe, listen," the sheriff, replied. "I'm gonna explain all that. That's why I wanted you here. I want to explain some things to you and have you hear everything. But, you gotta calm down. We're gonna make this right. I told dispatch to get Rogers over here, too. We'll get together and figure this all out."

"Why Rogers? Why are we meeting here? What the hell's going on?" Joe demanded.

"I gotta ask Rogers some questions. There are some things that Scott Miller told me that I gotta ask Rogers about."

"Why here?' Joe demanded again.

"This is best, Joe. It's best that we get this mess straightened out. You know…away from the press and everyone. Believe me, this'll all make sense to you when…

"What did Scott tell you?" Joe forcefully interrupted.

"You gotta understand," the sheriff parried. "You know Scott was a drunk. You saw him the night that I talked to him. There was no reason for me to believe anything he had to say. Hell, he couldn't even stand up, Joe."

"Tell me what he said, now!" Joe shouted. "Tell me now, Mike or I'll beat it out of you."

"You can't talk to me like that," the sheriff replied defiantly.

"Fuck you, Sheriff! That's Katie out there. I'll break every bone in your goddamn body," Joe threatened, grabbing the sheriff's shirt with both hands. "You tell me. You tell me first. I have a right to know. You tell me now!"

"OK, Joe! OK! Let go of me. I'll tell you. But listen good. I'm telling you up front and I'm being honest. I had no reason to believe what Scott told me. But, I'll tell you now. Sit down and listen. You'll see what's happened. You'll understand."

Joe released the sheriff from his grasp, and the two men sat down at the table. Sheriff Armstrong hesitated for a moment trying to compose himself.

"You know, Joe, this is hard for me, too," he said. "I'm the one who is gonna be hurt most by all of this. Maybe we can help each other out of this mess."

"You'd better understand something, Mike. I don't give a damn about the mess you're in. I just wanna know why Katie's out there at that quarry site."

"OK, Joe. OK," the sheriff replied. "I understand what you're after. Believe me I wanna get everything straightened out, too. That's why I asked you to come here. You sure you don't wanna wait until Rogers gets here? He might be able to answer some of your questions."

"Fuck Rogers! Tell me what I want to know now!"

"You gotta calm down, Joe," the sheriff advised. "You gotta listen carefully to what I have to tell you. If you listen carefully, you'll see that I couldn't open up Katie's case just on the story of the town drunk. And when Scott went and got himself killed, there just wasn't anything I could do about what he said. You're gonna see that when you hear my side."

Although Joe was enraged, he focused all of his attention on Sheriff Armstrong. Years of police work had taught him to recognize traits exhibited by liars and thieves. He saw some of those traits in Armstrong's mannerisms.

"I'm gonna listen," he said "I'm gonna be listening real good, but I wanna hear everything Scott told you that night in jailhouse. Everything!"

You will, Joe. You will," the sheriff replied. "I promise. I'll tell you everything. But, Joe...you gotta keep an open mind about all this stuff. You're gonna see that we need to work together here. That's why I picked you, Joe. You're a team player. I know it."

Joe listened intently as the sheriff began to tell him what Scott Miller had said in his jailhouse confession.

CHAPTER FORTY-ONE

"L arry Karver killed Katie," Scott Miller had told Sheriff Armstrong on the last evening of Miller's life.

"Why would Larry kill his wife?" Sheriff Armstrong demanded.

A sly smile came over Scott Miller's face.

"He killed her because he found out about her and Joe," Scott said. "You didn't know about them, did you, sheriff? None of you knew about that. I knew. I saw them kissing one time. I know lots of things that you don't know."

"When did you see them kissing?" Armstrong insisted.

"I don't know. It was a long time ago," Scott recalled slowly. "It was before Katie and Larry got hitched, I know that. But when I told Larry about it, he got real angry. He said that he had always wondered about Joe and Katie."

"Why would you be talking to Larry about Joe?"

"Larry and me, we're drinking buddies," Scott announced.

There was a touch of pride in Scott's voice.

"You wouldn't think that a guy like me drinks with high society, but I do. We'd drink in the Karver warehouse cause Larry always wanted to protect his family name. He didn't want to be seen drinking. He gave me money, and I brought the booze. We'd mostly drink there when old man Karver went out of town, or when the old man was busy with his clubs. You think I'm a lush, don't you, sheriff? Well, Larry's as big a lush as me. He's just got money to cover it up."

The sheriff had heard stories about Larry and Scott leaving the Karver warehouse in the late evening hours. The Kewanee police had taken Scott in a couple of times when he was found asleep in his car outside the warehouse. Armstrong suspected the two men used their drinking to complain to each other about how they had been unfairly treated in the world. And, Armstrong was right in his assessment. Scott Miller and Larry Karver frequently met in one of the Karver's storage areas, where they would pour whiskey down their throats, while whining over each other's failures and proclaiming their bitterness towards an unfair world.

"You're right, Scott. A lot of important people around here drink. You're right. But tell me about this kissing. I mean...so several years ago Joe kissed Katie...big fucking deal. Why would Larry care about that?" Armstrong queried further.

"Lots of reasons," Scott replied. "Larry cared cause Katie was supposed to be his. He cared cause she had the Karver brand on her. He cared cause old man Karver loved her more than he loved him. And, he cared cause he found an email from Joe."

"What email? When did Larry find the email?" Armstrong demanded.

"I don't know when he found it," Scott said. "I think sometime right before Katie was killed. Maybe about a week before she was killed."

A puzzled look came over Scott's face and then disappeared. His face lit up, and an expression of discovery replaced his previous bewilderment.

"Yeah…that's why we were talking about Joe," Scott remembered. "Yeah…Larry asked me why Katie would be emailing Joe. He said he found an email on Katie's computer, and that the email was from Joe. He said the email was a reply to something Katie had sent to Joe."

"Did Larry tell you what was in the email? What was the message?" Armstrong asked.

I don't know that," Scott replied. "Larry just said he found the email, and he wanted to know why Joe would email Katie. I told him maybe Joe wanted to make out with her. We were bombed, and I was being funny. I was just joking around. But, Larry got mad and told me that I had to explain what I meant. That's when I told him about Joe."

Armstrong looked hard into Scott's eyes.

"Think Scott," he said. "Did you tell Larry when you saw Joe kissing Katie? Did you tell him it was years ago?"

"Larry never asked *when* they were kissing," Scott exclaimed. "He just got real mad and stormed out of the warehouse. He had me by my shirt when he asked me about Joe. He can get mean when he drinks. He was gonna hit me if I didn't tell him."

"Alright, Larry got mad about Joe kissing Katie. That doesn't mean that he killed her," Armstrong concluded.

"He told me that he killed her," Scott blurted out.

The look on Scott's face became pensive. His body began to shrink back against the cell wall. He literally began to shrivel up with guilt in front of the sheriff's eyes.

"I helped Scott get rid of the body," he whimpered. "I helped him hide Katie's body."

The sheriff jumped up off the bunk. His voice exploded with surprise and rage, causing Scott to shiver with fear.

"You did what?" the sheriff bellowed. "Tell me what you did, Scott?"

Armstrong paced back and forth and then stopped in front of the jailhouse bed. As he stood towering over Scott, his mind raced with the implications of what could happen if any of what Scott had said was true. He struggled with the rage he felt. He wanted to grab Scott and toss him around the jail cell. But in the end, his years of police work gained control, and he continued questioning Scott. The sheriff began to concentrate on his breathing, taking in measured breaths and exhaling slowly as he looked at Scott scrunched up on the bed. He cleared his head of the anger and focused on plying more information from Scott.

"Alright, Scott. OK. Let's get this out in the open," Armstrong said calmly. "You're not to blame here. Tell me about what Larry did."

The sheriff sat back down on the cell bed. He moved slowly, not wanting to frighten Scott into silence.

"It was an accident. Larry told me so," Scott pleaded. "Larry was mad and drunk. He didn't mean to hurt Katie. I wouldn't have helped him if he'd just killed her. It was an accident. You gotta believe me."

"I believe you, Scott. I do believe you. I know you and Larry wouldn't murder anyone, especially Katie. I run into these things all the time. People get mad, and they do some things that are wrong. You just gotta make it right. I can help you if you make it right," Armstrong promised.

"I'm doing the right thing. I'm telling you," Scott continued. "I'll tell you what happened, and you'll help me. Isn't that right, sheriff? Isn't that the way this'll work? You'll tell people I was just trying to help? You'll explain it to Joe, too, right? I'm gonna do the right thing and you're gonna help me."

The sheriff patted Scott on his right knee.

"I'll tell everyone," the sheriff agreed. "They'll understand," he assured Scott. "I've seen this kinda thing a thousand times, but you gotta tell me what happened."

Scott lifted his face up and gazed into the darkness, staring toward the ceiling of the cell. He folded his hands together in a prayer-like manner and spoke softly as if he were confessing his sins and seeking forgiveness.

"Larry hit Katie," Scott said. "He'd hit her before, and she never died. He must of hit her too hard this time. Larry was going to call for help, but he was afraid of his old man. And then when Katie never got back up…well, Larry got afraid of everything."

"Where's Katie's body, Scott? What did he do with her body?"

"Larry hid it in the warehouse. He showed it to me when he told me about everything. It was on ice. That was the weirdest thing I've ever seen. I…I was scared, but Larry said I had to help him. He said I was the only person who could help him…he was crying, and he said he needed my help. I knew it was wrong, but Christ, Larry and me were always being dealt a bad hand. I just wanted to help. You gotta believe that, sheriff," Scott pleaded.

"What'd you do with Katie? Where is she now?" Armstrong pressed on.

"I want ya to know, I didn't have anything to do with cutting her. She wasn't really cut up, you know…it was just her leg. Larry cut her leg off," Scott said desperately. "That was Larry's idea…he said doing that would throw everyone off. He said the cops always look at the husband first. Larry said no one would think he'd do something like that. But he did all of that by himself. He cut her leg off and threw it in the canal. I didn't want no part of that. I just helped him bury her body."

Scott crossed his arms on top of his knees and buried his head on his arms. He began to weep and then to sob.

"It ain't fair," he cried. "It ain't fair. Larry's the one to blame, not me. I was just trying to help."

Sheriff Armstrong waited patiently for Scott to drain his soul. He knew that once he stopped crying, he would be anxious to tell the Sheriff everything. He had seen jail cells become confessionals hundreds of times before.

Armstrong placed his hand on Scott's shoulder.

"Get a hold of yourself, Scott. You're not to blame," Armstrong assured him. "This was a domestic quarrel that went bad. That's all. You were just trying to help a friend, and no one's gonna hold that against you. But, you gotta tell me everything. You gotta tell me everything, Scott," Armstrong repeated.

Scott shuffled his position on the cell bed. He straightened up and pushed his shoulders against the cell wall. He shook his head and rubbed his face. He was ready to talk again.

"Katie's body is buried off Billy Wolf Road back near some trees. I don't know where anymore. I know it was near Cleveland Road. We did it at night...we were drunk...we put her in a plastic bag and buried her. Larry was right, no one would look for her there."

"And you and Larry...you're the only ones who know about this?" Armstrong questioned further. "You told Joe that we had the wrong guy, but you didn't tell him any more than that. Is that right?"

"I don't think I told Joe any more. I was drunk and I think I passed out," Scott answered. "But there is someone else who knows."

The sheriff's eyes grew wider.

"Who else knows?" he asked.

"Old man Karver knows. He found out about what Larry did. He knows, too."

Scott was hoping this ordeal of confession would now be over. He hoped he had given the sheriff everything he needed to know, but he was wrong.

"Gerald Karver! You're telling me that Gerald Karver knows about this!" Armstrong exploded again. "Goddamn it! You're saying Gerald Karver knows his son killed Katie!"

The sheriff's renewed outrage terrified Scott.

"He didn't know right away...he found out later. It was long after you convicted that Stablein guy. He didn't find out until this July," Scott said hurriedly. "Larry was drunk in the warehouse...and the old man caught him there. They fought, and Larry threw all this in his old man's face. Old man Karver got hit hard by that."

Sheriff Armstrong sat up rigid on the edge of the bed. The sheriff's fingers gripped tightly onto the edge of the mattress.

"And you were there in the warehouse? You saw them fighting?" Armstrong asked in disbelief.

"No…I wasn't exactly there," Scott replied. "Not in the room. I…I wasn't in the room. I came over to drink with Larry, but I saw his old man going in the warehouse. So I snuck up around by the window…I was gonna warn Larry, but the old man got to him first. Old man Karver was really pissed off cause Larry was already drunk. He started shoving Larry around the room and calling him a worthless son of a bitch. He said Larry never did anything right and he slapped him twice. He said Katie had been more of a man than him. I saw it all."

"What did Larry say to his father?" the sheriff demanded. "How did old man Karver find out about the killing?"

Scott tilted his head back against the wall and laughed faintly.

"Larry bragged about it. He told old man Karver he knew how to handle things. He said, 'I took care of my wife's cheating, didn't I?' "

Scott shook his head back and forth.

"Shit! Old man Karver about went through the roof when Larry said that. The old man grabbed Larry and hit him hard. He kept jerking Larry around and yelling at him. 'What cheating? What did you do to Katie?' The old man just kept yelling at Larry. That's when Larry broke down and told him everything."

"That's why Larry's in Arizona?" Armstrong asked quietly.

"Yeah," Scott said. "That's right. Old man Karver told Larry that very night that he would be leaving Kewanee. The old man said he would set Larry up with a motorcycle business in Phoenix. He told him to never come back. Larry cried and pleaded, but the old man said he was done with him. Hell, he told Larry that the Karvers would raise Larry's daughter. And, he threatened to kill Larry if any of this got out."

"Did Gerald Karver find out about your part in all of this?" Armstrong asked.

"Yeah," Scott replied. "Larry told him about me. Old man Karver told Larry he would take care of everything. I'm supposed to go to Phoenix and help Larry. We'll be partners in the motorcycle business. Larry's gonna contact me and send me some money."

Sheriff Armstrong sat motionless and silent on the cell bed. His anger had turned into an exhaustive recognition of the truth Scott was telling.

This is a damn nightmare, and I'm screwed, the sheriff thought. Screwed by these three idiots!

Scott fidgeted around on the bed and smiled while remembering the Karver feud.

"But, ya know what made old man Karver the maddest, sheriff?"

"What, Scott? What got the old man's goat?" Armstrong probed.

Scott laughed again, but slightly louder than last time. His laugh became sustained as he recalled what he saw as a joke on old man Karver. He gained his composure, but chuckled as he continued to talk.

"Larry's old man got angry as hell when Larry told him where we buried the body," Scott continued. "You know why sheriff? You know why he got mad?"

Armstrong knew what Scott was going to say.

"You tell me, Scott," Sheriff Armstrong said. "What got old man Karver mad?"

"Well, the old man blew his stack, that's for sure. Larry told the old man that we buried her on a piece of land owned by the Karvers because Larry knew he could control the area. But, old man Karver went and sold the property. Larry didn't know that when we buried her there, but he sure found out that night in the warehouse. You should've seen the look on both of their faces."

"Karver sold the land to River Bend Quarry," Armstrong confirmed.

Scott slapped his hands together.

"Yeah, that's right," he said. Old man Karver sold the land to the quarry people. Sold the land and the body to the quarry."

Then a serious look spread over Scott's face.

"Hey, Sheriff, what's this I hear about the quarry wanting to expand?" he asked. "Where they gonna expand?

"Not where you put Katie," Armstrong lied. "They're thinking about expanding below the bluff. You buried Katie above the bluff, right?"

"Yeah, above the bluff by some trees," Scott replied.

The weight of what he had just confessed began to sink into Scott's mind. His manner became sober and remorseful. He covered his face with his hands, trying to hide from the sheriff.

"One more thing, Scott," Armstrong continued. "What about Stablein? Did Larry have you set him up?"

Scott uncovered his face and looked at the sheriff. His voice was faint.

"No…really no," Scott said. "When Katie was first missing, I told Deputy Rogers that Stablein had the hots for Katie, and he asked me to tell Joe. I just did what Deputy Rogers told me to do. But, everyone looked at Katie. I didn't set Stablein up."

The sheriff sat silent. He knew Scott was lying about Stablein, but he didn't care. Only thirty seconds passed before Scott decided to speak again, but it was a long thirty seconds for both men.

"What's gonna happen now, Sheriff," he asked.

"Nothing right now," Armstrong responded. "I'll have to look into this. But I have to be sure about something…and I want you to be sure about this…you haven't told any one else about these things, have you?"

"Honest Sheriff. I haven't told nobody," Scott confided. "But you gotta know, it's those Karvers that are to blame. I was just trying to help. I liked Katie. You gotta tell everyone I didn't hurt her."

"You just keep quiet about all this," the sheriff said. "I'll handle it, and I'll make sure everyone knows who's to blame. You understand, Scott? You gotta keep this thing to yourself until you and I can talk again. You gotta promise me that."

"I won't tell anybody," Scott agreed. " I promise. You can count on me. I'll keep my mouth shut."

"OK, Scott," the sheriff said. "That's good. I know I can trust you. I'll get you outta here soon, and you can go home. You go home and rest and forget about all this for right now."

"I might need a drink before I go home," Scott mumbled.

CHAPTER FORTY-TWO

The sheriff had finished telling Joe everything about Scott's confession. He sat at the table and looked at Deputy Lambert, trying to read his thoughts.

"That's what Scott told me, Joe. You know Scott got himself killed that very next day."

"Yeah I know," Joe replied. "You sent Rogers to my house to tell me about it."

"Course I did," Armstrong answered. "I thought you'd wanna know about it right away. And, Rogers told me he wanted to tell you."

"Rogers is a prick," Joe responded. "I don't need him telling me anything, and I don't want him in my house."

"I'm sorry. I didn't know you and Rogers didn't get along. How would I know that? Anyway with this Scott Miller thing, all I had was a drunk telling a story in a jail cell. I mean hell…Scott was accusing Larry Karver of murder, and he was accusing Gerald Karver of being an accomplice! I needed time. I couldn't act on that information just on the say of Scott. I needed to think about all of this."

"You needed time?" Joe responded indignantly.

"Yeah, that's right! I needed time. I needed to check all of this out with a new investigation. I was gonna include you in the investigation. But, this stuff is all sensitive. Hell, you got the town drunk making accusations against the Karvers for Christ's sake! I needed to proceed on all this stuff in a methodical manner. I had to go slow."

"What kind of time were you thinking about, Mike?" Joe scoffed. "Maybe you were gonna *methodically* wait until after the election? This is pathetic!"

Unable to remain still, Joe stood up and stared aggressively at Armstrong.

"You left something out of your story," Joe said. "Tell me about Scott's death. How did he really die?"

"Hey! You just hold up on that!" Armstrong replied. "Read the report. Read the tox report! Scott killed himself. The record on that is one hundred percent accurate. Scott was a Goddamn drunk and he killed himself! End of story."

Joe turned his back on the sheriff and walked a few steps away from the table. He stared out of a window and felt his body filling with anger and resentment. He turned and faced Sheriff Armstrong again.

"You mean the report that was written by Rogers, right? You really believe that, Mike?" Joe questioned. "Christ, I think you do. Goddamn pathetic! This whole thing is goddamn pathetic. This fucking meeting is pathetic!"

"Hey listen up deputy! I not taking this crap from you," Armstrong angrily replied.

The sheriff rose up from his chair and pointed a finger at Deputy Lambert.

"I'm the sheriff here," he bellowed. "This is my county. I'm the law here. If you know what is good for you, you'd better be on the right side of this. It's the Karvers we're after."

Fuming with anger, Deputy Lambert moved to within inches of the sheriff. He stood a full head taller than Armstrong and pointed his finger directly in the sheriff's face. His gestures were menacing and the full power of his physical strength exploded in front of the sheriff.

"Fuck you, Armstrong! Fuck you!" Joe yelled. "There's a whole line of people in this mess. Damn it! Katie's dead, and we sent the wrong man to jail for it. What the fuck is wrong with you?"

Joe's body shook with anger. His hand impulsively dropped down to his belt, and he felt his right hand resting on the butt of his pistol. Instinctively, he unsnapped his holster strap and the thought of killing the sheriff passed through his mind.

Sheriff Armstrong immediately saw Joe's hand move toward his weapon. His face contorted in fear. His mind and his body froze. The two men glared at each other, speculating for an instant about what would happen next.

"You gonna kill me, Joe?" Armstrong asked quietly.

Joe moved his hand up away from his sidearm.

"No," he said. "You're already dead. I think you know it."

Sheriff Armstrong sat back down, and Deputy Lambert continued to stare at him. Armstrong did not look like a sheriff any more; all the fight had been taken out of him. He was a man crushed by exposure.

"What are you gonna do, Joe?" Armstrong asked.

Joe's voice became calm and methodical.

"I'm gonna get the Coroner," he said. "He's over at the quarry site right now."

"The Coroner?" What'd you need him for?"

"I know the law, Sheriff. You know it, too. The Coroner is the only official in the county who is authorized to remove you from office. I'm gonna have him remove you, and then I'm going to get warrants for the arrests of Gerald and Larry Karver. And, I'll have Rogers investigated, too."

Deputy Lambert turned away from the sheriff, disgusted at seeing the man he had admired become a self-pitying wreck. He paused for an instant, turned slightly toward the sheriff, and then continued to vocalize his plan.

"After you're removed from office, you'll be arrested too," he said.

"Wait, Joe. Wait. You can't," the sheriff pleaded. "Don't do this to me."

"To hell with you," Joe said as he moved toward the office door.

"Wait!" the sheriff frantically cried out.

Desperately, the sheriff charged toward Deputy Lambert. His hand grabbed at Joe's pistol, and a feeling of dread engulfed the deputy as he felt his pistol sliding from his holster. He whirled around to face the sheriff only to hear the explosive sound of his own weapon thundering inside the small room.

"God, no!" Joe exclaimed.

The deputy plunged backward. The weight of his body banged loudly against the office wall and his eyes stared deeply into the sheriff's face. His hands pressed on the gaping wound in his chest as he slowly slid down to the floor, his body crumpling in an unconscious heap.

Stunned by what he had done, Sheriff Armstrong watched in disbelief as Joe fell to the floor. He knew immediately that the deputy was dead. His shot had hit the mark. The sheriff fell to his knees beside the fallen deputy and felt Joe's neck, searching for a pulse, but finding only death.

"Joe," the sheriff said to the lifeless deputy. "God damn it, Joe, I didn't want this. This isn't what was supposed to happen. You should've listened. I just wanted to work this all out. Damn it! I can't be removed from office! You should've known that."

Instantly, the sheriff's calculating mind dominated his actions. Armstrong knew there was no time to be remorseful, and he hurriedly moved to cover his tracks.

The sheriff placed Joe's pistol on the floor next to the dead deputy, then he pulled the office door up against him in order to obscure the body from view. Armstrong paused and examined what he had done. A shiver of regret ran down his back, and his body shook as he looked at Joe's lifeless face.

"I didn't want this, Joe," he whispered. "I really liked you, but I can't lose, Joe. I can't lose. Not now. Not like this."

Tears welled up in the sheriff's eyes. He shook his head back and forth and continued to talk with the dead deputy.

"It's Rogers and those goddamn Karvers," he said. "They're the ones who did this. I'll get 'em back for this. I'll make 'em pay."

Sheriff Armstrong got back up on his feet. He looked at Deputy Lambert one more time, and then walked quickly out of the warehouse to his squad car. Somehow he had to salvage himself from the mess he had just made.

CHAPTER FORTY-THREE

"**D**ispatch," the sheriff barked into the mike of his squad car.

"Roger, Sheriff," the dispatcher responded.

"Have you contacted Rogers and Lambert for me?"

"That's an affirmative, Sheriff. Both men were directed to meet you at the Karver warehouse on the west side of town. They should have been there by now. Want me to contact them again?"

"Cancel that dispatch," the sheriff replied. "I see Joe's car headed this way. I'm sure Rogers will be here soon. We'll be here thirty minutes or so and then we'll head over to the quarry site. Any news on the remains found there?"

"Negative on anything new, Sheriff," the dispatcher reported. "But every law enforcement agency in a twenty-mile radius is there helping. Sheriff...you know that there are reports that the remains are Katie Karver's?"

"Yeah, I know that," the sheriff replied in an irritated voice. "That's why I've got Rogers and Lambert meeting me here. We'll be heading over there after we rehash the case. You call me if any developments come up that I should know about."

"Roger that," the dispatcher responded.

As he replaced the mike on the dash, Sheriff Armstrong saw Deputy Rogers' squad car entering the warehouse parking lot. He waved the deputy toward him and pointed to the area where he wanted Rogers to park.

Rogers parked his squad car next to Deputy Lambert's car, climbed out of his car, and walked rapidly to Sheriff Armstrong.

"Hey, Mike. What's going on over at the quarry site?" Rogers said. "I hear they've found Katie Karver's remains there."

"We don't know that for sure, Neil," the sheriff said. "But it might be so. We need to talk about some things. I've got Joe here, and I want us to put our heads together on this thing. You know, like a think tank. There's going to be a lot of questions asked if those are Katie's remains. And a lot of those questions are gonna be directed at you."

Rogers' body fell back hard against the sheriff's vehicle. He turned his face up towards the sky.

"What the hell are we gonna do now?" Neil exclaimed. "Shit! Those fucking Karvers!"

A feeling of anger and loathing for Rogers swept through the sheriff's body. He hated Rogers now, but he maintained control of his emotions and proceeded with his plan.

"Forget about the Karvers. We'll get it all figured out," the sheriff assured. "Joe and I have been talking. We think we've got some ideas. Joe's in the bathroom now, but lets you and me go in, and I'll brief you on what we've come up with so far. Maybe you can help clarify some things for us. Does that sound good to you, Neil?"

"Yeah, yeah, that's probably the best approach," Neil agreed. "But, is Joe on board?"

"Joe's loyal," the sheriff replied. "He knows what's right here. He'll protect the department. And you have to tell us everything you know. It's important we get our stories straight. After that, we can work everything out."

"It's the press we gotta watch out for," Rogers said. You're right…we gotta get our stories straight before those bastards try to screw us over. And, we gotta look out for Taylor, too."

"Yeah, we gotta be ready for the press," the sheriff said.

The two men walked into the warehouse, and the sheriff paused at a pop machine in the hallway. He dropped two quarters into the machine and turned to face Deputy Rogers.

"Want a coke, Neil," the sheriff asked. "It's on me."

"Sure. Actually, I could use something stronger."

"Don't worry. We'll get this worked out,' the sheriff replied. "Right now we need clear heads. I'll get a coke for Joe, too."

Armstrong put more money into the machine. He pulled three cans out of the machine and handed them all to Neil.

"Put 'em on the table in the office, Neil," he said. "I'm going to let Joe know you're here."

Deputy Rogers walked into the office and put the three coke cans down on the table. Hearing a noise at the door, he turned and saw the sheriff standing in the doorway with his pistol drawn. In the same instant, he noticed a portion of Deputy Lambert's body protruding from behind the office door.

"What's this?" Rogers called out. "What the hell's going on?"

"It's enough to tell you that once you were a help for me, Neil," the Sheriff said calmly. "But, you're a liability now."

Once again an explosive thunder filled the small office. Deputy Rogers' body fell back, slamming against the wall opposite of the doorway. He clutched at his chest, and his eyes stared at the sheriff in disbelief.

"Sheriff," Rogers uttered in disbelief.

He sank to his knees and fell forward onto the floor.

"Son of a bitch," the sheriff said aloud.

Armstrong stared at Rogers' body lying on the floor.

"Son of a bitch," he said again.

Sheriff Armstrong walked over to Rogers' body, bent down, and checked for a pulse. Finding none, he straightened up and looked down at the deputy.

"You were good, Neil," he said to the dead deputy. "But, you fucked up. I told you before, in this business you can't fuck up."

The sheriff walked over to Joe's body, picked the deputy's pistol up off of the floor, wiped it clean with a handkerchief, and put the pistol in Rogers' lifeless hand. Placing a finger from the dead deputy's hand on the trigger and pointing the pistol towards the office door, Armstrong pressed on the deputy's finger and fired a round from the weapon into the wall. He then allowed the pistol to fall from the deputy's hand.

Armstrong paused only momentarily to reflect upon his actions and to think about what he needed to do in order to pull himself out of the mess that surrounded him.

"God damn," he said aloud. "God damn, it wasn't supposed to turn out like this. That goddamn quarry expansion and those goddamn Karvers! That's what caused all of this."

Sheriff Armstrong had been a cop for almost two-thirds of his life, and his mind quickly processed what he needed to do. He knew he had two significant advantages in dodging any responsibility for the dead deputies: his experience and the authority of his office. Once again, he moved briskly to his squad car and radioed his dispatcher.

"Dispatch," he called into the mike.

"Roger, sheriff," the dispatcher immediately responded.

"Get an ambulance to the west Karver warehouse now," the sheriff ordered. "Two officers are down. Send me back up for assistance only. All hostilities are over, but I need immediate medical assistance for the officers. And, notify the Kewanee cops."

"Roger, Sheriff," the dispatcher responded sharply.

Armstrong left his car, walked back inside the office, and checked out the crime scene. He wanted to assure himself that everything was in place to reinforce the version of the killings that he had composed in his head. He pulled a small measuring tape from his pocket to check the distance between the two fallen deputies. He felt for their pulses again, guaranteeing that they were dead. He moved to the three coke cans on the table, popped open one of them, and took a sip.

"Damn," he said softly, looking at the two dead deputies.

Suddenly, Armstrong heard the wail of sirens moving rapidly in his direction. Within another instant, the sound of spraying gravel and sliding tires penetrated the warehouse walls as a Kewanee police car sped through the parking lot and headed toward the three parked squad cars. Oscillating flashes of bright red and white lights bounced off the office walls, and the heavy slamming of car doors broke the silence of the empty warehouse.

The sheriff hastily put the coke can back down on the table and moved toward the middle of the room. Immediately, he heard the pounding thud of hurried boots and the apprehensive voices of two men preparing to assault the tiny room.

"Sheriff Armstrong!" a voice called out. "You in there?"

"That you, Mike?" the sheriff called out. "It's alright. Everything is secure in here."

The two Kewanee cops cautiously entered the room with their guns drawn and spotted the two downed officers.

"Christ! What happened?" Officer Mike Free exclaimed.

The Kewanee officer's head spun back and forth as he looked at both of the bodies.

Sheriff Armstrong pointed to the body of Deputy Rogers.

"Rogers went berserk," the sheriff responded. "He killed Joe, and he took a shot at me. I had to shoot him. Where are the medics?"

Just as the sheriff's brief description ended, the men heard another vehicle pulling up alongside the four cars.

"That must be them now," Officer Free speculated.

"You OK, Sheriff?" the second Kewanee cop asked.

"Yeah, I'm fine," the sheriff replied.

Two medics came rushing up to the office door.

"Jesus, is that Joe?" one of the medics cried out.

The medic dropped down to the floor and knelt beside the deputy's body.

More sirens screeched through the night air and the parking lot cried out again under urgent tires. A tangle of flashing lights illuminated the warehouse parking lot, making it look like it was the center of a thunderstorm. Inside, the dancing lights continued to sway back and forth on the office walls, covering the gruesome deaths in a wild, carnival-like atmosphere.

"Check my two men out," the sheriff commanded. "I'm sure they're dead, but check them out. And, don't mess up the scene."

Turning to the Kewanee cops, he slowly pulled his pistol out of his holster and carefully handed it to Mike Free.

"This is your jurisdiction, Mike," the sheriff said. "But, I want my men treated right. You got investigators coming here?"

"Yeah, of course," Officer Free said.

The bewildered Kewanee police officer awkwardly reached for the sheriff's pistol.

"But you know Sheriff, we can check your weapon later," Officer Free said. "You don't need to turn it in to me."

"I want everything done by the book, Mike," the Armstrong replied. "Get pictures all over this warehouse area…inside and out. And run every test there is. I'll be making a statement to Chief Metternich as soon as I can, but I want a favor from you first."

"Sure, Sheriff," Mike Free replied. "We're here to help you."

"I want to get back to my office and notify my people about all of this before they hear a hundred different stories," the sheriff said. "My people have a right to hear what happened from me. And, they have a right to know the truth. I want you to keep the television people away from this building. I don't want any statements to the press until I have time to talk with my men. Can you do that for me?"

"Of course," Officer Free replied. "I'll square it with the chief. There shouldn't be any problem, but you gotta get that statement to Metternich ASAP. We'll handle everything else here. You go on back to Cambridge and be with your men. You gonna be OK, Sheriff?"

Armstrong stared down at the body of Deputy Lambert.

"I lost a good man here today," he said. "You take care of Deputy Lambert. I'll be all right as long as I can talk with my people. This is a hell of a mess."

The sheriff walked outside, wanting to get away from the carnage he had made in the small room, hoping that distance from the scene would help him keep a clear mind. Spotting one of his county squad cars pulling into the parking lot, Armstrong abandoned his hope of finding any immediate tranquility and, instead, wound up barking orders at the rookie deputy in the squad car.

"Boone! I want you to block the entrance to this parking lot," the sheriff commanded. "No one else needs to get close to the warehouse, and I want you to keep the Goddamn press out!"

The sheriff pointed toward the warehouse.

"Joe and Neil are in there dead. Let's show them some respect."

"Joe and Neil!" the stunned deputy responded in disbelief. "Dead?"

"Yeah, both of them are dead. You call dispatch. Tell them I'm heading back to the office to explain everything. Have dispatch get a hold of as many deputies as they can. I want a meeting set up in the large courthouse room in an hour. As soon as you can, turn your job over to one of the Kewanee cops and get back to the office. This is a shit day, Boone," the sheriff said.

Not wanting to engage in any explanations, Armstrong quickly turned away from Deputy Boone and marched rapidly toward his own car.

"You OK, Sheriff," Deputy Boone called out.

Realizing he had to say more, Armstrong turned towards Boone, put his hands on his hips, and bowed his head slightly. He shook his head back and forth and then looked up at Boone.

"It's a shit day, Boone," the sheriff repeated. "I hope you'll never have to go through anything like this, but I'll be alright as long as you do what I instructed you to do. We lost a good man today. In times like this, we gotta make sure we pull together as a team. We gotta do that for Joe."

Without waiting for a reply, Sheriff Armstrong turned away and headed to his own car, hoping to escape from what he had done.

CHAPTER FORTY-FOUR

Driving west on Illinois 81 toward Cambridge, the sheriff began to analyze his recent performance at the warehouse.

I think I did good, he reflected. And, I gotta keep in mind that this isn't my fault. Rogers and the Karvers are at fault here. They messed everything up. Damn it! Why the hell couldn't Joe see that? I'm sorry about Joe, but what did he expect me to do? Did he really think that I would let the Coroner arrest me? And, that Goddamn, kiss-ass Rogers, it's his fault that Joe is dead. He got Joe killed by screwing up the Karver case. And that pompous, Goddamn Karver, he brought all this on. I'll make sure that bastard pays. I owe that to Joe. What I said to Boone was right...we all gotta pull together as a team for Joe. We can make this right for him if we just all work together. Joe would want those Karvers put away for what they did to Katie. That's gonna be my main point...let's get this done for Joe.

Sheriff Armstrong arrived at the Cambridge jailhouse twenty minutes after departing from Kewanee and found his office area filled with people. The room buzzed with speculation about the quarry discovery and the Kewanee warehouse. All eyes turned on the sheriff as he walked through the outer room, heading toward his office.

"Marshall! I want to see you in my office," the sheriff barked at the watch commander.

Armstrong stopped at his office door and turned to face the crowd of employees who had assembled in his office.

"The rest of you clear out of here," he told them. "We're gonna be meeting in the courtroom in about forty minutes. And, I don't want anyone talking to the press. Marshall and I will handle all of the press releases from this office. I want the rest of you people thinking about Joe. We need to pull together for Joe and, right now, that means keeping your mouths shut and waiting until you hear from me and Marshall!"

Armstrong turned and moved into his private office, followed closely behind by Bob Marshall.

"Close the door, Bob," Armstrong told Deputy Marshall, "and sit down. We got a lot of planning to do."

Sheriff Armstrong walked briskly behind his desk, stood there for a moment, and then shook his head back and forth while looking directly at Deputy Marshall.

"God damn it. God damn it, Bob!" He said.

The sheriff picked up a pile of mail on his desk and threw it back down. The pile of mail hit with a loud thud, scattering across the desk and falling to the floor.

"This is one Goddamn mess, Bob," the sheriff groaned. "One Goddamn, fucking mess!"

Armstrong fell back into his chair, biting his lip, and continually shaking his head. He placed his hands over his face and sat quietly. Marshall remained quiet and attentive, watching the sheriff's anguish.

Sheriff Armstrong spoke first, but seemed to be speaking more to himself than to Deputy Marshall.

"I had to turn my side weapon into the Kewanee police," the sheriff said. "I killed Neil Rogers."

The sheriff uncovered his face and looked at Marshall.

"You heard what I said, Bob?"

"Yeah, we know about it, Mike. I mean…that's what people are saying."

Armstrong looked deeply into Marshall's eyes.

"What've they been saying?" the sheriff demanded.

"Mike, I don't know what happened over in Kewanee," Bob exclaimed. "I mean…I just heard that you shot Neil because he went crazy. Is it true that Neil killed Joe? Is Joe dead?"

"Yeah, that's all true. Christ…that son of a bitch Rogers killed Joe!" the sheriff cried out.

Tears welled up in the Armstrong's eyes.

"Does everyone know?" he asked. "Do they know what happened in Kewanee?"

"Well everyone knows what's being said," Marshall replied. "Christ, I can't believe that Joe's dead."

Marshall shook his head in disbelief.

"God damn it, I just talked to him this morning when he began his shift. Why the hell would Neil kill Joe?" Marshall asked.

"I'm gonnna tell everyone at once, Bob," the sheriff responded. "This is hard, and I don't want to have to repeat it over and over again. But, I'm gonna tell you some things first. I'm gonna need your help, so I'm telling you this confidentially. You understand what I'm saying, Bob?"

"You can trust me, Mike. You know you can," he replied.

"Yeah, I do know that. You're a good man, Bob. Let me tell you what happened. I really need to share with someone…someone like you…a veteran…a veteran who'll understand all of this."

"You should, Mike. You should get it all out," Bob said. "You've been through a lot."

Armstrong stood up and paced back and forth behind his desk. He turned and faced Bob Marshall.

"This is the worst day of my life," the sheriff confessed. "Seeing Joe shot and having to shoot Rogers. I never saw anything like this coming. Christ, Bob! Rogers could just as easily have killed me, too."

"Take your time, Mike. We're all here for you," Bob said. "I know all of this has gotta be painful for you."

Armstrong sat back down in his chair and sighed heavily. When he spoke, there was anguish in his voice.

"Christ, its painful!" he said. "Painful as hell, but I need to talk with someone about it. Here's what happened. Joe and I found out that Neil screwed up the Karver case. He screwed it up badly. We think he even used Scott Miller to frame Brad Stablein."

Deputy Marshall's face seethed with anger.

"Neil! That bastard," he said. "That no good son of a bitch! I knew he would cause us all trouble some day. Why the hell did he frame Stablein though? What was in it for Neil?"

"Joe believed Neil framed Stablein because he wanted the chief's job in Kewanee," the sheriff explained. "Neil wanted to get a quick conviction to please Gerald Karver. Joe and I, we had good information that the whole case was screwed up, but until Katie's remains were found, we had no real hard evidence to go up against the case Neil had built with Stablein. All we really had was a rambling statement Scott Miller made to us when he was drunk."

"But if Stablein didn't murder Katie, who did?" Bob asked.

"Larry Karver murdered Katie," the sheriff answered. "He killed his own wife and then hid her body over there off of Billy Wolf Road. The bastard cut her leg off and threw it into the canal to divert the investigation away from him. Then he used Neil to frame Stablein."

"God, Mike! Larry Karver! Holy Christ! Was Rogers being duped or do you think he was covering up for Larry?"

"Joe and I think he knew. We think he was covering up to protect the whole Karver family…sucking up to them to get the chief's job in Kewanee."

Bob Marshall shook his head back and forth.

"Rogers! That goddamn bastard! He's really screwed us all with this mess!" Marshall exclaimed.

The sheriff paused for a moment letting the accusation sink into the deputy's mind and watching Marshall's face fill with anger.

"Neil was a bastard," Armstrong agreed.

The sheriff eagerly wanted to reinforce any negative image of Deputy Rogers.

"When I heard the remains at the quarry might be Katie's, I had Joe and Neil meet me at the Karver warehouse," Armstrong said. "I wanted to confront Neil and get ahead of what the news people would be asking. Finding her remains over there just didn't jive with the case Neil built against Stablein. All I wanted to do was protect the department. I thought we could deal with Neil there and get all our facts straight."

"Yeah, that was a smart thing to do," Marshall agreed.

"Things were going good at first," the sheriff said. "We met in an office over in the warehouse. I got there before Neil and Joe. I bought some cokes from a machine in the warehouse so the meeting would look real casual. Joe showed up just a little bit before Rogers. He had just come from the quarry, and he was real upset. He was taking it real hard. I told him to calm down. When Neil arrived, I told him we just wanted to rehash some things about the Karver case."

"Neil must've been worried then, huh?" Bob observed.

"Not really," Armstrong said. "I mean, Neil's a cool customer, you know. And, I don't think he had heard anything about Katie being found at the quarry. I was more worried about Joe than I was about Neil. Joe can be hard to read sometimes because he's so quiet. I had thought about not having Joe come there, but I knew that wouldn't be fair to him."

"Yeah, I know Joe and Katie were good friends at one time," Bob said. "And, I know there wasn't any love between him and Rogers. That would be a tough call."

"Yeah, it was a tough call, and that's where I screwed up," the sheriff said. "I should've known Joe would lose it and confront Neil. And I shouldn't have left those two guys alone, but while I was waiting for them to get to the warehouse, I drank too much coke. As soon as we sat down for our meeting, I had to go to the john. Hell, I wasn't gonna be gone that long, so I figured everything would be alright. But while I was pissing, I heard Neil yelling at Joe. Joe must have said something to set him off. I headed back for the office right away, but I heard a gun shot before I could get there."

"Oh Jesus," Marshall said.

"I couldn't believe it. I drew my weapon and went into the office. There was Neil with a pistol in his hand and Joe on the floor. He looked crazy, and he pointed the pistol at me, but I shot him first. He got one round off before he went down. When he was down, I saw the pistol he was holding was Joe's. I don't know how he got Joe's weapon, but there must've been a struggle or something."

The sheriff covered his face again and then slammed his hands down hard onto his desk.

"Rogers! That bastard!" Armstrong shouted. "He shot Joe! I had to shoot him and I'm glad I did. I'm glad I killed the bastard."

"Sure, Mike," Bob said. "You did the right thing. I understand. Everybody's gonna understand. This must be real hard on you, but you did the right thing. I mean, hell the guy would've killed you, and you've been with Joe for a long time. It must've been tough to see him shot like that. Are you all right? Can I get you anything?"

"No…I'm…fine. I'm fine," the sheriff said. "I'm just mad as hell about all of this. Poor Joe, he didn't deserve to die like that. And, I'm the one who put him in that situation. I should have seen this coming. Hell, I've been doing this job for twenty years, Bob, and I've only pulled my weapon four times. I've never had to shoot anybody. Now, the first time I do, I have to kill a cop. I mean I know I had to kill Rogers, but still…"

"None of this is your fault, Mike," Marshall said, trying to comfort the sheriff. "You did what you had to do. I know you liked Neil, but I've never trusted him and a lot of guys around here didn't like him. He was always out for himself. And now, the bastard's killed Joe. You did the right thing."

"Thanks, Bob. Your support means a lot to me".

Armstrong stood up and reached across his desk to shake Marshall's hand.

"I appreciate your help in all of this," he said. "It's not going to be easy, but we've always done the right thing in this office, and we've always pulled together in hard times. I want to keep that tradition alive, and now we've gotta pull together for Joe and for Katie. Hey, is there news from the quarry?"

"They've taken the remains in for testing," Marshall replied. "It's pretty certain that it's Katie. Joe found her wallet over there."

"Yeah…that's what he told me," the sheriff said "I'm sure he was mad as hell with Neil about that. I'm pretty sure that's why Neil killed him. But, Christ, there was no reason to kill Joe. That bastard Neil, he was always out for himself."

The sheriff fell back into his chair, swiveled the chair away from Bob Marshall, and stared at a blank wall. Deputy Marshall cast his eyes down on the floor and cupped his hands in his lap. A brief period of silence fell over the two men as they thought about what had happened. Then Marshall lifted his head up, cleared his throat, and brought the conversation back to the planning they needed to do.

"Listen, Mike," the deputy said. "I know this is a bad time for you, but the news people are after a statement of some kind. It's gonna be a circus out there, what with the quarry and what's happened in Kewanee. They'll be falling on us like locusts."

Sheriff Armstrong swung his chair back to face Marshall, and he nodded in agreement.

"Yeah, I saw a television truck setting up outside when I pulled up," the sheriff sighed. "Keep them at bay, Bob. And, tell them I will be making a statement after I meet with our people…we don't want any names released until after the next of kin have been notified. At least, until we notify Joe's people. Neil's not from around here anyway. And, you make sure that Joe's folks are notified before I speak to the press. As soon as we're done in the courtroom, I want a warrant for the arrest of Gerald Karver and Larry Karver."

"Gerald Karver!" Marshall shot back. "What the hell does he have to do with this?"

"You'll find out soon," the sheriff said. "But, you listen good to what I tell our people, and then you go and arrest both of them. I want both of those bastards in cuffs and sitting in a jail cell. Larry's in Phoenix, but we can arrest the old man tonight, and we can get the Phoenix cops to pick up Larry. That bastard Gerald killed Joe just as much as Rogers did. We're going to make 'em pay for what they did to Joe."

"You got it, sheriff," Bob replied.

The watch commander was initially dumbfounded by the idea of arresting Gerald Karver, but he immediately shook off of his apprehensions.

"I'll tell you this," Marshall said, "if Gerald Karver had anything to do with hurting Joe, there'll be a lot of guys wanting to cuff him."

"Old man Karver is as guilty as Neil Rogers and Larry Karver," the sheriff said. "You have some of the guys bring him in, Bob."

Armstrong pointed at Bob and stared into his eyes.

"I'm giving him to you, and putting my trust in you on this one," he said.

"Thanks, Mike. I'll get started on it right now. You can count on me. I'll get it all done."

"OK, Bob. I know I can always count on you. Guys like you and me…we've made this department what it is today. Listen, why don't you go get started on the warrants right now? I'm gonna need some time alone before we go meet with our people."

"Sure, Mike. I'll get started now," Bob said. "You sure I can't get you anything. I mean…you'll be alright here?"

"Yeah, I'll be fine," Armstrong answered. "I just have to clear my head a little. Just keep what we said in here to yourself. I only want one message coming out of this office, and I need to tell the men myself. You understand?"

"Sure."

"And, Bob," the sheriff said, "I need something else from you."

"Anything, Mike. Whatever you need, just ask."

"Well, I'm kind of shook up by all this mess. The statement I make to the press has to be good…I can answer any questions about what happened, but the statement has to be good. Maybe you could write something up for me?"

"Of course," Bob responded. "I can do that. Don't worry about anything. You take some time to relax."

When Deputy Marshall left the office, Sheriff Armstrong went over their conversation in his mind, making sure that what he told Marshall fit in with what he planned to say in the courtroom, and what he planned to say to the news media.

Everything has to jive, the sheriff thought. I can't be changing my story. Rogers and the Karvers…they're the villains here. No one ever liked that weasel Rogers anyway. He was always such a kiss-ass. And, there'll be a lot of people happy to see the Karvers fall. Stablein shouldn't be any problem. That dumb ass confessed, and if he sings that he was forced to confess, I'll blame all that on Rogers. This all can be turned into a plus if I get the right spin on it. Hell, I'm about to solve the Karver murder case, free an innocent man, and put the responsible people in jail. Maybe this could turn out real good in the election. I just gotta get the right spin on it all. Bob seemed to buy it, and I should have the rest of the department behind me. Just gotta get the right spin on it. Of course, my real problem's gonna be with my worthy opponent. Taylor's gotta be circling like a vulture right now, but the press has always liked me. I gotta get to them first and give them my version of what's happened here. Goddamn Taylor! Hell! Why'd that son of a bitch have to pick this time to run? That goddamn Ted Chapman is behind all that.

A knock on his office door interrupted the sheriff's thoughts.

Sheriff," Deputy Marshall said. "Everyone's ready for you in the courtroom. And, there are four network television crews parked outside. We've roped off an area to contain them and told 'em that you'll be making a statement in about thirty minutes. I've got an opening statement written for you."

Sheriff Armstrong quickly looked over the brief statement Deputy Marshall had written for him.

"This looks good," Armstrong said. "The press…they're vultures. Thanks for writing this. I gotta talk with them sometime, and its best to get it over with quick. Make sure you get those warrants. I'm gonna tell the press we're about to make some new arrests in the Karver case, and I want that to happen immediately."

"I already called the State's Attorney to begin the process," Marshall said. "I'll be sending our men to Kewanee to get old man Karver while you're handling the press."

"That's great!" the sheriff said. "Good job. Now let's get over to the courtroom. I want you beside me when I explain everything to the staff. I'm going to tell them to contact you if they have any questions. You'll be my right hand man on this thing, OK?"

"You got it, Mike," Marshall replied. "Hey! Just so you know, everyone's concerned about you. They all know how rough this must be on you. We're all with you on this."

"That means a lot to me, Bob," the sheriff said. "I need you guys with me."

Bob Marshall and Sheriff Armstrong left the county jailhouse, heading for their meeting with all the personnel of the sheriff's department. It made Sheriff Armstrong feel good to have Marshall walking closely by his side as they entered the courtroom.

This is all gonna work out, the sheriff thought.

CHAPTER FORTY-FIVE

Deputy Marshall appeared to be right in his assessment of the department's support for the sheriff. When comrades fall, the bond between warriors becomes stronger, and support for one another becomes a central part of their group dynamics. So it was with the staff of the sheriff's department. While the sheriff explained the situation, the department became a tight-knit unit whose solidarity was bolstered by a show of support from the deputies who were veteran department members. After the meeting in the courtroom, the deputies clustered together in three small groups, each group representing one of the three work shifts.

"We all need to help the sheriff on this thing," Deputy Borkgren said to the deputies who worked the third shift. "The Goddamn Quad-City press will try to fry us all over this thing. There will be all sorts of comments about us being 'hick' cops. You know how they love to find trouble in Henry County."

"We gotta do it for Joe too," a young deputy chimed in. "I talked with Joe during the Karver investigation. I don't think he liked what Neil was doing. He told me he thought the investigation was all going too fast. And, we all know that Neil was a suck-up."

"Yeah, Joe was right about all that," Borkgren added. "That bastard Neil was always looking out for himself, and now the son of a bitch has shot Joe. And those Karvers! They think they own the county. I knew Katie. She was a wonderful woman, and those bastards killed her and got Joe killed. We've all gotta stand with the sheriff."

When the clusters broke up, the deputies began walking out of the courthouse and forming new clusters, which were now based on age and seniority. A group of younger deputies gathered together and looked over at the area that had been given to the news media.

"The news people are fast," Deputy Erickson commented. "It'd be good it they could be as accurate in covering a story as they are quick."

"Yeah," Deputy Johnson agreed. "But, I gotta tell you, there are some things I still don't understand...and don't get me wrong...I'm with the sheriff here, but I don't understand a lot of the things that have been going on. Joe wasn't the kind of guy to get himself killed in a heated argument. And, Neil killing Joe with the sheriff in the same building? That doesn't make sense to me."

"Well, for sure the Karver murder investigation is turning into a big fuck up," Erickson added. "There's going to be an awful lot of questions to answer on that one. And, I agree about the warehouse situation. I didn't know Rogers very well, but he seemed to be an awful cool character. I wonder what could have made him fly off the handle like that. I mean killing another cop! And like you say…killing him with the sheriff in the same building? Man that's strange. I just hope Armstrong has all the right answers…keep in mind, it's an election year and something like this could get Taylor elected."

"We all gotta be careful," another young deputy added. "We don't have any seniority here. I want to support the sheriff as much as anyone, but I don't want my tit getting caught in a ringer either."

As the young deputies watched, the sheriff went to face the news media with a small group of veteran staff members who walked along side of him. The media rushed to question him about the two events.

The sheriff told the news media that he would make an opening statement and then allow time for questions. Cameras focused and lights shone on the sheriff as he stood in front of a temporary stand of nine mikes that had been assembled to record what the he had to say.

"You news people know that two deputies from this department are gone," the sheriff began.

Armstrong then pulled Marshall's written statement from his pocket and read it to the press.

"This is a sad day for Henry County. In all of my years in office, I can't remember a worse day. We have lost a friend and a loyal deputy. Deputy Lambert served the people of Henry County for over eight years and was one of the best officers in the department. And, he was my good friend. We are all saddened by his death. And, we are shocked and deeply disgusted by the actions of Deputy Rogers. It appears that Deputy Rogers manipulated the law to serve his own ambitions. He may have caused the conviction of a man we now believe to be innocent, and worst of all, he took the life of an honorable police officer. I am personally distressed by the events of today. However, I am proud of the officers who serve with me and who have given me their full support in this difficult time of my life. I will now take questions."

"Sheriff!" five television reporters screamed out in unison.

"I'll take the first question from the Channel Four reporter," the sheriff responded.

"We understand that you shot Deputy Neil Rogers. Is that true and how do you feel about it?"

"The deaths of Deputies Lambert and Rogers are currently under investigation by the Kewanee Police Department," the sheriff stated. "It would be inappropriate for me to comment while the investigation is being conducted.

But, I can tell you this. We are examining the conduct of Deputy Rogers. I mean we're looking at how he acted in the investigation of Katie Karver's death. There could be some things that went wrong there."

"Sheriff, what about the remains found at the quarry," a reporter from Channel Eight interjected. "We understand they're the remains of Katie Karver. What can you tell us about that situation?"

"We can't be sure if those remains belong to Ms. Karver," the sheriff said. "We're waiting for the forensic report. But, I'll tell you this…there is enough information about those remains that it has caused me to have warrants issued for the arrests of two very important people in the county…two people who we now think had a part in the death of Katie Karver."

"Who are the two people, sheriff?" another reporter shouted out.

"I can't tell you that at this time," the sheriff replied. "I know you're in a hurry to ask questions about all of this, but it is too early for me to give you detailed answers."

Sheriff Armstrong momentarily turned away from the mike stand and put his right hand on Bob Marshall's shoulder. He gently tugged on Marshall, pulling him slightly towards the mikes.

"I want you to know that I've made Deputy Marshall the point man in all of this. He will be happy to answer your questions when we get more information. Right now I have a lot of work to attend to, so you'll have to excuse all of us. But, we'll be back to you real soon. You can count on that!"

Sheriff Armstrong moved out from behind the mikes and fell in behind five deputies who escorted him toward his office building.

"Officer Taylor!" Armstrong heard a news reporter call out.

Sheriff Armstrong and his men paused and turned to see Jim Taylor moving behind the temporary mike stand with reporters crushing toward him, ready to pepper candidate Taylor with questions about the day's events.

"Damn it! Let's get into the office," Armstrong said.

The sheriff increased his pace, marching quickly away from the news media's obvious attraction for his political opponent.

"Officer Taylor," the news reporter repeated. "Do you have any comments on the events that have occurred at the rock quarry and in Kewanee?"

Officer Taylor approached the mikes and slowly scanned the group of reporters who anxiously awaited his take on what had happened in Henry County.

"I am sure that the sheriff has expressed to you his concerns over the events of today," he said. "I am also sure that he was cautious in his comments. It would be rash to draw conclusions without having the facts. It will take time and serious investigation to sort out everything that has happened. However, I can state that I am very concerned about the possibility of Ms. Karver's remains being found at the quarry site. If the remains are those of

Ms. Karver, then there are a number of serious questions that must be asked about the conviction of Brad Stablein...and questions about who is really responsible for Katie Karver's death. It may be that there is a murderer still loose in Henry County."

"Officer Taylor!" another news reporter shouted. "Do you think that the Sheriff Armstrong mishandled the Karver case?"

"Look," Taylor replied. "I'm running for Sheriff of Henry County because I believe that I can do a better job than Sheriff Armstrong. That means that I think I can do a better job in every aspect of the sheriff's department. From what has happened today, I would say that some very important responsibilities have been mismanaged. Two deputies are dead, and the Karver case...a case that was supposed to have been solved over a year ago...is open again. And, it looks like Sheriff Armstrong has assisted in putting an innocent man in prison and has allowed the real murderer to roam free."

"Do you have proof that Brad Stablein is innocent?" another reporter questioned.

"I just heard Sheriff Armstrong tell you that he has warrants to arrest two prominent residents of Henry County in connection with the Karver murder," Taylor responded. "All of the information we have been getting today seems very peculiar to me. Over a year ago, the sheriff's department declared that a drifter was guilty of Katie Karver's murder, and now warrants are being issued for two prominent residents? What was the involvement of these two people in this murder? How come we have never heard about them before? This new information sounds like either a cover up or some very sloppy police work. We need to have a lot of questions answered here."

"Are you saying that the sheriff protected the real murderers and framed Brad Stablein?" a reporter asked.

"As I said before," Taylor responded, "we have to wait for the facts. But, Katie Karver's remains have been found at the quarry site, and two officers have been killed in a shootout with the sheriff...and all of this happens on the same day! And further, one of the dead officers was the man who made the case against Brad Stablein. These events seems very strange to me. I think you reporters will have a lot of tough questions to ask this sheriff. And, Sheriff Armstrong has a lot of explaining to do to the citizens of Henry County."

"What do you think the sheriff should do at this time?" a television reporter asked.

"I think that the Sheriff Armstrong should resign," Taylor said.

"Wait a minute," the television reporter interrupted. "Would you make that statement again?"

"Sure," Taylor calmly asserted. "I think that Sheriff Armstrong should resign from his office. I heard his statement about today's events, and it is obvious he is trying to make this mess go away by stonewalling. The people of Henry County need new management in the sheriff's office. A murder case has been mishandled, and two deputies are dead. All of this has to be laid on the shoulders of the sheriff. It is his department, and he has the ultimate responsibility for everything that happens in the department."

"Sheriff Armstrong claims that Deputy Rogers is at fault for what happened today," another reporter stated.

"Sheriff Armstrong is scapegoating when he makes such statements," Taylor responded. "I repeat...the sheriff is responsible for everything that happens in the department. However, he is right about one thing...this is a bad day for him and for his department. He could resolve all of these problems by stepping down and by withdrawing from the election."

"Wouldn't that assure you a victory at the polls?" a newspaper reporter asked.

"I am the better man for the job," Taylor said. "It is obvious from what has happened here today that the people of Henry County deserve a new sheriff. If Sheriff Armstrong won't step down, then the people should vote him out. When I am sheriff, you can be assured that I will fully answer all of your questions any time of the day. But right now, I am heading over to Kewanee to look into these situations for myself. I will be very happy to answer any questions you have after I am able to do a little investigating of my own. Let's talk about all of this again real soon."

CHAPTER FORTY-SIX

When Sheriff Armstrong reached the jailhouse complex, he immediately retreated to the security of his private office, sat down at his desk, and began fuming over the press' interest in Jim Taylor.

I can imagine what that bastard Taylor is saying to the press right now, the sheriff speculated. God damn him! And, the damn press will eat it all up. Shit! I solve the Karver case and Taylor's gonna make it look like I screwed everything up. It's that bastard Rogers that screwed everything up. Hell, I would've loved to arrest that little Karver weasel if Rogers would've done the right thing with the investigation. Rogers was a maverick cop, and that's not my fault. If that damn quarry would've stayed below the bluff, then no one would've known about all of this. And, that sorry-ass pervert Stablein deserves to be in jail…that son of a bitch would've wound up in prison anyway. Letting an idiot like Stablein out of jail is a recipe for disaster. God damn it all!

After sitting at his desk and ranting for a few moments, the sheriff tried to calm down and focus on his goal of re-election. He stood up, walked around to the front of his desk and leaned against it by placing both of his hands flat down on the desktop.

Well…maybe arresting the Karvers will change all of this trouble, he thought. Their arrests should be a real splash in the news, and I can still say that it was Rogers fault. I gotta make this all work. Goddamn Taylor! The timing of these things is really screwed up…what with Taylor running for office right now. Why did all of this have to come up when I face my strongest opponent? It's that goddamn Chapman's fault. I know that bastard talked Taylor into running for my office. Goddamn Chapman! But hell, there's gotta be a way of making this work for me. There's almost a month left until the election. Could be a lot of this will blow over. Voters forget things, and Taylor could stumble. Christ, if only the County Board would've delayed the quarry expansion. Goddamn County Board! This never would've happened if it weren't for the County Board.

In a short time, the sheriff's thoughts were interrupted by a knock on the door and Deputy Marshall sticking his head into the sheriff's office.

"Got a minute, Mike?" Marshall asked.

Sheriff Armstrong moved back behind his desk and sat down in his chair.

"Sure, Bob. Come on in," the sheriff replied. "Have we been on the television news yet?"

"Yeah, and Taylor was too," Marshall said reluctantly.

Sheriff Armstrong leaned back in his chair and frowned.

"I can imagine what that bastard is saying. Well, the hell with him. What have you got for me?"

"We picked up Gerald Karver," Bob reported. "You should know though, he's mad as hell, and he's threatening to sue everyone. Karver is saying we've got no reason to be holding him."

"Oh, the hell with him," the sheriff replied in disgust. "I'll talk to him. He'll break when he hears that we're arresting Larry. The old man knows that Larry will spill his guts as soon as we lock him up. You notified the people in Phoenix, right?"

"Yep, I think we'll be hearing from them within the hour," Marshall replied.

"Pretty soon we'll get this wrapped up. And then we'll let people know how Rogers screwed all of us. I think everyone will understand. Don't you?" the sheriff asked.

"Sure, Mike."

Armstrong detected that Marshall's reply was less assured than before.

"Anything wrong, Bob?" the sheriff asked.

"No, I...Huh...I just think Taylor sounded pretty good on television. I think a lot of people are gonna be asking some tough questions of us."

The sheriff quickly got out of his chair, moved towards Marshall, and looked him squarely in the eyes.

"You got questions?" the sheriff said, moving closer to the deputy.

"Hey Mike, I'm with you on this," Bob shot back. "It's just that the perception of this is gonna be bad. You gotta know that. And, Taylor's going to take advantage of everything that's happened today. Taylor's pretty good with words."

"Tell me this, Bob...do you think I can win re-election?" the sheriff asked.

"I don't know, Mike," Marshall replied softly. "I'm not a politician. I mean...a lotta stuff has happened today. And you know...now don't get upset...but you were on the losing side of the quarry issue. I mean...I just don't know."

"What about the rest of the guys?" the sheriff asked.

"They're all with you, Mike. We're all with you. At least I'm sure the veterans are. You never can tell about the new guys."

Armstrong moved back away from Marshall and leaned against his desk. It was obvious that the he was processing everything that had just been said.

Marshall was hoping to see a look of confidence or defiance appear on the sheriff's face. It never did.

"Yeah...the new guys," Armstrong muttered. "There are a lot of new people in the county. Lotta Democrats I bet. Taylor's a new guy, too."

Deputy Marshall decided it was time to change the direction of the conversation.

"Where do you want us to take Karver so you can question him?" Marshall asked.

"Just take him to the office in cell block three," the sheriff answered. "We won't be able to hold him long. His lawyer will get him out of here in a couple of hours. But, when Larry breaks, we'll charge the old man with conspiracy and obstruction. You get Gerald Karver in the office, and I'll be down to talk with him shortly."

"OK, Sheriff. Don't worry...everything's gonna work out," Marshall said as he left the room.

Sheriff Armstrong remained leaning against his desk as the door shut behind Marshall. He stared at the closed door without seeing it. The sheriff had just received a dose of reality from Deputy Marshall. The more he thought about it, the more he realized that the meeting in the courtroom had not gone as well as he had hoped. The men had seemed supportive, but there was a peculiar feel about all of it. It wasn't like the old days when a sheriff's voice commanded immediate respect.

Could they tell, the sheriff wondered? Were they able to see holes in my story? Damn! Maybe nothing's gonna work out...maybe I've been kidding myself all along. Hell, my election is screwed. Rogers...the Karvers...Miller...Taylor ...Chapman....they all got me. They got me good. After the election, I won't be sheriff anymore. Hell after the election, I'll just be Mike Armstrong...just another citizen. Those bastards got me right where they want me.

CHAPTER FORTY-SEVEN

After leaving the sheriff's office, Deputy Marshall went back to his desk and looked at the phone. He moved his hand toward it, but stopped with his hand resting on top of it. The strong sense of loyalty he had initially felt toward the sheriff was beginning to fade away as the reality of the situation became clearer.

Damn, none of this feels right, Marshall thought. None of it. I know Joe…he'd never let a guy like Rogers get the drop on him. He didn't trust Rogers enough to let something like that happen. And, how the hell would Rogers get Joe's gun. That'd never happen either! Something's screwed up here. And, Katie…her remains buried there in that field all this time? Joe wouldn't have left her remains over there. If he had any information she was there, he would've been over there digging up that field with just his bare hands.

Shaking his head to try and clear his mind, Marshall picked up the phone and called down to cell block three.

"Reese," he said into the phone. "Get Gerald Karver out of his cell and take him to room 324. The sheriff will be coming to talk with him. And, tell Karver his lawyer called and is on the way over here. Sheriff Armstrong and I should be there in about fifteen minutes."

"You got it," Reese replied. "Hey, did you see Taylor on the news tonight? I gotta tell you, he's gonna have people talking about all of this, and he's gonna be asking a lotta questions. That's for sure."

"You just get Karver ready," Marshall growled into the phone. "We'll let the sheriff handle all that other stuff."

"Hey, I'm just saying a lot of guys are wondering about some things," Reese said. "You know a lot of guys respect Taylor. He's been a good cop."

"You get Karver ready, and we'll be down in just a little bit," Marshall repeated. "If you got questions, you can ask the sheriff then."

"I got no questions," Reese replied. "Karver will be in room 324."

Bob Marshall hung up the phone and stared towards the closed door of the sheriff's office. He thought about going and talking to Armstrong, but his thoughts were interrupted by the voice of a freshman deputy.

"Hey, Bob. Did you want to see me?" the deputy said from behind Bob's chair.

Marshall swiveled his chair around to see Deputy Matt Boone standing behind him.

"Yeah, Matt," Marshall replied. "You weren't at the meeting, how come?"

"I was over at the warehouse," Matt answered. "The sheriff told me to stay there and keep the press out. I tried to get back, but it was busy over there."

"OK, Matt, that's no problem," Marshall said. "I'm just trying to account for everyone and get everyone caught up on everything. Have you talked with the guys about what happened at the meeting?"

"Yeah, I have," Matt answered. "I talked with a bunch of the guys outside."

"You got any questions?" Marshall asked.

"No," Matt replied. "I'm just minding my own business concerning all of this stuff, and I'm waiting to hear from the sheriff again. I mean, I think the sheriff will be telling us more, right?"

"Yeah, I'm sure he will. Hey, let me ask you something. Did you see anything over at the warehouse that I should know about?" Marshall asked.

"Nah, it's all wrapped up over there now. But, it was weird to be in the room where Joe and Rogers got killed."

"You went in the warehouse office?" Marshall asked.

"Yeah," Boone responded. "Two of the Kewanee cops needed some help at the scene, so they asked me. Everyone else had left."

"Did you see anything there?"

"Not really," Boone replied. "Kind of eerie though…there were these three coke cans just sitting on a table in the room. Those cans sort of made me think of our three guys. I guess they didn't have time to drink them. Two of the cans were unopened, and the other one was opened, but still full."

"Wait a minute," Marshall said. "Did you say the opened can was full? How full?"

"It was full to the top. If anyone drank out of it, it was only a sip. I guess they never got to them, huh?" Boone observed. "Wonder why only one of them would be opened?"

"You didn't see a fourth can over there, did you Matt?" Marshall asked. "Maybe an empty can in the trash or someplace else?"

"No. No way," Boone replied. "The Kewanee cops had bagged everything in the trash cans. Nope. There were just those three cans. I'm sure of that. Why do you ask? Is that important?"

Marshall was about to answer when he heard the sound of a muffled gunshot coming from the sheriff's office. He stared in disbelief toward the office door, his body became rigid, and he sat straight up in his chair.

"Oh, God," Marshall said quietly.

"What the hell was that?" Deputy Boone asked.

Boone reached for his holster, but looked toward Bob Marshall for directions as to what he should do.

Marshall sat further up in his chair, looked around the office, and saw the office personnel gazing towards the sheriff's door. Stillness reigned in the outer office as each person remained frozen in place, fearful any movement would give credence to what they knew the sound meant.

"What the hell was that?" Boone asked again.

Bob Marshall reached for the young deputy's wrist and held onto it. His eyes continued to stare at the sheriff's closed door.

"Just wait," Marshall replied.

The seconds that passed by seemed endless. No one in the office wanted to respond to the sound of the gunshot. Each person hoped the sheriff's door would fly open, announcing life, and providing some explanation for the noise, but only silence prevailed. Soon all eyes turned on Deputy Marshall, each stare appointing the deputy as the one to investigate the dreaded sound.

Deputy Marshall rose out of his chair and moved slowly toward the sheriff's door, frightened that every step he took would eventually confirm the painful thoughts that were racing through everyone's mind. When he reached the door, he looked back apprehensively at the office workers, placed his hand on the doorknob, and abruptly opened the door. He seemed to know that knocking or calling out to the sheriff would be a fruitless gesture.

Stepping inside the office, Marshall saw the sheriff in his chair, his upper torso sprawled across the desk, and his bloody face buried in a mass of papers. A revolver was in Armstrong's right hand, and his left hand clutched a piece of white typing paper.

The stillness that had consumed the office was now broken by the quiet shuffle of the office staff as they all moved cautiously toward the inner office. Bob Marshall stopped only two steps away from the sheriff's desk. He turned his head to look back at the office door and saw five office workers huddled together at the doorway, gawking at the horrible sight.

Marshall turned his eyes back upon the desk, staring at the body of Mike Armstrong. Although he knew it was hopeless, Marshall felt compelled to address the sheriff.

"Sheriff," Marshall said in a hushed tone.

"Mike," he called out a little louder.

Deputy Marshall took the last two steps needed in order to place him directly in front of the sheriff's desk. He slowly extended his hand and gently touched the side of Armstrong's neck with two fingers, but felt no pulse. With quiet reverence, he pulled the paper out of the grip of the sheriff's dead hand and read the words Mike Armstrong had scrawled on it.

Sheriff of the County
Law and Order